FORSAKING
ALL OTHERS

D1332873

9030 0000 248974

By the Author

Awake Unto Me

Forsaking All Others

Visit us at www.boldstrokesbooks.com

FORSAKING ALL OTHERS

by
Kathleen Knowles

2013

9030 0000248 974

FORSAKING ALL OTHERS

© 2013 BY KATHLEEN KNOWLES. ALL RIGHTS RESERVED.

ISBN 13: 978-1-60282-892-6

THIS TRADE PAPERBACK ORIGINAL IS PUBLISHED BY
BOLD STROKES BOOKS, INC.
P.O. BOX 249
VALLEY FALLS, NY 12185

FIRST EDITION: AUGUST 2013

THIS IS A WORK OF FICTION. NAMES, CHARACTERS, PLACES, AND
INCIDENTS ARE THE PRODUCT OF THE AUTHOR'S IMAGINATION OR
ARE USED FICTITIOUSLY. ANY RESEMBLANCE TO ACTUAL PERSONS,
LIVING OR DEAD, BUSINESS ESTABLISHMENTS, EVENTS, OR LOCALES
IS ENTIRELY COINCIDENTAL.

THIS BOOK, OR PARTS THEREOF, MAY NOT BE REPRODUCED IN ANY
FORM WITHOUT PERMISSION.

CREDITS
EDITORS: VICTORIA OLDHAM, SHELLEY THRASHER, AND STACIA SEAMAN
PRODUCTION DESIGN: STACIA SEAMAN
COVER DESIGN BY SHERI (GRAPHICARTIST2020@HOTMAIL.COM)

Acknowledgments

There are quite a few people who assisted me with information that helped me write this book.

My good friend Lydia Baldwin discussed polyamory and her experience of it at length and pointed me to the popular work on the subject, *The Ethical Slut*. Lydia also let me borrow her name for Jules's younger sister. No resemblance exists between the real and fictional Lydia.

Deborah Deegan talked about the ups and downs of dog walking with me. Rita Minero and Deborah Wyman-Dixon were generous in describing their jobs as social workers at UCSF's Community Focus/Community Forensics Clinic (Yes, it's the one in the book).

I was privileged to be able to screen Christie Herring's documentary work in progress, *The Campaign*, which yielded a treasure trove of details on the No on 8 campaign. Stuart Gaffney's recollections of his No on 8 campaign work were also hugely helpful.

My wife Jeanette and I spent a quite pleasant evening learning about Bakersfield with local LGBT activist Whitney Weddell. I'm sorry more of those details didn't make it into the final draft.

As always, I was supported in all ways by my spouse, Jeanette, and my sister, Karin. For this book especially, I'd like to thank my good friend Kent Bloom for always being there to listen to my angst-ridden monologues.

I am lucky to have two editors who helped make this book much much better than I could have on my own: Shelley Thrasher and Victoria Oldham. And my thanks to Radclyffe and everyone at BSB.

To Jeanette
There never will be any other

CHAPTER ONE

A woman stretched out a slim hand and drew Jules toward her. Their naked bodies touched and Jules gasped at the heat of contact. They kissed and fell into bed, not a sliver of space between their slick bodies.

Jules Marvin was jolted awake by the "William Tell Overture," the ringtone on her cell phone. Groaning, she groped for it, knowing it could only be one person: her mother. No one else had the nerve to ring her before nine thirty in the morning. A perk of her job as a dog walker was sleeping late, since she didn't need to begin picking up her charges until eleven or so, depending on who was on the schedule. Her mother's early-morning calls were yet another of her passive-aggressive methods of criticizing what she considered Jules's laziness and lack of a real job. Jules's mom thought she should be getting up at four in the morning like her workaholic sisters.

"Hi, Mom."

"Darling, I'm sorry to bother you so early, but I wanted to catch you before you went out."

"Mom, I have a cell phone so you can get hold of me anytime, even if you only call when you know I'm sleeping. And you don't seem to ever remember the time-zone difference."

"Julia, that isn't true." Jules's mother was prone to lying as well as using veiled criticism, and she never used Jules's nickname in spite of her many requests. Jules decided it wasn't worth fighting about.

"Whatever. Just tell me what's up." She liked to throw "whatever" into conversation to annoy her mother.

"Thalia is going to be out your way next month." Thalia, Jules's oldest sister, was an investment banker and marathon runner, and just being in the same room with her made Jules anxious.

"Why are you telling me this? Can't she call me herself?" Jules yawned, not bothering to hide her irritation. Her mother was always trying to get her together with Thalia, though they had nothing in common.

"I'm just helping. You know she's busy. I wanted to let you know."

"Is she going to want to stay with me?" Jules asked, already knowing the answer.

"No, dear, she'll stay in a hotel."

"Okay. What day?"

"Tuesday the fourth."

"Got it." Jules didn't bother writing it down because it was irrelevant. Thalia might text her to grab a drink, but more than likely, Jules wouldn't hear from her at all. That was the way it usually went, which was fine with her.

"That it, Mom?"

"Yes, Julia, dear, that is all. You should get to bed earlier, though, so you could get up earlier."

"Bye, Mom." She flipped her cell closed and snuggled back under the covers for another hour of sleep. With luck, she could pick up the dream where she'd left off.

❖

Jules stopped her Volvo on Castro Street near Nineteenth in front of the Edwardian house belonging to her third client, Elvis, the French bulldog. She thought of her dogs, not their owners, as the clients. She certainly spent more time with dogs than people, although she might share a quick hello and a bit of business chat with other dog walkers. With their funny and varied personalities, dogs were more relatable than people she knew. People came with problems, drama, and demands.

She bounded up the many steps to the front door. The house was set into the side of the hill that separated the Castro from Noe Valley and had been meticulously restored by its two male owners. Jules was used to seeing the fine houses of the owners of the dogs she walked. Her clients' families generally had to be well-off to afford full-time dog walkers. Jules didn't resent them for having money. In fact, she was grateful so many San Franciscans had dogs. It was, after all, the city of Saint Francis, the patron saint of animals, and it had the highest per-capita dog ownership of any large city. Only some of its fine houses had backyards, and even so, the conscientious dog owners still hired dog walkers. Jules performed a vital service. The dogs shouldn't be left to languish all day by themselves. Of course, the ones who lived in apartments had to be taken out, too. Hence, Jules and her colleagues were necessary and paid well for their services.

Jules opened the heavy oak door with its expensive beveled-glass window and bent down to pet Elvis. He was barking his little round head off, and the force of his barks made him look like he was bouncing straight up and down. Jules pulled his leash off the hook inside the door, snapped it on, and led him down the stairs.

She lifted him into the back of her Volvo and slid into the driver's seat to continue her rounds. She consulted her notebook to check the address for her next client, Barney, a mixed breed. His mom, Perla, was overseas and had left him in the care of a friend, someone named Sylvia, who lived not far from Perla. Jules had a soft spot for Barney, so she didn't charge Perla quite as much as she charged some other clients. Perla had a modest job and was a lesbian, so she deserved a break. Jules also admired her for adopting a mutt like Barney. He was a welcome change from the nervous, entitled purebreds she often took care of. Like Elvis, for instance.

Where did she want to go today? One of the many things Jules loved about San Francisco was its many city parks, as well as the Presidio spread over the northwest corner. She wasn't in the mood for chatter with the other dog walkers; she just wanted to be with the dogs, so she mentally mapped out the way to Sunset Heights Park. It was small and quiet, and she was unlikely to run into anyone other than a couple of moms with their kids in the tiny playground.

Jules had to pick up two more dogs after Barney to have her full complement for the day. She didn't like to have more than five at once, since the leashes became tangled and the dogs were harder to control. She also tended to concentrate on smaller and medium-sized breeds, since she didn't have much room in her Volvo station wagon, although its back area was good sized. She separated it from the front seat with a metal gate because some of the "kids," as she often thought of them, like Barney, wanted to climb into the front seat.

She tried to maintain a certain level of discipline with her group because it was good for them, and their owners were often uninterested in discipline and training. Jules required that the dogs be responsive to voice commands, and most of them were pretty good, but their other obedience skills could be sketchy. Jules didn't mind. She was fond of them all. It wasn't an intellectual job, but she spent most of her days outdoors, free from office drudgery. Her time was her own and she answered to no one, which suited her perfectly.

She reached the park around noon and started throwing balls for the ball chasers. Snips and Elvis ran around after each other. Jules decided to take a walk along the paths in the park with the group to give them plenty of space and time to run. A couple of them, Barney and Maggie, tended to not want to chase balls, so she needed to walk them to give them exercise. She decided to take the paths down around the southern end of the park, where she let them all off their leashes and draped the leashes around her neck, leaving her hands free.

"Ugh." Jules sighed, reminded of the one negative of her job. Maggie had a bout of diarrhea and Jules had to focus on her for a few minutes. When she finished cleaning up, she stood and looked around but couldn't see Barney. She started down to the dead end of the lowest part of the path, calling out to him, and heard a familiar yelp. She turned to the group. "Stay!" They all stopped and plopped their butts on the ground.

Barney was whining in the bushes to the right side of the cul-de-sac. She went toward the sound, and as she came to the end she saw it. A large skunk stood with his tail in air, his butt pointing right at Barney's face. The skunk twitched, and Barney yelped and backed away. The pungently bitter, intense smell of skunk juice reached Jules, and she gagged. She was too late. Barney had gotten a blast right in his face.

Crap.

❖

Sylvia Ramirez checked her calendar. William Noonan was due to come by in a half hour to discuss his job search with her. Sylvia, a clinical social worker, helped mentally ill people adjust to life once they were released from the hospital. San Francisco had three psychiatric inpatient wards: San Francisco General Hospital, Langley Porter Psychiatric Institute at UCSF Medical Center, and Saint Mary's Hospital. It offered, however, few places for follow-up care, so Sylvia and her coworkers at the Community Focus Clinic counseled the former psych patients and assisted them in assembling a life outside the psych wards.

William was a schizophrenic, but his disease was well controlled as long as he took his meds. He was actually a big flirt, and Sylvia enjoyed the verbal sparring with him as long as she didn't let it go too far. She smiled to herself because she liked William. Really, she liked most of her clients. Their resilience and courage greatly moved her, and she considered it an honor to assist them.

She pulled William's record from her meticulously maintained files. Keeping her work as well organized as possible was her nature, and she figured her clients needed her to help them structure their lives. She was neat and methodical in all parts of her life, though, not just at work. She loved routine. She'd agreed to care for her best friend Perla's dog, Barney, for six weeks purely out of love for Perla, not because she particularly liked dogs. She found, however, that she liked the routine of walking Barney. Walking was her favorite exercise, and she had, in the past few weeks, grown fond of his company. He gave her something in her life to focus on other than her clients.

She flipped open William's file and pushed a strand of hair away from her face, then glanced at the candy bar on the edge of her desk and tucked it in the drawer before she gave in to temptation. She had to fight a tendency to gain weight. Real women did have curves, but she didn't want to let her weight get away from her. With a deep sigh, she focused on the file.

❖

Jules quickly hauled Barney away from the skunk so she wouldn't get skunked as well. She mentally ran through the procedure for de-skunking. Grabbing the water bottle she carried on her belt, she lifted Barney's chin and sprayed water into his eyes to wash out the skunk oil. He whimpered and tried to back away from her, and she cursed her choice of Sunset Park. If she were anywhere else, she could have gotten one or more of a dozen other dog walkers to help her. Here she was on her own and she needed at least one more hand.

Jules held Barney's collar and drenched his face with water

again. His head whipped from side to side and, in his distress, he tried to bite her hand. She called all the dogs to her, snapped on their leashes, and sprinted back to where she'd parked her car. After she ordered them all into the back except Barney, she looped his leash around her wrist and rummaged in her glove box. There she grabbed her notebook and found the number for Sunset Animal Hospital, Perla's vet.

"I've got a dog who's been skunked. Barney Naguit." The vet routinely gave a pet the owner's last name, like the family members they truly were.

"In his eyes?" the vet tech asked.

"Yeah. He took a direct hit to the face, and I tried to rinse his eyes out with water."

"Good. You need to bring him in. We'll look at him."

"Right." Stress knotted her stomach. She didn't have a credit card, and vets required payment up front. *Oh, shit.* Perla was gone and she had someone named Sylvia looking after Barney.

Jules looked at her notebook again and found Sylvia's cellphone number. She keyed it in and prayed Sylvia would answer.

❖

Sylvia's cell phone rang, startling her since she'd been completely immersed in formulating a plan for a new client.

"Hello, this is Sylvia. Can I help you?" She spoke in a practiced customer-service voice.

"This is Jules Marvin." Sylvia didn't recognize the voice or the name, although the caller sounded as if she expected Sylvia to know who she was.

"I'm sorry. Who are you?"

"Jules Marvin, Barney's dog walker."

"Oh." Sylvia gripped the phone and her shoulders seized from anxiety. "Has something happened?"

"Yes. Look, can you meet me at Sunset Animal Hospital?"

"I'm at work. Downtown. What's happened to Barney?"

"He's not hurt. He's okay but he has to go to the vet. He's been skunked."

"What?" Sylvia was finding it difficult to redirect her focus.

"Skunked! He got sprayed by a skunk." The voice sounded impatient, which increased Sylvia's annoyance.

"Look, I need to get going. The vet promised to squeeze him in," Jules said. "Can you meet me at Sunset Animal Hospital on Eleventh Avenue?"

"Meet? Why? I thought you said he wasn't hurt."

"Not really. But they need to flush his eyes out, and I need to get stuff to clean him up."

"Then just go ahead and do it."

"I need you to meet me, you know, to pay them."

"I don't know if I can leave work, and I don't have a car." Sylvia finally comprehended the problem. The dog walker didn't have any money, or at least not any she wanted to spend. There was an awkward pause.

"Where's the vet?" Sylvia asked. It was Barney, after all, and Perla would want *her* to look after him, not the dog walker. Sylvia forced herself to adjust to this sudden turn of events.

"Sunset Animal at Eleventh and Lincoln. Near the park." Jules repeated herself, obviously still trying to hold her temper in check.

"I'll get the next bus and meet you there as soon as I can."

"Okay. Thanks. See you."

Sylvia asked her coworker in the next cube to look after her client, sent an e-mail to her supervisor, grabbed her coat and backpack, and practically sprinted the two blocks to Market Street.

Sylvia was able to get a Haight number 72 bus relatively easily and made it to Sunset Animal Hospital within twenty-five minutes. As she walked in the front door she could smell the skunk's odor. *Talk about chemical warfare*, she thought with grim amusement. She didn't see Barney in the waiting room, so she approached the desk, and the scrubs-clad girl looked up.

"I'm here for Barney—Perla Naguit's Barney."

"He's in exam room one, right around the corner. Go ahead in."

Sylvia opened the door and the smell nearly knocked her over. Barney would have literally jumped into her arms if a blonde in jeans and a hooded sweatshirt hadn't had a death grip on his leash.

"Barney! Down."

Barney obeyed immediately. Maybe his skunking had had an effect on him. He was looking up at her hopefully and she wanted to comfort him, but he reeked so badly, she really didn't want to touch him.

"What happened to you, you crazy dog?" She spoke to him gently and glared at the dog walker.

"How did you let this happen? I thought skunks only came out at night." She knew her tone was accusatory but she wasn't in the mood for diplomacy.

"I—" The door opened and the vet walked in.

"Hello. I'm Dr. Helms. I can tell from the stench what happened to Barney. And you two are?"

Jules and Sylvia looked confusedly at each other. Sylvia registered that Jules had eyes an amazing shade of blue that were focused on her with a worried expression.

Jules looked back at Dr. Helms. "I'm the dog walker."

"Ah," Dr. Helms said, and then turned to Sylvia. "And you?"

"I'm Perla's friend and I'm dog-sitting for Barney."

The vet raised her eyebrows. "I see. All right, let's take a look at him. Can I get one of you to lift him up on the table?" she asked sweetly. It was clear to Sylvia that Dr. Helms wasn't going to risk getting skunk juice on her clean purple scrubs if she could avoid it.

Sylvia and Jules again looked at each other.

"I'll do it," Jules said, and scooped Barney up and deposited him on the exam table.

Sylvia was impressed that Jules lifted him easily, since Barney weighed a good forty pounds. Barney was surprisingly cooperative while Dr. Helms checked him over. but he attempted to pull his head away as she shined her penlight into his eyes.

Dr. Helms snapped her light off and replaced it in her pocket, then scratched Barney behind his shoulder. "His eyes aren't too bad, not terribly irritated. That skunk juice is quite irritating to some dogs, but he seems to have weathered it well. We'll irrigate his eyes and I'll give you the recipe for the solution to get the stink off him. Please wait in the waiting room and we'll take care of him. Have a good day."

She left the room, and once again, Sylvia and Jules looked at each other. They didn't have a chance to say anything else before a young tech came in and put Barney on the floor.

"Don't worry, he'll be fine." She smiled first at Jules and then at Sylvia, apparently considering them a couple. Under other circumstances Sylvia might find the assumption funny, but the smell and the stress combined to make it irritating instead. As the tech led Barney away, she said to him, "Boy, you got a good snootful, didn't you? Poor guy. That'll teach you to go after skunks."

Jules and Sylvia went out to the lobby, where a woman with a cat inside a carrier looked at them with distaste. After a moment, Sylvia realized *they* must smell like skunk, too. They sat down on the uncomfortable wooden bench and experienced another beat of silence. Sylvia felt bad about her attitude and comments to Jules, but it didn't seem like a good place to talk, with the cat lady giving them the evil eye. The door opened and someone with a dog walked in, and cat lady was immediately occupied with soothing her kitty as best she could while he hissed inside his cat carrier.

Jules turned to Sylvia. "Look, I'm really sorry this happened.

I couldn't get to him in time. I had to deal with another dog. He'd gotten hit before I could get him away."

Sylvia was again looking into those remarkable blue eyes. Jules seemed genuinely contrite and Sylvia felt worse.

"I thought skunks were only out at night," she said, her tone even.

"Normally, yes. I guess this skunk didn't get the memo."

"I'm glad Perla's not here. She'd be crazy." Sylvia was unsure where to take the conversation.

"Yeah." They sat in silence for a few more minutes until Barney came bounding out, wagging his tail. He seemed quite pleased with himself, though he was still really smelly. The two people in the waiting room looked at each other and rolled their eyes. In the manner of strangers caught in a disaster, they had obviously bonded over their shared disgust at Barney's smell.

Jules stood up. "We'll wait outside for you."

Sylvia paid the outrageously large bill and got a sheet of detailed directions from the tech on how to de-skunk Barney.

Out on the sidewalk, Jules leaned against a telephone pole while Barney sniffed around the street debris. Sylvia registered that Jules was slightly taller than her, by an inch maybe, and that she was wearing old-fashioned, straight-legged Levi's 501s that fit her athletic body perfectly. She wore a stained down vest over her gray hooded sweatshirt, and with her short blond hair ruffled by the wind, she looked scruffy but wholesome.

"I can't take him back to the apartment as he is. Do you know where we can clean him up?"

"My house has a backyard. We can do it there," Jules said, quietly. "But I'm afraid we'll have to endure him in the car."

"I'll survive," Sylvia said.

"My car's over here. I still have all the dogs to drop off, but we can take you and Barney over to my house, and you can get started."

"That's fine, Jules. Oh, we have to get this stuff to clean him up. Can you take me to a store first?"

"Sure." Jules let Barney out of the car and strolled around the parking lot of the drugstore near her house while Sylvia shopped for the necessary components. As Sylvia exited the store, Jules was bending over to pet Barney, and when she neared, Jules looked up suddenly and grinned. Sylvia was a bit ashamed at how angry and unhelpful she'd been. Her mood lifted and she decided to apologize.

Back in the car, Sylvia swallowed. "Uh. Look. I'm sorry I lost my temper. It isn't your fault he got skunked."

"Well, thanks, but it kind of is since I was distracted."

"Must be hard to deal with more than one dog."

"It's usually okay, but today was one of those days." They fell silent again. The skunk smell was truly overwhelming in the confined space of the Volvo, even with all the windows open and the chilly March breeze blowing through.

A few minutes later, they pulled up in front of a big Victorian duplex. Jules parked in the driveway, and they went straight through the house to a back door that led into a spacious backyard.

They read the sheet from the vet together.

De-skunking solution—1 quart hydrogen peroxide, ¼ cup baking soda, 2 tablespoons Dawn dishwashing soap

Jules went into the garage and returned with a bucket.

"Could you go ahead in and make this up? Everything you need in the way of measuring tools is in the kitchen. I'll be back to help in about a half hour, I think. Hey, do you want a sweatshirt or something? You don't want to get your shirt dirty."

Sylvia was again struck by Jules's sensitivity but also embarrassed. "Um, sure, but I don't think you'd have anything to fit me." She flushed. Great, she'd just made it clear she'd checked Jules out.

Jules raised her eyebrows, obviously trying not to smile.

"I've got something that might work." She disappeared into the house and returned with a sweatshirt.

Sylvia shook it out. It was faded, oversized, and very soft. She put it on and grinned. "This'll work. Thanks."

❖

Jules delivered her dogs back to their homes, and the burst of adrenaline followed by crisis mode left her exhausted. She rushed through her rounds and got back to her house as quickly as possible, feeling guilty about leaving Sylvia to deal with the smelly dog on her own. The dog was, technically, still Jules's responsibility. And there was no denying Sylvia looked terrific in that sweatshirt. It slid over those perfect curves just right. Jules practically ran back to her car after dropping off the last dog, eager to get back.

When she walked into the backyard, Sylvia stood by a very wet Barney wearing rubber dishwashing gloves, her hair tied back but not staying in place, with wisps stuck to her cheeks. Her nicely tailored gray pinstriped trousers were spotted with water, and her face was a little flushed. The slight pinkness under Sylvia's caramel complexion was especially alluring. Jules took a breath. It felt odd to see this stranger in her backyard, garden hose in hand. *Attractive stranger. In Mira's old sweatshirt.*

"Hey. How's it going?" Jules said, attempting to cover up her inexplicable discomfort.

"Not bad, but I need help. Barney's not enjoying this."

As Sylvia turned around and walked back toward the kitchen, Jules watched her shapely rear end in the fitted wool trousers and gulped at a sudden spike of arousal.

"We're ready for the second treatment," Sylvia said. "If you'll hold on to him, I'll pour it over him and work it into his fur."

She was busily mixing the de-skunking solution in the sink, and Jules was charmed, and a bit unnerved, that Sylvia looked so normal standing in her kitchen as though it were her own. She'd even found the dishwashing gloves. "Sure."

They went back outside and Jules took hold of Barney's collar once again, but he only struggled a little.

Sylvia poured the skunk solution over his head, expertly shielding his eyes and focusing on Barney as though there was nothing else in the world. She gazed sweetly at damp, bedraggled Barney, and Jules's heart turned over. Considering how irritated Sylvia had seemed at the beginning of their acquaintance, she'd clearly gotten over it. Women who loved animals were irresistible.

They poured more solution on Barney and worked it into his fur.

Sylvia read from the directions. "It says to wait ten minutes. Do you have some old towels so we can dry him off?"

"Yeah, be right back."

Sylvia nodded.

Barney was shivering so Jules hurried, and after she returned, together they toweled Barney down vigorously. Everywhere their hands and arms brushed, Jules tingled.

Sylvia leaned close to smell Barney's head, then looked at Jules. "Still there, but much better."

"I'm so glad. Well. Shall I take you two home? It's getting late."

"That would be wonderful." Sylvia stripped off the gloves and dried her hands, then removed the band from her hair, shook it out, and ran her hands through it. Jules couldn't tear her gaze away from Sylvia. She'd seen that gesture before but never done so gracefully. Sylvia turned and seemed confused. Jules glanced away, embarrassed to be caught staring. Sylvia pulled the sweatshirt over her head, and Jules shivered as she got a brief look at Sylvia's smooth midriff before she tugged her shirt back down.

"I'm ready to go," Sylvia said quietly, putting her coat on and snapping on Barney's leash.

"Right. Sure." Jules dropped the sweatshirt on her kitchen chair and turned away.

They drove to Bartlett Street in almost complete silence. Inside Jules's beat-up Volvo, the smell of skunk still hung about the air, and in the silence, they could hear Barney panting in the back. "This is it," Sylvia said. "The building with the tree in front. Oh, but you know that." Jules nodded. "Well. It's been interesting," Sylvia said, almost to herself.

"I wouldn't describe it as interesting. Stressful. Dramatic, maybe. Thanks for coming to the vet to help."

"No problem. I'm glad you knew what to do. I wouldn't have."

"You'd have thought of it."

"Maybe. Again, I really am sorry about how I acted at the beginning. I'm glad you were there."

"Apology accepted. Really. You don't have to apologize anymore. Anyone would have reacted badly to suddenly getting a call like that at work." Jules was rewarded when Sylvia's beautiful dark eyes showed gratitude.

They sat in the car for a moment longer, the awkward feeling intensifying by the second.

"Well, Barney buddy, let's go get dinner. Thanks, Jules. See you."

Jules noted the breezy tone and felt unaccountably sad. *Well, that's that, I guess.* "Bye, take care. Bye, Barney boy. See you next week." Sylvia got Barney out of the car and disappeared into the house.

CHAPTER TWO

When her phone rang late Sunday morning, Sylvia looked at the number but couldn't place it. She instantly recognized the voice, though.

"Hi, this is Jules Marvin." It was the same as it was in the dream she'd just woken from—smooth, laconic, and soothing.

"Hello, Jules. This is a surprise." Sylvia tightened her grip on her phone and her heart rate increased a couple notches.

"I was wondering, how's Barney?"

Jules sounded rather too casual to Sylvia, like she was nervous or uncertain. "He's good, really, he's fine. How are you?"

"Oh, good, good. You?"

This has got to be the world's most inane conversation. "Me? Oh, I'm good." There was a pause. "So can I ask you a question about Barney?" Sylvia scrunched her face, thinking she sounded silly.

"Sure. What's up?"

"I was wondering, well. Barney pulls on the leash a lot when we walk, and I wondered if he does that with you?"

"Yeah, a little. I don't think Perla has ever leash trained him properly."

Hearing this made Sylvia feel defensive on Perla's behalf, though Jules had not spoken unkindly. "I don't think she knows what to do." Sylvia's tone was harsher than she meant it to be and she winced.

Jules seemed unconcerned, though, because all she said was, "I could show you and then you could show her."

"Oh. I…Okay. I guess. If it's no trouble."

"It's no bother, believe me. I'd be happy to do it."

Sylvia hesitated, unsure if she should accept Jules's offer. She wanted to see her again and that scared her.

"We could even start today," Jules said. "We can go to Crissy Field for a walk. It'll be nice. Good weather."

Sylvia found her enthusiasm endearing. *I certainly have nothing better to do.* "Sounds great."

"I'll pick you up in an hour. Wear something warm. It might be a little windy."

"I will. Thanks." Sylvia realized she was feeling something she hadn't felt in a long time: anticipation. She looked at Barney. "We're going out with your friend Jules. How about that?" He, naturally, wagged his tail and panted, maybe at the sound of happiness in her voice.

❖

After parking, they started down the path that stretched between the salt marsh on the left and the bay on the right. In the distance, the Golden Gate Bridge's international orange towers loomed, wisps of fog around their summits. Sylvia looked around with interest as they ambled along with dozens of dog walkers, kids, runners, and bicyclists. She knew vaguely about the Presidio. She had only seen Crissy Field from the bridge and it hadn't really registered in her consciousness. Jules had Barney in hand and was telling Sylvia, "When he pulls, you need to stop. Just stop. Don't pull backward on him. When the leash goes slack, start again." She demonstrated. Barney looked back at her accusingly when he couldn't move forward. Sylvia snickered at his apparent dismay. They started forward again. He lunged, trying to go as fast as possible, but imperturbably, Jules stopped dead and waited. This went on for a full five minutes.

"He's got no idea what to think, does he?" Sylvia asked.

"Nope, not a clue. But watch, he'll get it pretty soon."

Jules was right. Barney's pulling gradually diminished and he didn't glance backward any longer. Jules's patience had worn him down.

"Here, you try." Jules handed Sylvia the leash and they continued walking. Barney immediately reverted to his old ways and took off. Sylvia glanced at Jules, who nodded and they stopped. Barney walked sideways.

"Wait," Jules said, gently. Sylvia didn't move until Barney was still. They resumed the stutter-stop movement, but it took less time for Barney to fall into the proper gait.

"He gets it. He understands he has to match our pace or we won't go anywhere."

"Wow. You're right. He's much better." Sylvia glanced at Jules, grateful and impressed. "I can get Perla to practice with him."

"Yep. You'll need to keep it up. He'll still want to go back to his usual MO, but if you reinforce it consistently, it'll become a habit for him."

"How come you haven't taught him this already?"

"I've worked with him a little, but I have less time to work with individual dogs. With my other dogs, I have my hands full."

Jules sounded uncomfortable, prompting Sylvia to ask, "So why did you decide to help me train him?"

"I wanted to see you again."

"I see." Sylvia kept her voice impersonal. Truthfully she had no real reason to object. It was flattering for sure, and there was nothing wrong with Jules being interested. But there was everything wrong with encouraging her if they had no chance of actually being together. Sylvia tended to go on a date and then find a reason not to go further. It had something to do with her need to protect herself after the misery of Elena.

They walked in a somewhat uncomfortable silence for

another moment. Sylvia turned and looked Jules directly in the eye. "I'm glad you called and I'm happy to see you again. This"—she gestured, taking in the view, the bay, the other people—"is wonderful. Thank you for bringing me out here and for teaching me how to walk Barney." She was gratified when Jules's glacier-blue eyes lit up. They matched the blue of the San Francisco Bay and the sky, and she looked lovely. Her teeth were white and nearly perfect, but one was slightly crooked. Sylvia was absurdly glad about that. Otherwise they might be too perfect. Elena's teeth had also been dazzling white and perfectly even. She berated herself for thinking of Elena again.

"This is one of my favorite spots for dog walking. But it's a national park and the park police aren't really tolerant of dog walkers. They ticket us for having the dogs off leash. That's only allowed up on the grass." Jules gestured toward the grassy expanse to their left where dozens of dogs ran free, chasing balls and Frisbees.

"Would you like something to drink?" Jules asked as they passed a café opposite the fishing pier.

"Not right now, maybe on the way back." Sylvia wanted to avoid an awkward moment of who would pay for their drinks. "Look."

Jules followed her finger toward the bridge, where a huge container ship was coming in. It was too early in the season for many sailboats, but they could see the Red and White Ferry boat heading for the Golden Gate. They stopped to look and Sylvia took in the whole scene: the water, the locals with their dogs, the tourists snapping pictures of one another with the bridge as backdrop, and the people fishing. She felt a moment of uncomplicated happiness, something she hadn't experienced in a long time. Did being with Jules in this magnificent setting have something to do with it?

"So what is it you do for a living?" Jules asked. "Sorry if you said already. I forgot."

"No worries, I don't believe I've told you. I'm a social worker. I work for UCSF, well, sort of for the city. It's complicated. It's a city clinic but UCSF staffs it."

"What kind of clinic?"

"For people with mental illness. It's downtown on Mission Street."

"Holy crap! What do you do?"

"I counsel them, I get them reintegrated into society, reunited with their families, housing, a job, whatever they need."

"Wow. And they're mentally ill? Are they difficult?"

"If they take their drugs as prescribed, they're pretty normal." Sylvia stopped talking and glanced at Jules, glad to find she looked inquisitive rather than repulsed. "It's just that if someone has a psychotic break in their twenties and ends up in the hospital, it can take years to get them to a place where they can be released. Once they get out, they lack the basic social skills we all learn, so I help them."

"That's amazing. I'm really impressed you have the patience to do that. It must be discouraging."

"Sometimes, but not always. I like it. I like making a difference. Someone has to care about these people. Not many people do." Sylvia laughed at Jules's expression. "I'm not some kind of saint, though."

"I wouldn't imagine you are," Jules said softly, scrutinizing her.

Sylvia shivered at the look in Jules's eyes. Hunger and something else, something deeper and softer. She picked up a stone and rolled it in her hand, trying to focus on something other than the long-dormant feelings Jules was stirring up. "Have you always been a dog walker?"

"Nope. I've had a lot of different jobs. I just kind of fell into this. I started taking care of my friends' pets when they went away, and one thing led to another..." Jules shrugged, seemingly uninterested in going into more detail.

"Are you from here or elsewhere? Where did you go to school?"

"I'm from New Jersey. I went to a small liberal-arts college back there—Simmons. I have a degree in psychology. I came out here for vacation in 2000 and basically never left."

"Psychology? Really?"

"Yep. What about you?"

"I'm from the San Joaquin Valley, Bakersfield. I couldn't wait to get out so I escaped to go to school at SF State. My brother still lives there. My grandparents brought my parents here from Mexico in the early sixties to work on the fields."

"They were migrant workers?" Jules asked.

"Uh-huh. My grandparents were illiterate. They never learned to read or speak English but made sure my parents did. My parents in turn saw both of their children go to college. My brother works as a manager for Home Depot."

"That's great. They must be very proud."

"They're dead," Sylvia stated flatly. "Car accident. Their car collided with a truck on the interstate late one night when I was in college."

"Gosh. I'm sorry to hear that. That's awful."

"It was, but it happened a long time ago, so I'm sort of over it. I still miss them, though."

"Were they okay with you and the gay thing?" Jules asked.

"Sort of. The whole family, Grandma, Grandpa, they all were followers of Cesar Chavez, so they were kind of liberal because of his example. When I came out, they had a bit of a hard time because of the Catholic Church, but they came around."

Jules drove Sylvia and Barney home through the Haight Ashbury and then the Castro and pointed out the homes of her clients along the way, making Sylvia laugh at her descriptions of the dogs and their owners.

When they stopped in front of Sylvia's building, Jules took a breath. "Would you like to have dinner with me sometime?"

In spite of her sudden panic, Sylvia nodded. "Yes. Thanks, I would. Can I get back to you on when?"

"Sure. That's fine, Have a good evening."

"Thanks. You, too, and thanks for the obedience lesson."

❖

Later, Jules sat in her favorite chair, sipping a cup of green tea and replaying the walk with Sylvia. The outing had been successful on one level, two if she counted beginning Barney on the path to learning to heel properly. She and Sylvia connected well as friends, which was gratifying. *Now, don't get all excited. Then you'll have to get all deflated when you find out she's not interested in you or has a girlfriend or something. And I don't want anything serious anyway. But I don't think she has a girlfriend. If she had one, she wouldn't be alone on a Sunday, would she? Of course she could be. The girlfriend could be anywhere today.*

Jules shook her head. She had no business wanting to date the likes of Sylvia. It never worked when she tried to meet people casually. Once they found out the truth about her they shut down and backed off so quickly it made Jules's head spin. It really only worked if she met women who ran in the same social circles as she did.

Besides, as far as Jules could see, Sylvia's response to her indicated nothing beyond friendship. That was too bad, but in the end, Jules thought, it was probably just as well. Most women she met came with too many relationship issues, and Jules hated the complications. Something about Sylvia drew her attention, though. She didn't know what it was exactly, but against her better judgment, she wanted to find out. Hopefully Sylvia would call her back soon.

❖

Sylvia grabbed a soda out the fridge and settled herself in the armchair in the living room. She preferred when possible to use the computer comfortably; she owned a desk but kept it as a sort of giant filing cabinet. She had to use a desk at work. Work was work and home was home, and Sylvia didn't believe in mixing the two. She occasionally took emergency calls at home because that was part of the job; otherwise she didn't bring her work home.

She opened her Skype program and found Perla's name, then waited happily as the phone rang. Perla's light and cheerful voice sounded as though she was just across town rather than across several thousand miles of ocean. It was early evening in San Francisco but midmorning of the next day in the Philippines.

"Hello, sweetie. How are you doing?" Sylvia asked.

"Hey. I'm doing fine except Mama is making me crazy and it's only been three weeks."

Sylvia laughed but she knew it must be hard on Perla, who didn't get along very well with her neurotic mom. "What's going on?"

"She's moaning about being over the hill after her hysterectomy because she can't have babies anymore. She's fifty-five already!"

Sylvia laughed again but then turned serious. "Really, Perls, how are you holding up?"

"I should be used to it and just tune her out, but it's hard. Let's change the subject. How's my boy?"

"Good. We had a little problem last week, but he's fine."

"What happened? Is he hurt? My God! Tell me what happened."

"Take it easy, he's fine, really. He just got skunked and Jules had—"

"What? What do you mean, 'skunked'?"

"Jules called me at work. I didn't understand what it meant at first either. It means he got sprayed by a skunk." Sylvia told Perla the whole story.

"So Jules took us to her house and we got the stuff to clean him up. Then she drove us home. He smelled horrible. I don't think I've ever in my life smelled anything quite like that. Even the San Joaquin Valley farms don't smell that bad." Sylvia wrinkled her nose at the memory. "Jules was wonderful. I probably wasn't very nice to her at first because I was scared and her phone call came out of the blue, but I apologized and she was cool."

"Well, good. Is he still going to be stinky when I get home?"

"I doubt it, Perls. You can barely tell now and you still have another two weeks, right?"

"Something like that. It's okay as long as he's okay."

"And he is, thanks to Jules mostly, but I helped."

Perla laughed. "Jules is nice and she gives me a good price for her services. She seems like a great person. She's very good to the dogs, very professional. You know, I don't know why I didn't think of this before. I think she's single."

"Hmm. She asked me out on a date."

"No kidding! Are you going?"

"I said yes but we didn't set a time. I'm not sure I want to now. I do and I don't, you know?"

Perla's tone turned serious. "I don't want to nag you, sweetheart, but really, you need to get out more, meet more people. It would be great for you to get to know Jules, whether you date her or not. But what's wrong with dating her? Not everyone's going to turn out like the Princess of Darkness."

Perla had made up that name for Sylvia's ex, Elena, for whom she had no love. It normally made Sylvia snicker but now it didn't. Sylvia wasn't in the mood for another lecture about how she should get out and date. She'd tried and it hadn't worked. The moment things started to get a teeny bit serious, she wanted to run in the other direction. Her therapist friends at work told her it was akin to post-traumatic stress. She knew intellectually what Perla said was true, but her gut said, *No, not now. Maybe not ever...* She reluctantly acknowledged she was interested in Jules—as a friend. That was probably all. She flashed on the image of Jules at Crissy Field, holding on to Barney's leash, her short blond hair windblown.

"Okay. I won't nag or tease you about it anymore. I know when you're not listening to me, even on the phone."

"Thanks, Perls. I'll consider it. I really will." They chatted a while longer and then said good-bye. Sylvia closed her laptop and made herself carne asada and a salad, which she ate while she watched a movie. When had she become such an antisocial loner? She was friendly to the people she worked with. She had her volunteer work with Marriage Equality California, and she had Perla. But that was it.

It hadn't always been that way, though. Once upon a time, she had been intoxicated with San Francisco and freedom and social possibilities. She and her grad-school friends spent their weekends and their meager disposable incomes looking for a good time in the gay clubs and bars, and they usually found it. That was how she had met Elena. But that had fallen apart and the experience had made Sylvia reluctant to open herself up to a relationship. She feared the recurrence of that enormous pain and sense of futility.

CHAPTER THREE

By Friday, Jules still hadn't heard from Sylvia, and she was anxious and wondering whether to call her. As she was dropping her dogs off after their Friday walk, her phone chirped. She snickered at the text message: *din 7pm*. Claire never ever left anything to chance. Jules had enjoyed a standing date with the Bernstein-Nakamuras every Friday for the last two years. Most people would say "let us know if you can't make it," but not Claire Nakamura. She was an architect whose attention to detail was breathtaking, and her lover, Toni, often teased her about it.

Jules finished delivering her dogs and went home to clean up. She hummed to herself in the shower. Fridays with Claire and Toni put her in a good mood.

They lived in a work/live loft in a nondescript part of the South of Market district. It was severely modern with an open floor plan, poured-concrete floors, and exposed beams. Jules pressed the bell and the door buzzed open. Toni greeted her with a nice kiss and hug, and as she stepped back, Jules touched Toni's cheek. Toni had dark curly brown hair and a somewhat mournful expression when her face was at rest. She was a bit under the thumb of her controlling lover, which made Jules feel tender toward her.

"Smells great. What're we having?"

"Indian." Toni wrinkled her nose. She dutifully went along

with Claire's vegetarian diet but tended to be passive-aggressive about her displeasure.

"Jules! Hello!" Standing in their loft, Jules could see Claire in the kitchen. From there, you could see everything from everywhere. There were two floors; the sleeping area was upstairs but featured a balcony overlooking the downstairs living area.

"Hey, Claire." Jules grinned at Claire in her immaculate apron. The kitchen was so clean it would appear to the untrained eye that no cooking whatsoever was going on. Toni took Jules by the hand and led her over to the couch. They sat down close together and Toni gazed into Jules's eyes with her head cocked.

"You're looking good." Toni flicked a few strands of Jules's hair away from her face.

"Feeling good, too. How are you?" Jules looked seductively at Toni, thinking how sweet and pretty she was.

"Oh, fine. It's the same. The kids are either awful or needy or both. The parents are demanding. We just get no support from admin." Toni taught middle school for the SF Unified School District. "What was your week like? Are the doggies behaving?" She chuckled and Jules laughed with her, but before she could answer, Claire appeared in front of them, spoon in hand and with a tense expression. Jules loved Claire as much as she loved Toni, but Claire could suck all the oxygen out of a room in a nanosecond with her intensity.

"Toni. I need your help. Now." Toni slid off the couch and followed her lover to the kitchen with an amused backward glance at Jules. Jules leaned back on the couch, blew out a breath, and looked at the ceiling. Then she got up and went to put some music on. She chose modern jazz, knowing that would most likely be acceptable to Claire. She could hear their low voices in the kitchen.

She sat back down and, sure enough, in a moment, their cat Chloe sauntered out from wherever she'd been hiding, looked up at Jules, and mewed loudly. She was a lilac-point Siamese. Jules greeted her. "Hi, beautiful." Chloe was a purebred with papers listing her distinguished lineage and giving her some impossibly long and ostentatious name.

She had been Claire's choice: Claire wanted a show cat but couldn't be bothered with showing her, even though Chloe's regal attitude would have stood her well in the show ring. She was slender and slinky and had the demanding personality of the Siamese breed. Jules looked into Chloe's enormous round blue eyes and asked her, "How's it going?" For a response, Chloe paced back and forth over Jules's lap and head-butted her hand as Jules petted her. Her breeding was so severe she looked like an ancient Egyptian statue of the cat goddess Bast.

Jules had met Claire and Toni because of Chloe. Her business card was on their vet's bulletin board, and two years previously, they had called her for pet-sitting. One thank-you dinner was followed by a couple more, and then one evening when they all were drinking a bit more than usual, things had changed. As she stroked Chloe's slender furry body and Chloe purred and kneaded her thigh, she thought back to the night they'd made their proposal.

"Have another?" Claire asked as she held up the bottle of zinfandel.

"Sure, why not?" Jules was feeling no pain; she wasn't much of a drinker. For some reason, tension hung thick in the air, something that hadn't happened in the few times they had hung out before. They'd kept the wine flowing through dinner, and now they were all sitting on the sofa. Jules was between Claire and Toni, and she realized they were both sitting rather close to her. It wasn't unpleasant in the least, but something was going on. They were all giggling over nothing in particular.

"So, Jules," Claire asked. "Do you have a girlfriend?"

"No. Not at the moment. I was seeing someone a couple months ago but it didn't work out."

"So you don't have much sex?" Claire asked.

Jules thought it was an odd question but she answered truthfully. "No. I guess not, not really. I've only had a few girlfriends. I don't sleep around, if that's what you mean." She saw a look pass between Toni and Claire that signaled some sort of nonverbal agreement.

After a big pause, Toni said, "We were wondering, Claire and I, if you might be open to playing with us?"

"Playing?" Jules was feeling a bit fuzzy and all she could think they meant by "playing" was card games, which she loathed.

"Mmm-hmm." Claire was smiling into her eyes and reached up to stroke her hair. "You have the prettiest blond hair." Jules's stomach flipped over. She's coming on to me. What? She turned to her other side to look at Toni. Toni was also smiling and nodding slowly.

"Playing?" Jules asked again, and looked down when she felt a hand on her leg. It was Toni's.

"Yes," Claire said, softly, continuing to play with Jules's hair. "We'd like for you to spend the night with us. We like to share sex with other women. We like you. You're very cute, very sexy." Jules turned and Toni kissed her, and they both kept their hands on her. Jules didn't even think about it. She simply kissed Toni back. They were both stunning women. Claire was sleek and dark with sharp Japanese features, and Toni had large brown eyes and a peaches-and-cream complexion. Jules was astonished and quite flattered.

"I've never done anything like this, but sure, all right." The three of them stood and they led her to the sleeping loft. As they climbed the stairs, Jules focused on Toni's beautiful ass and wondered how it would feel to touch her. Claire and Toni slowly took off Jules's clothes, kissing and fondling her as they did so. It was dreamy. Everyone's actions seemed to be in slow motion. Once they had all gotten undressed and into bed, Claire said, "Just one last thing, Jules, and this isn't to offend you, but just for now, there's no oral sex." In a cloud of lust, Jules just nodded *and murmured, "Sure. No problem." She sank back into the pillows and reveled in their touches. Even with her eyes closed, she knew which one was kissing her. Claire's kisses were harder, more intense, and Toni's were more sweet and sensual. She felt like an observer of the scene as well as participant. She stopped thinking at all as Claire pushed her legs apart and entered her with first one, then two fingers. Toni kissed her neck and sucked her nipples as she rubbed her crotch against Jules's leg, leaving evidence of her arousal on Jules's thigh. Jules came quickly, but they didn't stop until she came again. She nuzzled Claire's neck, inhaling her slightly nutty smell. When she tried to sit up, Claire pushed her back down again gently. Jules relaxed and let whatever happened, happen. She let Claire guide her to making love to Toni while she watched, alternately touching Jules and Toni. Throughout the night, they took turns pleasing one another, pleasure cresting over and over again, their cries of satisfaction echoing through the room.*

The next morning, they got up and fixed breakfast and sat around drinking coffee and eating eggs and toast like they'd done it together forever. It was a sunny June day and the huge windows of their loft let the light pour in. Jules had no clue about the etiquette of a situation like this. She'd been in a few different beds and had to try to make conversation over breakfast after sex, often with disappointing results, but this was unique. Claire took charge much as she had in bed the night before.

"So you're probably wondering what this is and what's going to happen next." She neatly buttered a piece of toast.

"Um. Yes." Jules sipped orange juice and looked from Toni to Claire and back again. Toni was sitting back, drinking her coffee and looking completely relaxed.

"We practice polyamory. Have you heard of it?"

"Not exactly. Is it like swinging? Isn't that from the sixties or something?"

Claire laughed. "That's when it started and it's probably still going on, but this is different. We"—she nodded at Toni—"like to invite another lover into our relationship. We asked for no oral sex last night because we're a little cautious before we actually exchange body fluids. So we want to tell you a little about us and find out a little more about you. We like you very much and think you're beautiful, so…"

"I'm flattered." Jules was taken aback but not anxious. She liked both Toni and Claire and had certainly enjoyed sex with them. They were both attractive, and Jules found three-way sex remarkably arousing, with all those hands and lips everywhere. She looked from one to the other, thinking how they'd felt. She swallowed because the conversation was making her aroused again and it made it hard to think.

Claire continued. "We only have one lover at time, always a woman. We have no sexually transmitted diseases. How is your health?"

"Fine. I haven't gotten around enough to catch anything, I guess." Jules laughed.

"That's good because we'd like to have oral. But it's important for you to get tested, just so we're all safe."

Jules was both charmed and taken aback by the forthright but simple conversation. "Do you always spell things out so specifically?"

Claire let Toni take that question. Toni's serious, expressive brown eyes darkened somewhat and she looked sexy. Jules started to get hot looking at her and thinking about their lovemaking. The night before she'd been more passive than Claire and her manner was softer than Claire's clipped, straightforward personality. The combination was wonderful.

"Well. In polyamory, in order for everyone to be clear and get their needs met, we need to discuss things openly."

"We don't mind if you see other women. We just want you as part of our lives. We would want you to be attentive to health and safe-sex practices, though, if you're sleeping with someone else. We don't want to catch anything if the three of us are going to be together and fluid bonded."

"Polyamorous. Fluid bonded." Jules repeated the words thoughtfully. "So, what about jealousy? What if one of you gets more fond of me than the other, or what about my other girlfriends? Just hypothetically." She was envisioning some tense scenes and arguments, since it seemed too easy the way they described it.

"Well," Claire said, "it's not that jealousy isn't possible. It is, of course, but we have to talk about it. We basically have to do a lot of processing to make sure everyone is okay, so we need to all be honest with each other. In polyamory, we try to focus on making our lovers happy. It means that you're happy to see your lover experience love and pleasure with someone else. It's the opposite of jealousy. Last night, when you were making love to Toni, I felt happy for her. I wasn't mad. I enjoyed watching and helping. Watching my lover get off gets me off, too, so it works for both of us."

Jules looked from Claire to Toni and back again. They waited to see how she would respond.

"Okay. I'm in." They all clinked their coffee cups together and laughed. Toni came around the table and kissed Jules passionately. They kissed for a while with Claire watching. When Jules moved to include Claire, Toni whispered, "Let's go back to bed." Jules ended up staying with them until Sunday.

❖

As the three sat down to dinner, Claire squeezed Jules's shoulder and brought her back to the moment.

"So what are we having?" Jules asked.

"Lentil sambar," Claire replied. "It's a little like a masala." When Claire smiled, she softened so much she looked like a different person. It transformed her angular dusky features. Jules admired her looks and often thought she was as clean and precise as the lines of the buildings she designed. A timer went off on their stove.

"Tone, get the bread, please," Claire said. Toni leaped up from her chair without a word and went to the kitchen.

"Is this a new recipe?" Jules asked. She could see Claire glancing toward the kitchen and wanted to try to distract her so Toni could accomplish the task Claire had set her.

"Yep. I had something like it at Greens the other week for lunch." Claire referred to the most famous vegetarian restaurant in San Francisco. "Let's start. Toni will be back in a sec. I don't want this to get cold."

"It'll be fine," Jules said, not picking up her fork. Whenever possible, she tried to deflect Claire's perpetual impatience with Toni. "What kind of week did you have?"

"I've got another new project. If I was paid by the project, I'd be wealthy. It's a little hectic for me already. Sanders should have gotten this one, but he's such a fuck-up." Claire was coldly judgmental about her peers at the firm she worked for. Toni always said it was because she was the best they had and everybody knew it.

"You'll do fine," Jules said sincerely. She was awed by Claire's focus and ambition, both of which she lacked.

Toni came back to the table and they picked up slices of warm flatbread to go with their sambar. Jules listened to the two talk about their work for a while, and she shared some stories about her canine clients.

After they finished dinner, Jules and Toni, by custom, cleaned up while Claire relaxed with one more glass of wine in the living room, listening to music before the three of them went upstairs to the bedroom. Claire methodically lit candles, dimmed the light to its lowest setting, retrieved a few items from their toy drawer, and turned down the bed. Jules was deeply enamored of their bed, a Duxiana, made of some frightfully expensive Swedish steel, and it was enormous. Claire chose all the linen, which was in muted tones and exquisitely soft, as were the mattress covers.

Claire and Toni sat on the bed and watched Jules slowly take off her clothes. Their slight smiles and lowered eyelids gave away their emotions. Jules drew it out as long as she could until she was fully nude, and then she walked over to the bed and crawled between them. In the midst of them removing their own clothes, they kissed and fondled Jules. She lay back on the pillows and accepted their attention. The sensation of two sets of hands and lips was surreal, and it had taken some getting used to at first. Jules loved it now and loved being the focus of two attentive lovers who took their time. She kept her eyes closed, still able to guess who was touching her without having to look. Claire was kissing her face and neck and throat, and Toni was stroking her thighs and abdomen and gently passing over her pubic hair.

After two years in the relationship, she became aroused in no time at all by her dual lovers. In just a few minutes, she was silently praying for one of them to kick their lovemaking up a notch in intensity. She opened her eyes slightly as she felt the hand on her thigh replaced by lips. Toni slid between her legs and pressed them gently apart to go down on her. Claire embraced her and kissed her passionately. Jules had to close her eyes again as her arousal increased exponentially Toni was wonderful at oral sex. She had the right pressure, the right speed, and her little grunts of pleasure pleasantly filled Jules's ears Her tongue was alternately light and quick and then firm and slow. The muscles in Jules's legs tensed and her orgasm began to build.

"Uh-uh." Jules gasped involuntarily as the first orgasmic contractions started. She arched her back and came suddenly. Toni hung on until Jules could no longer tolerate the touch, and then she joined Claire at the head of the bed and they both embraced Jules as Toni kissed Claire to allow her to share the intimacy. After a few moments of rest, Toni and Jules turned their attention to Claire. Jules went down on Claire, and, as always, she enjoyed Claire's musky scent and sensuous writhing. It was the only time she seemed to let go of her need to control, and Toni often did little more than watch them and lightly caress her partner's breasts. She always said her favorite part was watching Jules give Claire so much pleasure.

Claire's body jerked, and she held the back of Jules's head as her orgasm washed through her. Jules held her tight, sucking her clit until she slumped back onto the bed. While she recovered, Jules turned and made love to Toni. Claire loved to have Jules fuck Toni with their modestly sized dildo, and Claire helped, playing with Toni's nipples and clit. Toni cried out as Claire pulled roughly on her nipples while Jules thrust into her, using her grip on Toni's hips to pull her down hard on the dildo. Toni's face, in the throes of ecstasy, morphed into Sylvia's. As Jules fell asleep, exhausted, the image of Sylvia lingered in her mind.

The next morning, they slept in and then made breakfast. Jules often wondered what the reactions of most people would be to a triadic relationship such as theirs. After her first sense of wonder at participating in something out of the mainstream, Jules now considered it ordinary. They prepared breakfast together as usual and sat down at Toni and Claire's dining-room table.

"I saw Sylvia last Sunday."

Claire swallowed the mouthful of food before speaking. "The one with the dog who got skunked?"

Jules had told them the story the Friday before. "Uh-huh. That one." Toni was looking at her expectantly, but Claire appeared indifferent.

Jules continued, unreasonably nervous about sharing what she was feeling. "We went out to Crissy Field and walked the promenade with Barney and taught him to heel." She knew what was coming next.

"So you think you like her?" Toni asked, her tone deliberately unconcerned. Even though they had an agreement, Toni sometimes got a little jealous of the women Jules dated though she sought to hide it and be positive in line with the philosophy of polyamory.

"I think so." Jules twisted her coffee cup around in her hands.

There was a beat of silence. Claire took another bite, another gulp of coffee, then dabbed her mouth delicately. Out of habit, Toni and Jules both waited for what she would say.

"It's up to you, but you know what happens," Claire said.

"It might be different this time." Jules realized she hoped it was true. Maybe dating Sylvia could be different somehow. Verbalizing her feelings to Claire and Toni made them more real. Their acceptance of Jules's other girlfriends had become so naturally a part of their relationship that Jules never hesitated to tell them about women she was interested in. Polyamory's emphasis on honesty was very helpful in that regard.

"Jules, darling, you've tried this. Once a non-poly finds out what you're into, she tends to run in the other direction." In the two years since Jules had taken up polyamory, she'd found out the hard way that it was far easier to date other polyamorists. She'd come to enjoy the easy sexual connection they could share. It was, as Claire and Toni explained to her, relatively free of jealousy. It all worked well until Jules had tried to date a monogamist. She was still inexperienced and had delayed explaining her polyamory lifestyle to the girl until after they made love, with painful results.

"I know that." Jules worked to keep her tone from being defensive, but it was hard. She was intellectually ready to hear what she knew Claire would say, but emotionally, it was another story. She drained her coffee and set the cup down a little harder than she meant to. Claire raised her eyebrows. Toni just looked concerned, the corners of her mouth turned down.

Claire asked, with a hint of challenge and the tiniest bit of condescension in her voice, "Have you told her?"

"No, we haven't even gone out on a real date yet. I asked but she said she'd get back to me. It may never go anywhere."

"Well," Claire said with an air of finality, "better spit it out sooner rather than later because it'll save a lot of heartache. Or you could just stick to the people we meet at the get-togethers. All that nonsense is out of the way right from the start." Toni nodded vigorously. The three of them attended social gatherings in the poly network that gave like-minded people the opportunity to meet and get to know each other. With the understanding up front, dating was *much* easier. Jules had had several pleasant encounters with other poly lesbians. Nevertheless, she was attracted to Sylvia in spite of what experience taught her would be the result.

"Thanks. I'll keep that in mind." She sighed and gathered her clothes, stuffing them into her duffel bag. They were right, of course. Trying to date Sylvia was probably a terrible idea. But it couldn't hurt to try just once. She'd tell her about polyamory and she'd see.

CHAPTER FOUR

Sylvia sat in her armchair with her phone and scrap of paper bearing Jules's phone number on the table at her elbow. In her primitive reptile brain, where the emotions of fight or flight lurked, the dark and frightening memories persisted. It had been so wonderful with Elena at the beginning and so miserable at the end. Elena had been charming and addictive at first, then became full of rage and unreasonable demands. Sylvia had to struggle to get free, just like an addict had to overcome addiction.

But Perla was right; she at least had to be a little bit open to seeing someone. Spending her life alone because of one terrible woman wasn't an option. Jules was gentle and sensitive, and she was also pretty damn cute, Sylvia had to admit, with her lazy grin and athletic build. Sylvia flashed on how Jules had looked during their walk at Crissy Field, with her eyes picking up the color of the sky as she gazed out over the bay.

Remembering the way she laughed made Sylvia's stomach flip just a little. Before her reptile brain could sabotage her, she dialed the number. Jules picked up on the third ring and her "hello" was breathless, as though she'd run to the phone.

"Hi. This is Sylvia."

"Hello, Sylvia." Jules sounded like she was laughing at something, and Sylvia decided she really wanted to be in on the joke, whatever it was.

Sylvia cleared her throat. "I wanted to get back to you about going out. Sorry it took me so long."

"No worries."

"So I was thinking of next Friday for dinner."

"Sorry. Fridays are always busy."

"I see."

"How about Saturday?" Jules asked.

"No, sorry. I'm getting together with my friends Hana and Elspeth."

"Okay. Sunday?"

"I have a meeting that night. I can't."

"Meeting?"

"Yeah. It's EQCA's regular Sunday-night meeting."

"EQCA?"

"Marriage Equality, California. You know, about the marriage cases?"

Jules never watched the news because it was all negative and depressing. "No. Actually, I don't know." During the pause that followed, Jules felt the rising tension.

"Well. Six couples are suing the state of California for the right to marry. They combined them in one case, and they've taken it all the way to the California Supreme Court."

"Still not tracking. Sorry."

"It's a long story. Basically, the hearing happened in March. We're going to be able to see the video next Sunday and hear from the attorneys who pled the case."

Sylvia's tone had gotten a little cool. *Well, excuse my ignorance.*

This wasn't going well at all, and after their splendid walk at Crissy Field, their conversation was more depressing than the news.

"Oh. Okay. Well, I have a standing appointment every Friday. But I guess I could rearrange my schedule," Jules said reluctantly. Claire and Toni would be unhappy, especially Claire.

So be it. She'd been unable to get Sylvia out of her mind all week, and she wanted to see if there was anything to it.

"I'd appreciate that. Where do you want to go?"

"How about Millennium?"

"What kind of food? I've never heard of it."

"It's vegan." Jules braced for the pushback. She somehow figured that Sylvia wasn't even vegetarian, never mind vegan. That was another wrinkle, good grief, to go along with the polyamory angle. She shook her head, glad Sylvia couldn't see her. Claire and Toni were right. It was a stupid idea to ask Sylvia out.

"Oh."

"Yeah. Is that a problem?"

"Oh, no. No problem."

Sylvia didn't sound very convincing. She supposed it was possible to pick a regular restaurant that might have a vegetable alternative on the menu so she wouldn't be reduced to eating salad and starch, as was often the case, but she didn't want to do that. Millennium was a classy restaurant with good food, and she was the one arranging the date. Goddamn it. Jules fought down her annoyance at the general presumption of the omnivore eaters, which she was projecting onto Sylvia.

"Do you want me to pick you up?" Jules asked.

"Sure, that would be wonderful."

"All right. I'll get us a seven p.m. reservation and pick you up around six thirty. It's a nice restaurant, I promise."

❖

On the way over to pick up Sylvia for their date, Jules considered what she knew already about her. She wasn't a vegetarian and she was political. Those could be negotiable, but she was almost certainly not poly. *This is probably futile.* But Jules wanted to take the chance anyhow. There was just something about Sylvia. It wasn't just her looks. Her energy, the way she talked to Barney, what she did for a living captivated Jules. Though she couldn't articulate the reason, she wasn't one to dwell on those sorts of musings. When she met someone she liked, she just went with her gut. On their way to the restaurant, she explained that vegans never ate any animal products. Ever. No eggs, no milk, no cheese.

"It's a much healthier way to live, but I can't handle no cheese or eggs, so I'm generally vegetarian instead of vegan." The previous year, Claire had decided to go vegan and had, naturally, pulled Toni and Jules along with her. They had retreated to ovo and lacto vegetarianism when Jules and Toni complained so much about the lack of protein.

Sylvia said, "I can see that, I guess. Heart attacks and all that."

Jules spared a glance to see how Sylvia was responding. Sylvia looked back at her, her expression unreadable. She did, however, look great in a fitted knit sweater and another pair of well-tailored wool trousers.

They were seated at a booth near the back. Sylvia looked around at the décor and the other diners. "Wow, this is quite elegant. Not what I expected."

"What did you expect?"

"Oh. I don't know. Lots of natural fibers and earthy-crunchy types in Birkenstocks and Mexican shirts. Bland, high-fiber food." Sylvia was smiling to show she was teasing, and Jules couldn't help grinning back.

"Vegetarian restaurants used to be like that, but not so much anymore. Do you know what you want?" Jules asked.

"Um. Nope. Not really. Can you help me?"

"I can try. What do you like?"

"Chicken wings and French fries."

Jules struggled to hide her reaction. *She's still joking. It's probably a nervous reaction.*

"It's not that kind of place."

"I know. I wanted to see your reaction, and you're good at keeping a straight face," Sylvia grinned and added, "so to speak."

"Good to know."

The waiter appeared and stood poised with his pad. "Are you ready to order?" Jules looked at Sylvia and raised her eyebrows. "Would you like a cocktail?"

"I'll have what you have," Sylvia said.

"Two glasses of white wine. Not too dry, please."

The waiter picked up the wine list and pointed to a sauvignon blanc that wasn't overly expensive. "Might I suggest this one?"

Jules read the entry and nodded to him. "Sure. Perfect." He went away. They were back to staring at each other, and Jules wondered if Sylvia was feeling the same level of discomfort that she felt. She wanted to get the date back on a better track but didn't know exactly how to do that. She looked across the table at Sylvia and a thought popped into her head.

"Did anyone ever mention that you look like Sara Ramirez from *Grey's Anatomy*?"

"Once in a while. I don't think I do, though." Sylvia tilted her head. "I think I'm better-looking," she said playfully.

Jules had to laugh. "Oh, I would agree." *Is she flirting with me?*

Sylvia's expression became serious again. "Would you order for me? Since you're the vegetarian, you know better."

"Let's see." She looked at the menu some more. "How about a black bean torte to start with?"

Sylvia read the description quickly. "Sure. It's Mexican. I guess I can't go wrong with that." She grinned and suddenly Jules felt more relaxed. It might be okay.

The wine arrived and the waiter took their order—a couple of entrees Jules had picked for them. After he left, they clinked glasses and each took a large sip.

Their food arrived and Jules watched anxiously as Sylvia tasted their appetizer. Her face relaxed and she closed her eyes as she chewed. Jules experienced a huge jolt of attraction as she watched Sylvia savor the black bean and whole-wheat tortilla as though it was the best thing she'd ever tasted.

"Oh, wow. This is great."

"You're surprised?"

"A bit, I admit it. I have an preconception about vegetarian food. I guess I'm wrong."

"Well. You may not be. It's just that this is the best. Some people think it's better than Greens. You've heard of Greens?"

"Yeah, I think so. Isn't it supposed to be the best vegetarian restaurant in San Francisco?"

"Yep, it is. But Millennium is different because it's totally vegan. Greens isn't."

"I see. So why did you become a vegetarian in the first place?"

"I love animals. I don't want to eat them," Jules said. The true explanation, that Claire had started it, crossed her mind. *Maybe later.*

"I can understand that. But we don't eat our pets. As far as I know, humans have always eaten all kinds of things. I like meat. I believe I always will."

"Lots of people feel that way. How about dessert?" Jules asked, realizing they would just have to agree to disagree, which in turn reminded her of the touchy subject they had yet to deal with now that they'd processed the vegetarian/carnivore issue, more or less.

They chose a sorbet/ice cream sampler with three different flavors and some decaf. Jules took a deep breath and a bite of the chocolate hazelnut. It was divine.

She leaned against the back of the booth. "So. I'm very glad you agreed to go on a date with me. I'm having a good time."

Sylvia's face softened. "I am, too. In spite of the smelly start we had."

"I don't know where we go next. I know I want to see you again. I want to see where this goes but…"

"But what?" Sylvia's expressive face went from serenity to confusion.

"I need to tell you something about myself. Something personal that's information you need to have as soon as possible." Sylvia gazed back at her intently and she gulped. She'd never been so nervous telling a date before.

"I'm polyamorous. I'm in a relationship with a couple." She stopped to let that sink in. As she feared, Sylvia's eyebrows came down, as did the corners of her lovely mouth.

"Really? Then what the fuck are we doing on a date?"

Jules was shocked at her harsh tone and language. *Uh-oh. She's really pissed off.*

Jules held up her hand. "Please let me explain. I'm sorry. I'm not handling this very well. I don't live with them but I see them every Friday. We have an understanding. I do date other women."

"Really?" Sylvia repeated. Her body language telegraphed clearly what she was feeling. She was sitting up straight, rigid, her hands on the edge of the table, her jaw set. Her dark-brown eyes were sending out sparks, but not the kind that Jules had hoped to see.

"I know how this must sound. And you're right to be confused—"

"I'm not confused. I understand what you're saying. You already have two lovers and you cheat on both of them."

"That's not it, exactly."

"Oh? That's what it looks like. Well, you're not going to be cheating on them with me, because this relationship is definitely not going anywhere. If you wouldn't mind, I'd like to go home as soon as possible."

The hope of the evening drained from Jules. They weren't going to get anywhere unless Sylvia cooled down some, if she ever did. That thought hit her hard and she remembered Claire's lecture. She took care of the check, and they drove from downtown to Bartlett Street in stony silence.

❖

Sylvia flopped down on the couch and flipped on the TV. It was only about nine thirty, and she wanted to watch something and try to take her mind off the disastrous date with Jules. *To think I was even entertaining the idea of dating her. Polyamory, my ass. Let's try calling it what it is. Promiscuity. Sleeping around. Two girlfriends already? God, what the hell is that?* Sylvia suddenly realized what the "every Friday night" thing meant. She got up and paced.

She didn't know which was making her madder, Jules's confession or her own reaction. Overreaction was more like it. Jules was attempting to be honest. She wasn't hiding anything. Well, that was in her favor but still wouldn't help. Sylvia had to admit she was disappointed as well as relieved that the relationship would never go anywhere. Dating Jules was off the table. Moot. Done deal. Kaput. Dead as a doornail. She started to smile a little as she thought of the various synonyms for "over."

As she got ready for bed, her mind wouldn't stop. She had the nagging feeling she'd overreacted by abruptly demanding they leave. Jules hadn't really done anything wrong. She owed Jules an apology, and if she was honest with herself, she knew next to nothing about polyamory, other than what she had read in erotic novels. It was kind of like vegetarianism. *I went ahead and ate the food and it* was *tasty.* Granted, polyamory was more complicated than vegetarianism, but she liked Jules, and even if they had totally different lifestyles, throwing away a friendship would be silly. And now there was no question. It would have to be friends or nothing.

She tugged the covers up to her chin and closed her eyes. She was back at Crissy Field and watching Jules's face as they looked at the scenery—her serious concentration as they worked with Barney, when Sylvia had told her she wasn't a saint and heard Jules's unexpected response. Sylvia felt like she was being understood in a way she never had before. Jules was present, perceptive, and empathetic. Her casual, devil-may-care persona was deceptive, Sylvia decided. Elena's intense focus and histrionic personality, Sylvia recalled, had excited her at first, but things had become so toxic. Low-key and sympathetic was what she certainly needed. As she drifted off to sleep, Sylvia was maybe more regretful than relieved they would never be more than friends.

CHAPTER FIVE

On Sunday evening, Sylvia and Perla, who'd arrived home two days before, walked down Market Street from the Church Street Muni stop in the dusk to the LGBTQ Center and continued their postmortem examination of Sylvia's date with Jules.

Sylvia said, "The place was so fancy it was hard to believe it was a vegan restaurant. I can't imagine a life without chicken enchiladas or medium-rare hamburgers. Or carne asada or even fish, for God's sake. But the food was good, even without meat."

"I know a vegetarian at work, and she's the most boring and self-righteous person I've ever met."

"Well, Jules isn't boring. Or self-righteous. But she *is* polyamorous." Sylvia rolled that last word off her tongue, making it sound like a disease.

"Tell me again what the rationale is for all that sluttiness?"

"Well, according to the sites I've looked at, they believe there's more than enough love to go around and no reason people have to be monogamous. They say monogamy is a social convention, another one of those 'shoulds' in life people think they have to adhere to. The polys think you can have relationships with more than one person because people are capable of having emotional attachments to several people, not just one particular one."

"Hmm. That's a nice rationale for promiscuity."

"Well, not the way Jules tells it, but still, I'm not going there. Besides, she probably comes from money. I saw the prices at the restaurant. And she's too white." Sylvia knew she was probably way off base and sounded like a prejudiced asshole. She was probably trying to find more reasons to not date Jules because she didn't want to deal with the fact that she found Jules attractive in a lot of ways. She kept trying to concentrate on how much she disliked the idea of polyamory, but she really wanted Perla to talk her into changing her mind.

"Oh, come on. That's not you, Syl. Elena used to say shit like that all the time, but I know you don't really think that." Perla was looking at her closely.

"No. It's not me, but still. We have nothing in common. She's completely different from me."

"Right. What's the issue? You aren't going to date her. Case closed."

"Yes, but I don't want to cut her off completely. And I owe her an apology for how I acted."

"So call her."

"We can't go on another date."

"Ask her to take a walk with Barney. Like you did when I was gone. That's not a date. That's taking a walk."

"I'll think about it." They turned in the front door and made their way to the meeting room in the back. As soon as they entered, their friend Hana spotted them and waved. She was deep in conversation with one of the staff liaisons for NCLR, the National Center for Lesbian Rights. Perla and Sylvia found a couple of seats and saved one for Hana, who joined them a few moments later.

They hugged and kissed. Hana said, "Hi, girls. Is this exciting or what?" Hana was an Israeli lesbian who had moved with her diplomat parents to San Francisco in the eighties. She'd been working in the marriage equality movement since she was a college student and was waiting impatiently to marry Elspeth, her girlfriend of five years.

The president of ECQA San Francisco called them to order and introduced attorney Lisa Moore. Those assembled in the room clapped enthusiastically. She acknowledged her reception with a nod and then dove right into business.

"We've mounted an incredibly strong case with two teams of attorneys from Los Angeles and SF." She grinned. It was San Francisco's show all the way, even though some of the plaintiffs were from Los Angeles. The rivalry between northern and southern California was alive and kicking in the biggest gay rights case California had ever seen.

Lisa continued. "I've seen the various briefs and filings the other side has offered, and I'm here to tell you, it's a joke." The people laughed and shouted encouragement. Lisa described the anti-marriage forces for a few minutes. Then she said, "Now, I know you all want to find out tonight how you're going to be able to see this."

The EQCA director, Mark, returned to the podium, cleared his throat, and leaned forward, his serious expression silencing the room. "I've been in touch with a few people from the LGBT center LA. A couple of their members, as you may have heard, make a point of going to some of those evangelical mega-churches they seem to have in abundance down there. Know your enemy, so to speak."

He paused for the boos and catcalls to subside. Sylvia knew from her attendance at many meetings and from watching the news that the religious right-wing types were the most vocal opponents of marriage equality. It was a sort of grim joke with everyone, but it struck a little too close to home with Sylvia because of her brother and, more specifically, because of her sister-in-law.

"They have stronger stomachs than me, that's for sure," Mark said to more laughter. "Anyway, all joking aside, I'm talking about this because the SoCal folks say the fundies are collecting signatures to get a referendum for an anti-marriage constitutional amendment on the ballot this year."

One guy called out, "Is that because of this court case?"

The room erupted with shouting and cursing. California had a law prohibiting same-sex marriage, the very law that the Supreme Court case was challenging. California's political system, however, allowed for citizen referenda on almost anything under the sun. A constitutional amendment would be next to impossible to get rid of.

"Yes, we believe that's true." The crowd erupted with more shouts and not a few curses. A couple people started to chant, "Two, four, six, eight, separate church and state."

"Take it easy." Mark held up his hands and the room settled down. "This is not confirmed and we don't need to get upset yet. The California Supreme Court won't issue their ruling for a few months. Those folks have a ways to go to collect enough signatures for the election this November. In the meantime, let's go watch the hearing. We're going to have equal marriage in California by this summer. Massachusetts may have been first, but we're going to be second. It's going to happen, people. I promise you. It's going to happen."

❖

After the disastrous date with Sylvia, Jules morosely went about her dog-walking chores for the week. She was hoping that Sylvia might call; she didn't dare call her. She also dreaded Claire's I-told-you-so smirk that would be forthcoming on Friday. It was odd for Sylvia's attitude to bother her so much. She'd encountered the same reaction on a few occasions. Claire and Toni had told her often enough that the mainstream monogamous folks, hypocrites that they were, were extremely contemptuous of poly folks. When the subject came up in the meetings and discussions, the general attitude was that the poly people would keep the high ground and continue to reiterate that monogamy was a perfectly valid relationship style. It was a personal choice that everyone got to make, and no one really had the right to look down on anyone else's harmless personal choices. Jules had gone from one end of the emotional spectrum to the other.

When she'd told Claire and Toni about the date with Sylvia, Claire was less smug than she usually was in reaction to one of Jules's tales of rejection, and Toni made sympathetic noises. Usually, Jules would just forget about whoever had rejected her because of the poly angle and go make love with her girls. But it wasn't working out quite that way this time. Although she realized they had no future, she had to know if Sylvia even had any sexual feelings for her. She was afraid, however, to call her and risk an unpleasant conversation.

She couldn't stop thinking about their dinner at Millennium. Watching Sylvia eat was a revelation, and Jules was sure she would approach sex the same way. Jules had suspected that once Sylvia succumbed, her surrender would be complete; she wouldn't be half-assed or tentative. That wasn't her. She would give herself to the experience wholeheartedly. Jules sighed, trying to accept that it wasn't to be.

Now it was a week and a half later, and she still hadn't heard from Sylvia. She sat down for a break at Fort Funston while her charges were getting their fill of treats from one of the many dog lovers who showed up during the day and her phone rang. Her heart nearly stopped; it was Sylvia's office number. She fumbled, trying to open the line, and nearly dropped her cell into the Fort Funston sand.

"Hello?" she said, somewhat breathlessly.

"Hi, this is Sylvia."

"Hello." Jules forced her voice into a neutral tone, though her emotions were churning. She was afraid but excited, exhilarated that Sylvia was calling her. She just hoped it wasn't to tell her off or berate her for her lifestyle.

"Hi, Jules. How are you?"

Jules shifted her phone to her other ear and patted one of her dogs to calm herself. "Oh, I'm fine. You?"

"I owe you another apology."

"No, you don't. I'm not angry."

"No. If I were you, I'd be. I was rude and I overreacted. And I'm sorry."

"Well, I'm not angry." And it was true. She was sad and disappointed more than anything else, with a bit of longing thrown in, maybe. Curiosity, sure. Lust, absolutely.

"So, let's not argue about this, too. Would you like to take a walk on Saturday? I can borrow Barney."

"Sure." Jules was taken aback. She was thrilled that Sylvia wanted to see her again, but somewhat mystified. Maybe she wouldn't be running away screaming after all.

"How about one? You pick the place since you know all the good ones."

"Sure thing. See you then." Jules snapped her phone shut and grinned. "All right, you mutts, let's go! Barney, Elvis, Maggie, Shadow, Snips, we're out of here!"

❖

"We seem to be on much surer ground when we do this," Sylvia said. "Take a walk with Barney, I mean." She favored Jules with a rueful one-sided grin. The overcast day rendered the ocean gray and depressing. The beach at Fort Funston was sparsely populated, and they walked along quietly for a moment.

"There's a storm out there somewhere," Jules said, looking toward the horizon. "Look at the breakers." The waves were choppy and crashed on the oily sand. Barney ran ahead, dodging the waves.

"Look. We need to talk about last week." Sylvia was on shaky ground and didn't really know what to say. She wanted to apologize and hoped Jules would accept and they could be friends.

"Okay."

"I'm sorry I reacted the way I did. I was surprised."

"Don't worry about it." Jules looked at the ground. She called, "Barney!" When he ran over, she playfully jumped to the side so he'd chase her.

She seemed unemotional, almost resigned, which irked Sylvia. She didn't know what she was expecting, but this distance wasn't it.

"Don't minimize this. Please, Jules. I was out of line. I have no right to judge you. Just understand that we aren't going to date."

"Could we date if I wasn't polyamorous?" Jules asked, her gaze bleak.

Sylvia stopped in her tracks mentally and almost echoed her motion physically. That was just the angle she was trying to avoid thinking about because she didn't know the answer. She didn't want to face how disappointed she was to have to reject Jules. She didn't want to look at how much she liked her.

"I don't know," Sylvia said truthfully. "I asked to see you today because I want to be friends."

"Ah, yes. The famous let's-be-friends speech."

"That's not fair."

"Sorry. It's just that I've heard it before."

"Have you really? Then it's not a surprise." Sylvia crossed her arms, hugging herself against the combined chill in the air from the coming storm and Jules's attitude.

"No. It's not, but it's still never easy to hear." She kicked a chunk of driftwood and sent wet sand flying behind it.

"Jules. I'm here to make peace, not to fight. I think we have a connection and I'd like to preserve it. It's just not going to be a romantic connection. You can understand that, right? Polyamory is you, but it's not me."

Jules persisted. "Are you attracted to me at all?"

"That's not relevant."

Jules stopped walking and got in front her. "It is to me."

They glared at each other for a full thirty seconds. Sylvia was surprised at Jules's reaction. She had, so far, been so distant she seemed emotionless. Now she looked ready for a confrontation.

"It's not relevant. You're poly. I'm not. That's the end of it." Sylvia looked out to sea, longing to be far away.

"It matters because if you aren't attracted to me, it makes it easier to let this go," Jules said, gently. "I am really attracted to you." She touched Sylvia's cheek, and Sylvia pressed her cheek into Jules's hand, warmed by the gesture, before she pulled away and stepped back to put some space between them. She didn't want to risk making eye contact. Instead, she girded herself with outrage.

"You have casual relationships that involve dating whoever you want, just because you want to. It's nice that you're attracted to me, but how can I take you seriously when you're already involved with two other people? They're your Friday-night appointment, aren't they?"

"Yes, Friday's the night."

"Yeah." Sylvia's sudden and totally inappropriate stab of jealousy surprised her. She looked out to sea to hide her feelings.

"I'm serious all right. Quite serious. I don't do mindless sex, in spite of what you might think," Jules said softly.

Sylvia's annoyance at herself and at Jules washed away. She turned around. "I believe you, but…"

"Never mind," Jules said. "You've let me know how you feel. Apology accepted. Friends?" She spoke sadly but kindly.

Sylvia met her gaze and nodded. She didn't seem angry, exactly, but her jaw was tight. She looked resigned.

They continued walking in silence down the nearly empty beach while Barney chased the waves and barked loudly as he evaded them. In the wet sand at the water's edge, his footprints and theirs mingled with dozens of others, both canine and human, which would be washed away as the tide came in.

Chapter Six

Of Jules's two sisters, it was the younger one, Lydia, that Jules got along with the best. Lydia was an attorney and as high-achieving as her other sister Thalia but, unlike Thalia, she had a sense of humor. Whenever Lydia came to San Francisco they met for drinks and caught up with each other. She was the only member of her family Jules felt was actually interested in her life.

By choosing polyamory, Jules was rebelling against her family's overachieving materialism and not really having to be responsible for half of a relationship. She had tried and failed at that a couple of times. Of course, the examples her parents and, later, her sisters provided had failed to inspire her to find her soul mate, one true lover, and life partner. Her parents' marriage appeared glacial. They seemed to lead completely separate lives, with only their three children in common. Jules watched her workaholic, self-involved sisters with their brittle, narcissistic boyfriends and had reached her conclusion. *Not for me.*

She got a text from Lydia asking to meet her for a drink at the Pied Piper Bar in the Palace Hotel on Friday. Jules sighed inwardly at the necessity of putting on good clothes and taking the Muni Metro subway into what she considered the alien territory of the Financial District, but Lydia was worth it. She put on her best slacks, a button-down shirt, and a tweed jacket.

When she walked into the bar, she spotted Lydia right away. She was sitting at the bar chatting with a fellow in a business suit. Making her way to her sister, she took in the luxurious surroundings of the Palace Hotel. With its dark wood paneling and giant Maxfield Parrish original mural behind the bar, the Pied Piper was of another, more elegant age.

Lydia personified the put-together young professional, her suit impeccable and her hair perfect. She sipped from a glass of red wine as she crinkled her eyes at whatever her companion was saying. Jules tapped her on the shoulder.

"Jules!" she cried, and putting her wineglass down, she slid off the bar stool to embrace her. They hugged for a moment and Lydia dropped back.

"Greg, this is my sister Jules. Greg is an associate at the Graham office I'm working on the merger agreement with."

"Very nice to meet you," Greg said.

"Nice to meet you, too."

Lydia turned back to Greg. "I'll see you at the crack of dawn tomorrow and we can wrap this up. Jules and I need to catch up."

Greg nodded. "Of course. I understand. See you in the morning. Nice to meet you, Jules." He walked away.

"Seems like a nice guy," Jules remarked after she sat next to Lydia and ordered a glass of white wine. Lydia's chief failing as far as she was concerned was her taste in men. Her current boyfriend, Howard, for instance was pretty much a jerk.

"Yeah. He's okay." Lydia was noncommittal. "So, sis. What's new? You're looking well, as usual. God, I wish I could spend all day outdoors. If I want a tan like yours, I have to spend hours at a salon."

"That's not a good idea, Lyd. Cancer?"

"They claim not, but whatever. I could just sue them if it came to that." Lydia laughed merrily. "Anyway, tell me, how are Claire and Toni?" Of her entire family, Lydia was the only one who knew about her polyamory. Their parents weren't especially concerned that she was a lesbian, only that she wasn't interested in settling down. Given their example, though, no one could blame her for taking a different path.

"They're fine. They're just the same."

Lydia must have picked up something in her tone, because she took a gulp of wine and cocked her head in the way she always did when she was in an inquiring mood.

"Yeah? What about you? You're still the same?"

"Yep. I met someone, though."

Lydia snorted. "Jeez, Jules, you've got two girlfriends already. What do you need with another one?" Lydia never criticized Jules for her life choices, but she reserved the right to tease her about them.

"It's not a question of needing another girlfriend. I met someone I really like. Someone I'd like to see more of."

"So what's the problem?"

"She's not poly. She wants nothing to do with me except as a friend."

"Oh. Tough. But, hey, you just move on to someone else, right? It's all good. At least that's what you tell me." Lydia looked at her sharply. Jules felt a bit defensive and a little embarrassed.

"Usually, but not this time. This time it really bothers me."

"So tell me." Lydia ordered them two more drinks and they pulled over the bowl of pretzels. Jules hadn't realized how much she wanted to talk about Sylvia and how reticent she'd been with Toni and Claire.

"Her name is Sylvia Ramirez. She's Latina."

Lydia snorted. "Duh!"

"She's a social worker. She's my opposite in every way."

"You know what they say about opposites." Lydia tossed down a gulp of wine and signaled the bartender for another.

"Yeah. I guess so."

"So what are you going to do about it?" Lydia was always ready with a direct question.

"I don't know. I want to see her, but she's made it crystal clear that we can't date."

"Well, shit, Jules. Do you blame her? This poly gig, so it works for you and for Toni and Claire, but it sure as hell doesn't work for a lot of other people."

"I know that." Jules blew out a breath, frustrated. "It just never mattered to me as much as it does with Sylvia."

"You've got a dilemma, then."

"I sure do. Let's change the subject." They went on to family gossip and Lydia's work.

"Jules, are you really happy being a dog walker?" Lydia had asked the question before and Jules always answered in the affirmative. She knew that Lydia only cared about her, but it still made her feel defensive, although she had to admit it might be getting a little bit less absorbing than it used to be.

"Yes. I am."

Lydia looked at her steadily and didn't say anything for a moment. "Okay. Just as long as *you're* happy."

Jules nodded but didn't really know how to respond.

By the time Jules got home, she was a little buzzed, in spite of having dinner with Lydia, and she couldn't get to sleep right away. She'd texted Claire on Thursday to say she would come over Saturday because of seeing her sister, but it felt strange being by herself in her own bed on a Friday night.

She lay there, staring at the ceiling and thinking about Sylvia. She'd told Lydia she was happy but she wasn't convinced. It didn't seem as true anymore, and she was afraid it had something to do with her unrequited lust for Sylvia. Sylvia's rejection had fueled her longing. In the past, someone declining sex just hadn't been that big a deal. She turned onto her side and punched her pillow, now fully awake. The only way to solve her problem was to act. Sylvia had said they'd be friends, so Jules was prepared to go forward on that basis. *Something could change.*

CHAPTER SEVEN

Sylvia pulled out her file on William Noonan; it was time for his regular check-in visit.

She waited for a half hour then called him. His cell went to voice mail. She tapped her pencil on the desk. What was up? It was unlike him to miss an appointment. She read her notes from the last visit. He'd been upbeat and talkative, as usual, and had gotten the job in the car wash he'd applied for. She closed the file, hoping he'd call back later. It wasn't unusual for most clients to blow off their appointments. Sometimes the explanation was simple, a mix-up of time or some other routine mishap. But it could also indicate trouble.

Her clients were fragile, their grip on reality dependent on so many factors: whether or not they took their meds, their family support. Their ability to adapt to the stresses of the world outside the psych ward was subject to change at any moment. In any case, in a half hour, she was due to see Tilly Mae Henson, a sweet-natured woman if she was sober but a holy terror if she wasn't. On any given day, it was impossible to predict if Tilly would show up sober and happy, or drunk and confused.

Sylvia knew she should make some calls to check on some of her other clients, but she was restless. She thought about Jules and their conversation at Fort Funston. In fact, she hadn't been able to stop thinking about it no matter how many stern mental directives she'd given herself. She thought about friendship, then about something deeper, and she was no longer as decisive as she had been on that day at the beach, which irritated her. Her cell rang, and when she saw the number on the display, her stomach did a little flip. It was Jules.

She steeled herself to wait for a couple rings before answering.

"Hello." She kept her voice cool.

"Hi. Is this a bad time?" Jules sounded like she was trying, as usual, to be casual and controlled.

"Nope, it's an okay time. I'm not involved in anything at the moment. If I was with a client, I wouldn't answer."

"Of course, that makes sense." After a short pause, Jules said, "I called to see if you wanted to get together."

"Um." Sylvia stalled for time, the desire to say yes at odds with her desire to keep her distance.

"If you don't, that's okay, too."

Jules was definitely trying to be accommodating, which was touching, and Sylvia's defenses crumbled. She wanted very much to see Jules again.

"Why don't we try resetting our relationship? Let's have dinner, but I'll pick the restaurant," Sylvia said impulsively.

"Absolutely, your call. What day were you thinking of?"

"Would Saturday work for you?"

"Sure."

"Great. Would you mind driving again?"

"No, not at all. What time?"

"I'll text you. I don't think we'll need a reservation, but I better check first." They said their good-byes and hung up. Sylvia sat staring at her phone and wondering why she felt like they were going out on a date. Again. She shook her head. *Not a* date. *Just a casual dinner with a friend.*

❖

They were circling the blocks around Noe and Market Street searching for a parking place. Sylvia said, "Perla has a little prayer she uses. 'Gladys, Gladys, full of grace, please find me a parking place.'"

Jules laughed heartily. "God, I hope it works. I'm usually pretty good."

"You've got parking karma, then?" She meant the magical combination of luck and vigilance that allowed drivers to find a parking space in San Francisco's overcrowded streets.

"Usually."

Jules spared a quick glance over at Sylvia, who seemed to be enjoying herself. Their gazes met and Sylvia's brown eyes sparkled, and Jules could see the little laugh wrinkles. Sylvia looked good tonight, younger, for some reason. She was in blue jeans and a bright-green sweater, and her tawny skin and dark-brown hair shone.

At dinner, Sylvia asked Jules, "How's your pasta?" They were at Pasta Pomodoro on Market Street. Jules was pleasantly surprised that Sylvia had picked it because she'd been expecting a steak or hamburger kind of place.

"It's very good. How's yours?" Jules grinned.

"Just fine, thanks. So tell me. How in the world did you end up in a ménage à trois?"

Jules nearly choked as she tried not to spit her pasta across the table. "You get right to the point, don't you?" She wiped her mouth with her napkin, wondering how to answer the question.

"We may as well talk about it, since it's already out there. I'm just curious. You don't have to tell me if you don't want to."

Sylvia's expression was dispassionate, and Jules wondered if she had some agenda with this but decided she'd probably find out in due time. She was fairly adept at seeing what was behind the things people said, an ability that had allowed her to conduct an essentially trouble-free relationship with Claire and Toni. Whatever tensions they experienced when they were together,

Jules was usually able to defuse, since she had discerned early on what lay behind most of their interactions and tailored her behavior accordingly. She'd had practice with her parents. When her parents weren't getting along, she strove to lighten the tension and distract them.

"I don't mind. It was pretty simple, really. I cat-sat for them, we became friends, and then one evening they asked me to sleep with them and I did."

"That's all?"

"Yes. That's all."

"They truly don't care if you have other girlfriends?"

Sylvia looked perplexed, a response Jules knew well. She and Claire and Toni could sort of make sense, but then when someone found out Jules was free to see other people outside their little trio as well, their preconceptions broke down. Claire was right. To most people, love was a zero-sum game, and if someone had your love, there was nothing for anyone else. It was the culture of scarcity whereas, in polyamory, people celebrated abundance. It was the contrast between possessiveness and generosity.

"No, they don't. They're happy for me. Our relationship is inclusive. Sometimes they sleep with other girls, but just casually."

"I find that hard to believe."

"I know. It's hard to grasp for lots of people. What do you believe?" Jules thought she knew the answer.

"I believe in one true love, one person you pledge yourself to completely without reservation, for the rest of your life."

"Marriage, in other words."

"Yes, if possible. If not, the commitment is still the same."

"You think that's the only way to live?"

Sylvia raised her chin and looked straight into Jules's eyes. "It's the only way for *me* to live." Her expression held a bit of a challenge but her conviction was compelling. There was, to Jules, just one thing wrong.

"So why don't you have that? Where is that one perfect person that's going to give you everything you need for the rest of your life?" She instantly regretted her words, because Sylvia's face fell.

"I thought I had that once. But it didn't work out."

"I'm sorry."

"It's not your fault. Don't be sorry. I'm not. She was far from perfect. Me either."

Jules felt bad for pointing out the inconsistency between Sylvia's life and her belief, since it was clearly a sore spot. It wasn't worth proving her point if it meant hurting Sylvia's feelings. She wanted to ask what happened but decided to drop it.

Sylvia said, "Let's pay the bill and take a walk."

They walked west on Market toward Castro Street and window-shopped. At the corner of Castro and Market, they stopped in front of the Twin Peaks Tavern. It was Saturday night, so it was packed. They could see the mature crowd through the huge glass window.

Sylvia said, "Someone told me this is the first gay bar to have windows like this. In the old days, no one wanted to be seen, so there were no windows. The bars were like dark caves."

Jules laughed. "I think some of them still are. Do you want to get a drink somewhere?"

"No, not tonight. I'd like to keep walking, if that's okay with you?"

They meandered down to the corner of Eighteenth Street and Castro and stopped to chat with the petitioners who stood by the Bank of America. Couples strolled by hand in hand, and a group of bedraggled teenagers panhandled in front of Walgreens. Jules and Sylvia wandered up the other side of the street back toward Market. The blue-and-red neon sign of the Castro Theater lit up the night, the marquee announcing that the Bette Davis movie *All About Eve* was showing for the weekend.

"So much history in this block," Sylvia said quietly.

"Yes, I've heard." Jules became uneasy because she was experiencing that fantasy again, the one that had started in the vet's office the day Barney got skunked nearly a month before, the one where she and Sylvia were lovers. She shook her head to get rid of it.

"I think we're about to make history again." She looked up toward the Castro Theater sign and its bright lights, and her eyes shone.

"What history is that?" Jules asked, distracted by the way the lights highlighted Sylvia's perfectly shaped lips.

Sylvia turned and looked at her, clearly aghast. "The marriage case, of course!" Her tone held an edge of reprimand.

"Oh, right. Of course. I knew that."

"Right."

"No, really, I read about the arguments in the online news. I think our side is expected to win." Jules had made an attempt to read about the marriage case because it was obviously so important to Sylvia, but it had been hard going until she found one article that explained the issues clearly.

"Yep, all true. Sorry, I judged you too quickly."

"You seem to do that."

"I apologize, though," Sylvia shot back.

"That you do. I would rather, however, that you stop judging me."

Sylvia looked at her calmly. "You're right. I need to do that. Here's a question for you, though. What do polyamorous people think of marriage equality?"

"You know, I've no idea. We've never discussed it."

"That tells me something right there. This is the biggest gay rights issue in a decade, but you didn't know anything about it before you met me."

"Well, I'm not sure about that." Jules figured Sylvia was probably right, but she didn't want to admit it.

"Why don't you come with me to the next EQCA meeting?" Sylvia asked. "Find out more about it."

"Nope, sorry. Not my thing."

"Oh, come on. I'll be open-minded if you'll be. We can learn more about each other. What do you say?"

"Okay, then. I will." Jules had no idea why she was agreeing, since politics truly bored the shit out of her. The electric touch of Sylvia's hand on her arm had something to do with it. They made their way back down Market Street to Noe Street, where Jules had parked, moving through the throngs of queer folk out enjoying their Saturday evening in their neighborhood. They looked in shop windows and at people dressed in full leather. Jules commented a few times on the breeds of dogs they came across. Jules was relieved that, in spite of their discussion, they hadn't gotten into an argument. For the time they strolled on Castro Street, Jules felt they were a normal couple, on a normal date. Why did she like the idea when it wasn't true on any level?

❖

The day of the EQCA meeting, Sylvia, Jules, and Perla met at La Cumbre Taqueria on Valencia Street. Jules had been there before, and she realized that the giant painting of the girl representing Mexican independence reminded her of Sylvia, with her dark hair, liquid-brown eyes, and nice curves. They sat down with their burritos and Perla, Sylvia's friend, looked at Jules with an expression of amused curiosity. How much had Sylvia told her about their interaction? In spite of their business arrangement, Jules and Perla hardly knew each other.

Jules decided to open with what she hoped was a safe subject, although she wasn't sure why she was feeling defensive and nervous. It wasn't as though she and Sylvia were dating and she had to pass muster with Perla, Sylvia's best friend. *No pressure,* she thought, *get over it.*

"How's Barney doing?"

Sylvia and Perla glanced at each other and Perla grinned. "You worked a miracle with him," she said, and Jules couldn't tell if she was joking or if she really meant it.

"I don't know about that. He just needed some practice heeling."

"He's much better now. Thanks for your help."

"You're welcome." And that exhausted that topic. Jules carefully unwrapped her burrito.

Sylvia turned to Perla. "Jules doesn't know anything about the marriage case. So I invited her to come with us."

Perla looked seriously at Jules. "This is Sylvia's cause, you know. She's very passionate about it."

Jules thought she detected a warning note somewhere in Perla's otherwise neutral tone. "Yep, I know it."

"It's so exciting, don't you think, Jules? California queers will be able to get married."

"Jules isn't really interested in marriage," Sylvia said suddenly. What was she driving at? Hadn't she agreed to come to the meeting to find out more about it?

"I mean for yourself." Sylvia amended her statement, and Jules realized she meant the polyamorous relationship.

"I've never thought about it." She had, of course, but the prospect of spending the rest of her life with someone she could barely stand to talk to just wasn't all that appealing. The three of them were quiet for seemed like an eternity until Perla finally broke the silence. "We better get going or we'll be late. Parking there is impossible." They dumped their dinner debris and drove over to the LGBT center, where Jules found a spot on Laguna Street, next to the old UC Extension building.

As they pulled in, Sylvia said, "Whoa. I knew you had parking karma, but this is amazing."

Jules, Perla, and Sylvia joined the crowd in the downstairs meeting room, where a screen was set up in the front. Jules looked around and wasn't sure what she'd expected, but what she saw surprised her. For one thing, the crowd was buoyant and noisy. For another, it included all age ranges, both genders and some none-of-the-above, all races, and, unexpectedly, heterosexual couples. Jules expected to see a slew of earnest, dull, political-type queers.

Perla and Sylvia greeted a good many people and were finally motioned over to sit next to an attractive young female couple. Sylvia introduced them as Hana and Elspeth.

"Not much longer now, right?" she asked them, laughing.

"Nope. We set the date for September. That'll give the relatives time to plan," Hana said gaily.

Sylvia turned to Jules and said, "Their wedding."

"Oh. Nice." Jules couldn't think of anything else to say. Hana and Elspeth looked like they were in their early twenties. Why in the world would they want to get married so young?

Sylvia and Perla discussed the wedding plans animatedly with them until the meeting was called to order. Jules was bemused: they seemed so terrifically confident that they would be getting married. Perla, Jules, Hana, and Elspeth discussed the court hearing, and Jules realized they had all been there for the actual hearing and were about to sit through at least part of it again, something Jules really didn't understand. She asked Sylvia quietly, "You already saw this, right? You were there?"

Sylvia looked at her curiously. "Uh-huh."

"But you're going to watch it again?"

"Just parts of it. Then the lawyers will talk about it and answer questions about all the legal stuff." Jules was mystified that so many people were so avidly interested in something as dry as a court hearing. Why did they apparently consider listening to lawyers as exciting as going to a rock concert?

Mark introduced the National Center for Lesbian Rights attorneys and the San Francisco assistant city attorney. They described the progress of the case up to the California Supreme court and explained, "We distilled this down because the whole thing is three hours long, and some of it is really boring." The audience laughed, and when he added, "And I think you know which parts," they laughed even harder. Jules saw Perla and Sylvia joining in and was irked because she didn't get the joke. She fought her boredom at the technical discussion, reminding herself she was there because of Sylvia.

One of the lawyers talked about the California Supreme Court justices and told everyone which justices' questions to listen to, and then they started the video. During the film, the noisy room got very quiet when either the lawyers or any of the judges were speaking, but when the other side was presenting, which was only shown for a few minutes, they booed loudly. Jules couldn't follow the thread very well because she was unused to legal arguments. Instead she watched Sylvia, and her facial expression spoke to Jules. Sylvia glowed with excitement, her lips parted slightly and her cheeks flushed. She was so rapt she could have been watching the most compelling mystery movie. Her absorption was uncanny, and though Jules didn't quite understand it, she was drawn to the woman beside her whose emotions were so profoundly stirred.

At the end, the three speakers fielded questions from the audience. Jules really tried to concentrate and understood that the attorneys were confident they were going to win the case and those present were overjoyed.

Back in the car, Jules listened to Perla and Sylvia discuss the meeting excitedly and again felt left out, though she was happy they were happy, especially Sylvia. They dropped Perla at home.

When they stopped at Sylvia's house, she hesitated for a moment and then said, "Would you like to come in for a drink?"

"Yeah, sure. Thanks." Jules couldn't help feeling a bit hopeful in spite of Sylvia's firm "just friends" edict. Sylvia made coffee while Jules looked around her apartment with interest. It was smallish but neat and tastefully decorated. Most of the art was Mexican, with even a beautiful serape covering one wall.

Sylvia came with cups of coffee and sat down beside her on the couch. They sipped from their cups in silence.

"What did you think?" Sylvia asked.

Jules shrugged. "It seemed like a good thing. They appear optimistic."

"I meant, what do *you* think?" It seemed to be another challenge.

"People who want to get married should be able to get married." She actually wasn't sure she thought it was *that* important, but she was reluctant to admit that to Sylvia.

"That's it?"

Jules shifted and looked into her cup of coffee as though the answer was swirling in its dark depths. "I'm impressed that it means so much to so many people and so many people are so dedicated to it."

"I see." Sylvia leaned back and looked at the ceiling. Jules wondered what she was thinking and felt like she was being judged. Again.

"I get it, Sylvia. I really do. This is a big deal for you."

"It's not just me. Don't you understand? This has the power to change the lives of thousands of people. It will change history."

Jules thought that was a little exaggerated, and her silence clearly disturbed Sylvia. Sylvia had withdrawn emotionally and Jules was sad—bereft, as a matter of fact. She wanted them to be closer, but it seemed they were still far apart.

"The meeting was interesting. I'd never even given the subject any thought before."

"And now?"

"I don't know. What do you want me to say? It's just a new idea for me. I'd like to know more, I guess."

Sylvia looked at her silently for a moment. "Well, okay. If you want to go with us to another meeting, you're welcome."

Jules pulled on her vest and turned to look once more into Sylvia's dark eyes, searching for what, she didn't know. Sylvia stepped forward and hugged her quickly, releasing her before Jules could truly experience the gesture.

"I'll see you soon," Sylvia said.

Jules nodded and walked back to her car, slightly more relaxed. They'd made some progress at least. In spite of her political ignorance, Sylvia was willing to see her again. Jules figured she would see how things went.

❖

"I think we're just going to be friends, nothing else," Jules told Claire and Toni the next Friday. Jules was dimly aware this wasn't what she really wanted, but she needed to blunt the expected criticism.

"It's about time, Jules," Claire said, and took a sip of wine. Jules almost wanted to slap her because of her infuriating "I told you so" attitude. "It just doesn't work, you know. Once they find out about the polyamory, they're done. You don't need that crap. We're not the ones who have a problem with *their* lifestyle."

Toni nodded in agreement and looked kindly at Jules. She, at least, seemed to have some sympathy, for which Jules was grateful. She didn't want to accept that she and Sylvia were probably too different to even have a friendship. But she didn't want to hear any more judgments from Claire and Toni, so she kept her hopes to herself.

Toni came around the table and gave Jules a very sweet, sensual kiss, and Jules gladly responded, drawing it out. Toni took Jules's hand and they climbed the stairs to the bedroom with Claire right behind them. In bed, Jules felt like her two lovers were being especially attentive. After her first orgasm she turned to Toni, but Toni gently pushed her back down and both of them continued to make love to her until she came again and then again.

At breakfast the next morning, after they finished eating and were sitting around with coffee, Toni and Claire looked at each other and then turned to Jules, both beaming.

"What's up, you two?" Jules grinned. "You look like Chloe would after she's eaten the canary." Jules looked down and Chloe was right by her chair looking up at her.

"Well," Toni said, "we've got something important to ask you." She glanced back at Claire, who nodded. Jules looked from one to the other. "We want you to move in with us."

Claire said, "We don't expect an answer from you today, but we wanted to put it out there and have you think it over. We both love you so much, it just seems right."

Jules knew her expression must be giving away her "Oh shit!" thought because Claire added, "Nothing else will change. We aren't planning to ask you to be exclusive. We'd just like you to be with us more often."

"Yeah. Okay. I'll think about it." It wasn't a good answer, but she was so taken aback she couldn't think of anything to say. "You know I love you two, but this is a huge step—"

"Uh-uh." Claire held up her hand. "Don't say anything. Just think about it."

"Sure. I'll do that. Hey, I better get going." Jules suddenly felt like it was hard to breathe and she needed to leave. Immediately.

They looked at her with concern and she felt guilty as she gathered her belongings, kissed them good-bye, and left. As she drove home, she wondered why she didn't feel more enthusiastic about Claire and Toni's offer.

CHAPTER EIGHT

That's exactly the point. Why *do* you care so much what she thinks?" Perla asked. They were eating lunch at a Filipino/Chinese greasy spoon on Folsom Street. It was their usual spot since it was midway between Sylvia's clinic on Mission Street at Ninth and Perla's graphic arts studio on Bryant Street near Sixth.

"I don't know," Sylvia said. She'd examined practically every conversation she'd had with Jules and was more confused than ever. She wanted to see Jules again, and since she couldn't explain it to herself, she tried to explain it to Perla, hoping she could find clarity. "She's quiet and she's funny, and it just makes me nuts that she's polyamorous and that automatically excludes her from being dating material. And there's something else."

Perla raised an eyebrow and motioned with her fork for her to continue.

"Jules asked me why, if I'm so committed to the idea of marriage equality, I'm not in a committed relationship. I got what she meant and I couldn't answer. I didn't want to tell her about Elena and go into that whole mess."

"What did you say?"

"I said that I thought I was once but it didn't work out."

"Uh-huh. That's a lame answer and you know it. I've been saying that for four years and you've ignored it. I'm impressed with Jules. I didn't know she was so smart." Perla was grinning triumphantly.

"Yeah." Sylvia took a big bite of chow mein, and Perla didn't say anything for a few moments. Then Sylvia took a huge gulp of Diet Coke and looked at Perla, who was gazing at her with an odd expression.

"What?" she asked, irritated.

"Syl. The whole time at La Cumbre the other night, she didn't take her eyes off you, not for a microsecond. And then at the meeting, she only looked at you. She was watching your face. She's got a thing for you."

"I noticed. But it's just not going to work. Vegetarianism, polyamory, politics. We both like Barney and that's about it."

"Why did you ask her to come to the meeting the other night? You intended to apologize for being so nasty about the polyamory confession and ended up inviting her to go with us. So? What's the story? What do you really think? What's the problem with being friends?"

"Perls."

"What? Why are you getting cranky with me? I'm just asking." Perla sat back, her eyes narrowed.

Sylvia looked at her, then glanced away. "Okay. There's nothing wrong with being friends with her. I'm just being…I don't know. I'm just being weird."

"There. That wasn't so complicated, was it?"

Sylvia nodded but wasn't sure if she agreed. "Complicated" was the word that described her feelings. "Ambivalent" was accurate, too. She was seriously starting to think her feelings for Jules wouldn't allow her to stay in the "just friends" zone.

❖

With five leashes wrapped around her hands, Jules marched her dogs down the Golden Gate Promenade at Crissy Field. She was concentrating so hard on keeping them in line, she couldn't spare even a glance at the monumental sight before her: the Golden Gate Bridge spanning the opening of the San Francisco Bay. She wanted the troops to walk a bit before she took them down to the water and off leash to play, and she most definitely still wanted to avoid a ticket from the U.S. Park Police. That kept her mind occupied until she veered off the path near the National Oceanic and Atmospheric Association facility in the old Coast Guard house. She unhooked all their leashes and watched them scatter in all directions, bounding and sprinting. They were so endearing, she thought fondly as she kept an eye on them. Oh, to have the simple life of a dog. Wouldn't it be nice?

Her thoughts drifted to the question Claire and Toni had posed to her. She had no idea what to do. She was fairly certain she didn't want to move in with them. She liked the status quo. She liked her independence. She liked them, loved them, even, but… But what? It was a natural step, at least to them, it appeared. Claire was fascinating on the one hand, but she was so controlling, it was hard to envision living with her on a daily basis. Toni, on the other hand, was sweet and sexy, but it seemed like, given half a chance, she might be too inclined to possessiveness. On the other hand, she wasn't getting anywhere with Sylvia, obviously. Considering her tepid interest in marriage equality, Sylvia might even find her lacking as a friend. They didn't have a chance of having a pleasant affair, even if Sylvia ever got past the poly barrier. Sylvia could not and would not entertain a relationship with someone with whom she had no intellectual or emotional connection. *We have no common ground.*

"But I really like her," Jules thought, speaking silently to the ocean, to the sand. To the universe. She couldn't discuss her feelings about Sylvia with Claire and Toni. They were her friends as well as her lovers, but somehow, she felt judged by them. As she felt judged by Sylvia. God damn it. *None of this is fair*, Jules thought, irritated. *Well, the hell with it.*

Her phone rang. The display said *Sylvia*.

Much to her dismay, she couldn't keep the eagerness from her voice when she picked up.

"Hi."

"Hello. Is this a bad time?" Sylvia's mellow contralto washed over Jules like the warm sea in Hawaii she remembered from a visit years before.

"Nope. Not at all. Just watching the kids play in the ocean."

"Great. Hey, I wanted to see if you wanted to get together week after next. I have to go out of town, but when I get back, let's do something."

Jules was astounded and overjoyed. Maybe it wasn't as bad as she thought. Sylvia taking the initiative to call her had to mean something, right?

"Sure. Anything in particular you want to do?"

"I'll let you choose, since last time we did what I wanted to."

"How about a movie?" Jules asked, holding her breath. The idea of sitting in a dark theater with Sylvia at her side made her dizzy. There was a short but significant pause.

"Sure." Sylvia seemed surprised but game.

"So let's be clear, this will be the second weekend of April."

"Yes."

"Right, well, I'll check out what's playing and give you a choice. How's that?"

"Wonderful. I'll call you after I get back in town."

Jules clicked her phone shut and looked out over the bay to the marina in Sausalito. *We are not going on a date. We're just going to the movies. Don't read anything into this. We're trying to be friends. We can surely manage that?*

❖

Jules had never visited Claire and Toni's house without a sense of calm and anticipation. She loved going to see them. She loved their home, their hospitality, their caring. She loved them. *Just not enough to move in.* She didn't want to hurt their feelings, but she had a gut feeling that if she tried to make it work it would end up being bad for all of them. After she parked her Volvo, she made her way to the front door and pressed the buzzer. Her palms were a little damp and her stomach a little nauseous. She told herself it would be okay. Dinner smelled good and she suddenly got very sad, wondering if she would ever be invited back. She walked inside and there sat Toni on the couch with Chloe, who was cuddled up next to her, looking regal and smug, her tail twitching. Toni smiled her warm smile. Jules dropped her bag by the door, sat down on the couch on the opposite side of Chloe, and gave Toni a lingering kiss. When the kiss broke, Claire appeared, clad in her apron, spatula in hand.

"Hello, Jules." Jules stood up and kissed Claire as she had Toni, enjoying the different feel of Claire's slightly harder kiss compared to Toni's sweet one.

Claire called them over to the table, and as they sat down to eat, Jules was struck again by how utterly routine it all felt, how right and comfortable. She thought, it would be like this every night. Cooking, eating dinner together, going to bed together, getting up and having breakfast. It was the same soothing domestic ritual millions of couples performed all the time. What was the difference if it involved three people instead of two? None. *But I can't do it. For whatever reason.*

After they finished eating, Toni and Claire were quiet and seemed to be waiting for Jules to bring up the subject. If Jules knew them, and she was fairly sure she did, they would want to know her answer sooner rather than later. They both thrived on routine, planning, and predictability. That was somewhat at odds with the polyamory lifestyle, which suggested more spontaneity or mystery, but not so for Toni and Claire. Jules fussed with her silverware, moving it from the empty plate to the table.

"So." Claire, inevitably, would be the one to speak up. "Have you thought about what we asked you?"

"Yes. I've hardly thought of anything else," Jules said, half truthfully. She had thought of it constantly when she wasn't thinking of Sylvia.

Claire raised her perfect black eyebrows. "Oh? Are you going to share?"

Jules exhaled with a bit of a laugh. "Sure. Look." She paused. Neither Toni nor Claire said a word or moved. "I love you both, really I do." She took a deep breath and scraped together her courage. "But I don't feel it's right for me to move in with you." Claire and Toni didn't move, their expressions unreadable. Jules sensed they wanted her to go on. "And it isn't because I don't love our time together."

Claire said, "But?"

"It's hard to explain, but I want to be on my own. Moving in feels like too big a commitment, like something I'm just not ready for yet."

"Nothing would change. Same rules," Claire said again. "You wouldn't even have to pay rent."

Jules looked away, slightly embarrassed. Claire and Toni knew she was occasionally short of money, since income in the dog-walking business wasn't consistent.

"That's great of you to offer, yet still…"

Claire and Toni traded a look and a slight nod.

"That's it, then," Claire said. "We'll talk about it again. Later."

Jules woke up in the middle of the night. Claire and Toni slept soundly on either side of her. Their lovemaking had been sweet but a little sad, like some unspoken sort of farewell. Jules knew she wouldn't stop seeing them because she didn't intend to disrupt the status quo. That had been the point of her refusal to move in with them. She *liked* the status quo. In the back of her mind was also the thought, though she didn't feel like examining it too closely, that it was better to keep the relationship with Claire and Toni a little looser. Moving in, even with the same expectations, felt much too much like a commitment, like something permanent, something that would be difficult to get out of. Jules couldn't handle that.

CHAPTER NINE

After the movie, Jules and Sylvia stood at the top of the second-floor escalator in the AMC Sundance Theater multiplex, surrounded by the milling patrons of eight movie theaters. The floor-to-ceiling glass walls faced the busy Post and Fillmore intersection of Japantown and the Fillmore District. It was Saturday evening, and it seemed to Sylvia that most of San Francisco, like them, had come out to see a movie.

They looked at each other, a bit at a loss. Sylvia finally spoke. "You want coffee?"

"Sure. Here?" There was a small coffee bar down the hall.

"Not really, let's get out of here. I don't mind crowds, but I hate the smell of stale popcorn and soda-machine gunk. I want some fresh air."

"Do you know of a place around here?" Jules asked.

"No, I don't. I thought we could just walk. I'm sure there's a place." They seemed to do best together when they were moving. It had been odd, sitting together in the dark watching the movie. She'd itched to take Jules's hand in the darkness but she'd resisted, keeping a firm grip on her bottle of water.

They turned right on Fillmore Street and walked north. Sure enough, they spotted a Starbucks a block away.

"Do you have political objections to Starbucks?" Jules asked, a trace of humor in her tone. Sylvia eyed her and decided she was being polite.

"I don't boycott them, if that's what you mean, but if I have the choice, I'd rather patronize a neighborhood café."

"Fair enough." They walked on. Fillmore Street was crowded with every conceivable sort of business, but there was no café in sight. In its superficial Hollywood sort of way, the movie's message of recovering from a bad relationship and taking a chance on new love had made Sylvia uncomfortable. But she'd decided not to voice her opinion and start some sort of argument with Jules because it was just as likely that Jules's pick for a movie had nothing to do with her and she was reading way too much into it. Why had she become so paranoid?

They finally resorted to asking a neighborhood guy with a dog for directions to a neighborhood coffeehouse and managed to snag a table at a homey place off the main street called the Grove. Sylvia ordered a mocha because she liked the concept of coffee as dessert. Jules ordered a house coffee. Sylvia was amused that Jules chose the most basic form of coffee; it fit her no-frills personality. They sipped their drinks contemplatively and absorbed the intimate ambience of the little coffeehouse.

Jules broke the silence. "What did you think of the movie?"

"Oh, I liked it. That boy, he was such a goofball. He was lucky to get a girl like that. That wouldn't happen in real life."

"No, probably not. I liked that she got him to jump off the cliff into the ocean. It showed so much courage and trust."

While Sylvia was charmed by Jules's enjoyment of the movie's conclusion, she couldn't resist saying, "That's not realistic. People don't just bounce back from a bad relationship and right away they're all fine and happy with their new love."

"No. I suppose not. You sound like you're speaking from experience."

"After I broke up with Elena, I didn't want to go out with *anyone*."

"How long ago was that and who's Elena? Your ex?"

Sylvia could tell Jules wasn't being pushy. "Almost four years, and yes. Elena was her name."

"What happened?"

Because Jules seemed so sincerely curious, Sylvia fought her usual reluctance to discuss her past and decided to try to explain Elena to her. "Well. She was difficult."

"Difficult?"

Sylvia's stomach clenched and she silently cursed the power the thought of Elena still had over her. Thinking of her brought back a lot of old horrible emotions.

"Elena was a seducer, very extravagant and ardent. She bowled me over. We started living together a month after we met. But it got really bad with her jealousy and accusations. She didn't want me to go see my family in Bakersfield very much. She was suspicious of our friends. She always made everything seem like it was my fault. I couldn't make her happy, ever. We went around in circles. I'd threaten to leave and she'd go into rages. I was so scared I'd stay. After that she'd be all lovey-dovey and attentive. Things would be fine for a while until she started acting out again. I loved her. I didn't want our relationship to fail."

Jules looked at her, her blue eyes grave. "Wow. That's awful. No wonder you left."

"It took me a long time but yes, I left, finally." Sylvia hesitated, unsure if she really wanted to say more. Had she had merely extricated herself physically and was still, in some way, mentally and emotionally chained to Elena? To her surprise, she wanted to tell Jules the rest.

"It was in 2004. We'd gotten married when it was legalized briefly."

Jules's eyebrows knitted. "Oh. Wait a sec. I sort of remember that."

"In February of 2004, Mayor Newsom decided that if Massachusetts could have marriage equality, so could San

Francisco." Sylvia remembered the day Elena had called her at work.

"Elena was really excited when she heard. She told me we should get married. We'd been fighting a lot. I thought maybe it would help." Sylvia grimaced at her naïveté. "We went down to City Hall on Valentine's Day. It was like this huge party, with tons of people there getting married. We stood in line and just had a blast. These young heterosexual couples would come around and hand everyone flowers or bagels or something. They were so adorable. Perla was there, and she and my friend Todd were our witnesses."

Sylvia teared up at the memory, Jules watching her closely. She swallowed.

"What happened?"

"The high from that lasted maybe a week. Two, at the most. Then we were back to having screaming fights." Sylvia was so choked up she wondered if she could go on. She wanted to say it. She wanted Jules to hear how it ended. "In August we got a letter from the city and county saying our marriage was null and void. We could ask for a refund of our fee."

"Null and void?"

"Yep. When we got that letter, I told Elena I was leaving. It took everything I had in me to do that. I thought it was my fault it didn't work."

"Doesn't sound like it was your fault."

"No, I know that now. I found out later Elena was crazy. I mean literally. Mentally ill."

"Wow. It's good you left, then."

After a pause Sylvia took a deep breath and pulled herself together and back into the present. "So when you asked me why I didn't have a committed relationship, why I'm not 'married,' that's the answer."

"I'm sorry. I didn't mean to hurt your feelings." Jules looked woebegone.

"No, it's okay. You're not to blame. A lot of the time I'm not willing to look at how ridiculous it is for me to work so hard for something I'm not able to have."

"Why do you think that? Not everyone's like Elena."

Sylvia snorted. "That's what Perla says."

"It's true. You should be able to have what you want. Someone to marry."

"I suppose. I just can't shake my own sense of failure. I can't seem to put myself in the mind-set or get to the place where I could meet someone, fall in love, and be married. For life. Forever. I thought I had it once. But you don't believe that's possible."

Jules looked surprised and confused. "No, no. It's not that I don't believe it's possible. I don't think it's for me. Ever."

"Ever?"

Jules paused. "No." There was another uncomfortable silence. "So what's up with the marriage case?"

"Any day now we'll get the Supreme Court decision."

"What happens then?"

"People can start getting married." Sylvia beamed at Jules. "Awesome."

Sylvia wondered just how sincere her interest was or if she was just being polite to keep the conversation going. Jules had seemed to know when to stop talking about Elena.

Jules looked at her thoughtfully. "It's wonderful you care so much about this."

Sylvia sensed the unspoken self-judgment. And to Sylvia's surprise, Jules added, "I don't think I care that much about *anything*."

"What about your family?"

"Oh. They're fine, but we don't have anything in common."

"Nothing in common? That doesn't matter. They're your blood. What does it matter what you have in common?" Sylvia honestly couldn't relate to that idea. She had almost nothing in common with her brother, but they were related at the most basic level and she loved him more than she loved anyone. She felt sorry for Jules. "I love my brother. It doesn't matter whether we agree on everything."

"You may be right. I do get along pretty well with my youngest sister."

"There you go." Sylvia looked right at Jules and thought she looked a bit sad. Jules wasn't even aware how her lack of connection to her family really affected her.

CHAPTER TEN

Sylvia and Perla were having dinner and discussing plans for Cinco de Mayo. Sylvia was wondering whether to ask Jules to join them for the celebration.

"You said you think she's too white," Perla said. "You think she's clueless when it comes to Latin culture. Here's your chance to get her clued in."

"You know that's so not my job, don't you?" Sylvia felt resentful for some reason, maybe because Perla knew she wanted to ask Jules but was still worrying about sending the wrong signal if they spent too much time together. Still, after the movie discussion the previous week, Sylvia wanted to see Jules again. They seemed to be getting along well as friends, finally. Jules was comfortable to be around, sweet and undemanding.

Perla raised her eyebrows. "You're full of shit. You say you like spending time with her but complain about her being too white, then refuse to do anything about it. You're not making sense."

Perla was well aware of her mixed feelings about Jules and never passed up an opportunity to point out Sylvia's inconsistencies. She was biding her time, waiting for the moment Sylvia proved her right.

"All right. I'll ask her." Cinco was one of her favorite events of the year, along with the pride parade in June. Like Pride, it was the perfect combination of politics, culture, and just ordinary fun. It was San Francisco in all its multicultural glory with a Latin flavor. Perla was in the women's drumming group, Sistah Boom, and they were performing.

Sylvia called Jules and asked her to come to Cinco de Mayo. "Why don't you get here early and I'll make you breakfast," she said. "Then we can walk over to Dolores Park."

❖

At nine a.m. on Saturday, May third, Jules rang Sylvia's doorbell, elated that Sylvia had asked her to this event. Sylvia's cultural background was evidently important to her, and Jules wanted to know about it.

When the door opened and Jules said, "Hi," Sylvia hugged her and kissed her on the cheek. It was over so quickly, Jules barely had time to notice the touch. The rich, dark aroma of coffee enveloped her as she followed Sylvia through the living room to her tiny kitchen. She sat down at the table that had a large plate of fruit in the middle. Sylvia poured two cups of coffee and sat down, too.

"This looks great. It's really nice of you to have me for breakfast."

Sylvia shrugged and sipped her coffee. "It's early in the morning for Saturday. I hope eggs and refried beans are okay."

Jules thought Sylvia was looking especially good and wanted to tell her so, but didn't want her to get the wrong idea. *Or the right one.* Sitting in Sylvia's kitchen and drinking coffee on a Saturday morning seemed natural, although Jules would have preferred that it to be after a night together. Of course she'd spent Friday night with Claire and Toni. She dismissed the odd shot of guilt she experienced and focused on Sylvia.

"I love beans, but I never thought of having them for breakfast." Jules grinned. "But, hey, why not?"

"Scrambled eggs okay?" Sylvia stood up.

"A-okay." Jules watched Sylvia methodically cook breakfast. She cleaned up as she went along, impressing the hell out of Jules, who felt like she got half of her dishes dirty just cooking for herself. She also admired the way Sylvia looked in jeans and a tight tan T-shirt advertising something called Mission Economic and Cultural Association. The color of the T-shirt deepened Sylvia's natural skin tone and fit perfectly over nice-sized breasts. From Jules's vantage point at the table, she could also ogle Sylvia's butt.

"So what is Cinco de Mayo, exactly? Besides the fifth of May. Even though it's only the third today."

"Well, some people think it's Mexican Independence Day, but it's not. During a battle at the town of Puebla way back in the eighteen hundreds, the poor, outgunned Mexicanos won against the big bad French army, and that's what Cinco de Mayo commemorates. It was the beginning of Mexican national pride, but we don't need much of an excuse to get together to eat, drink, and dance."

"Well, those things are good to do for anyone anytime."

"I like it because it reminds me of growing up in Bakersfield in the barrio and of my mom and dad and grandparents." Sylvia's eyes grew a little distant and misty.

"When exactly did your parents come to the U.S.?"

"Oh, I think Grandma and Grandpa, my dad's folks, started to make the trip every year around 1967. My mama's folks arrived a little later, around 1970."

"Did they all know each other?"

"Sure. They all came from the same village, and they traveled together and worked at the same farms."

"That must have been hard for them."

"Yes. Before the UFW, the landowners treated them like shit. They had terrible wages, no health care. The only good thing about picking in the San Joaquin Valley was it was better than Mexico, though that's not saying much." Sylvia cooked the beans and scrambled the eggs as she talked. She then pulled a plate of tortillas from the oven where they were warming and put them on the table, scooped the eggs and beans onto plates, and sat down. After she poured another cup of coffee she continued. "They fell in love when they were fifteen and always knew they would be together. And they knew they wanted to stay in the U.S. and have a family."

Jules followed her lead in constructing a breakfast burrito out of the eggs, beans, and cheese, then took a bite and moaned in appreciation. She suspected that was partly due to the lard that Sylvia had cooked the beans in and hoped her digestive system would be able to accommodate the unaccustomed animal fat.

"So your mom and dad knew each other when they were young."

It seemed that talking about her parents saddened Sylvia, and Jules wanted to hug her. The thought made her uncomfortable, so she changed the subject. "When should we go?"

"Pretty soon. Is it cold out?"

"Yeah. And kind of foggy."

Sylvia made a face. "Maybe it'll burn off later. Let's hope so."

They walked from Sylvia's apartment to Dolores Park, where a sizeable crowd had already gathered, even though things wouldn't get under way until eleven a.m. Jules and Sylvia found a place to sit and continued chatting.

"Tell me about your mom and dad," Sylvia said.

"Not much to tell. They met in college, got married right after, and had the three of us, bang, bang, bang." Jules laughed shortly.

"Do you think they still love each other?" Sylvia asked suddenly.

"I'm not sure they ever did, but I guess they did. They got married because it was just sort of the thing for their type of people to do."

"What's their 'type,' as you call it?"

"I don't know. Upper middle class? WASPs? Yuppies?"

"So. They have money?"

Aha, Jules thought, picking up an edge in Sylvia's tone. *She thinks I'm some spoiled rich kid.*

"Yes, I guess so. Not huge amounts, but enough, and they certainly seem to be pretty interested in making lots of it. The same with my sisters."

"But not you?"

"Not me, nope. I couldn't care less." Jules was growing uneasy with the direction the conversation was taking.

"Usually people who have money are the ones that don't care about it. If you don't have it, you sure as hell care," Sylvia said, her tone cold.

Jules made eye contact with her but couldn't read her expression exactly, though she heard, or thought she heard, judgment. She took a breath, struggling to not feel defensive and angry.

"I'm not interested in money because I have it. I don't. I support myself and I don't like to take money from my parents unless I absolutely have to. I don't think making money is the ultimate goal. I'm not saying anyone should be poor or be without, but you've got to have perspective. I'm different from my family. I don't consider making money or having a certain kind of job as my big goal in life."

"I'm sorry, Jules. It wasn't fair to assume something like that about you. When you said your parents have money, I automatically thought you do, too. It was dumb."

"It's okay. I get a whole lot of crap from my family for the way I choose to live my life, and it's not 'cause I'm a lesbian. It's because I don't have that big fancy job and I don't want one. They don't get it." Jules looked off in the distance, thinking about her family and their screwed-up point of view. "I understand why someone who grew up poor might have a different attitude about money."

"We weren't destitute but it was tough. I'm really glad my life and my brother's isn't like theirs and my grandparents'. I don't believe money should be the be-all and end-all of someone's existence either, but I also know what life is like without enough of it."

They were both silent for a while before Sylvia asked, "Are you happy doing what you do?"

"Yes, I am." But Jules wasn't exactly being truthful, not anymore. Lydia had asked the same question. It could have something to do with Lydia considering dog walking beneath Jules, and she resisted that judgment. She wanted to talk to Sylvia about it, but the performances were starting and they turned their attention to those. As they listened, Jules noticed Sylvia shivering in the thin hoodie she wore and wanted to hug her and warm her up.

Afterward, they wandered among the booths and sampled all kinds of foods, then searched for Perla to congratulate her on Sistah Boom's stellar performance. They found her, along with the rest of the troop, near the top border of Dolores Park by Twentieth Street. The hill provided a lovely view of downtown San Francisco, and the J Church Street car rumbled past every so often. People were sprawled everywhere on blankets, which amused Jules. Dolores Park was *the* place for sunbathing, but today, there wasn't any sun. Perhaps people were attempting to summon it, and it finally did come out in the late afternoon.

Perla looked good; she was wearing a sleeveless shirt, and her arms were buff after a few hours of drumming and she was flushed and happy. Jules and Sylvia complimented her on the performance, and then Sylvia asked, "So what's happening now?"

"A group of us are going over to Magda's house," Perla said.

Sylvia looked back at Jules uncertainly. "Do you want to go with them or just stay here?"

It seemed like Sylvia wanted her to make a decision, so she

said, "If you want to go with them, that's fine. Or you could come over to my house. I'll make you dinner."

Sylvia looked back at Perla, who grinned and said, "Sounds like a good idea."

Jules wasn't sure, but it seemed like Perla was throwing them together, which was an interesting thought.

After the slightest pause, Sylvia said, "Okay. Let's do that."

Jules was overjoyed that their day was going to be extended. "I have to do some shopping first," she said. "I hope you don't mind coming with me."

"Nope. That's fine. Let's wander around for a little while first." She kissed and hugged Perla good-bye, and then they walked amongst the booths scattered over the park. At times, Sylvia would speak briefly in Spanish to some of the people. In front of a booth advertising HIV prevention in both Spanish and English, she threw her arms around a white gay man about their age. She turned to the Latino man next to him and hugged him as well.

"Jules, this is my old friend from school, Todd, and his lover, Diego." Both of them hugged Jules and kissed her cheek.

"How's it going?" Sylvia asked them.

"Oh, it's pretty good, but you know these Latin boys. They like to pretend they aren't queer." Diego rolled his eyes. "But we know better." He grinned. "We've given away a ton of condoms."

Todd said to Sylvia, "How are you, love?" He flicked a glance at Jules and cocked an eyebrow.

"Oh, fine. I'm having a good day." And to Jules's surprise, she turned to her and smiled radiantly, which made her heart jump. "In spite of this no-sun thing. What's up with that?" They all laughed and Jules saw that the little moment had passed, but as short as it was, it made her wonder and it made her hopeful. Sylvia seemed to be sticking close enough to her that their arms would touch frequently. Every time it happened, it gave Jules a tingle.

They made their good-byes, wandered through the rest of the park and back to Sylvia's street to get Jules's car, and then drove over to the Rainbow Grocery on Folsom Street.

"So. Where's your fabulous parking karma now?" Sylvia teased her. They were at a dead stop at the entrance to the parking lot, where a fluorescent-orange-vested fellow stood guard and assigned parking spots.

As they waited, Jules ventured a question. "Was that the Todd who was a witness at your wedding?"

"Yup."

"When he asked how you were, it wasn't just the usual question, you know? It seemed like he was asking more than that. I don't want to be nosy, but…"

"Oh. Sorry, no. It's okay. Yes, he knew all about me and Elena, and he didn't like her. No one did, after they'd known her awhile. You picked up on that?"

"Well, not about your ex. Just the way he asked the 'How are you?' question, as though you maybe hadn't recovered from your breakup."

"He was. Is. Perla, too, because it's been so hard for me to get over Elena."

Jules wanted to ask more, but then they were being waved into the garage.

Sylvia trailed after Jules as they made their way through the crowded store. Jules was clearly on a mission, but various things kept snagging Sylvia's attention. She'd never been to Rainbow; it wasn't her kind of store. *No meat.*

They walked first to the bulk bins. Sylvia was unaware so many varieties of rice or flour or even beans existed. She looked through the various goods with interest while Jules was efficiently filling small envelopes of spices and scooping out a bag of brown rice and writing their numbers. A stern sign advised them, No GRAZING IN THE BULK BINS. Sylvia could easily see childish fingers covered with snot pawing through trail mix. Around the corner from the bulk bins, Sylvia found herself in front of gigantic barrels of peanut butter, apple butter, and almond butter, over which stood a shelf holding metal containers of at least six varieties of honey. The sheer quantity of food stopped her cold. She was staring and didn't notice Jules come to her side until she heard Jules's voice in her right ear.

"How about some organic peanut butter and jelly for dinner?" Jules asked in a low voice. "Crunchy or smooth?" To Sylvia, Jules seemed to be somehow talking about something else. The way she said "smooth" gave her goose bumps and put the thought of smooth skin into her mind.

She was afraid to turn but she responded, pitching her voice just as low as Jules had. "Smooth. Always smooth, for me." She dared to turn and look then, but Jules appeared innocent.

"Ah, good. Fortunately, we're having gumbo, a variation on that vegetarian standby, rice and beans." Jules tilted her head in a self-deprecating way, obviously apologizing for being vegetarian.

"Well, rice and beans are certainly familiar to me." Sylvia let her tone indicate that she was teasing.

"I'll try to make it at least a little exotic."

"I look forward to it," Sylvia said, and she meant it. It meant something for someone to cook for you; it was an act of love. She had certainly learned that at her mother's side in the kitchen, and she hadn't consciously thought of it while making breakfast that morning for Jules, but her mind now put that together. *We're just being nice*, she told herself. *It's what friends do for one another.*

At the produce bins, Sylvia could see more clearly the makeup of Rainbow's customers. They were mostly young, hipster Anglos: tattooed, dreadlocked, and pierced. The good number of Latinos, however, surprised her somewhat, but maybe it was merely their neighborhood store. She also saw trendy young Latinos, the intersection of the two groups. They all looked quite serious, carrying their cloth shopping bags and talking about varieties of kumquats with their companions. Sylvia started to develop a little attitude. Rainbow's customers seemed just a teeny bit self-righteous about their choices. They were, at least the Anglo ones, probably vegan or vegetarian, and they refused to patronize the nasty, price-gouging, corporate, non-organic, environment-raping supermarket. They were far too evolved.

"Come on, I want to show you something. It's my favorite part of the store." Jules touched her elbow to steer her. Sylvia's annoyance at Rainbow's customers ebbed in the face of Jules's enthusiasm.

Near the center of Rainbow were several aisles devoted to vitamins, supplements, minerals, amino acids, herbals, homeopathic meds, protein powders, and the like. Sylvia had never seen such an array. A rack held information sheets, and scattered about the aisles, comparably hip-looking Rainbow staff held detailed technical discussions on the various items with the patrons.

"Holy shit." That was all she could think of to say.

Jules grinned. "I know. It's all much too much, but I love it. I have to watch out in this area or I'll want to buy everything."

As they stood in a long line to check out, Sylvia couldn't resist saying, "This place is holier-than-thou to the max."

"That it is, but it's really a pretty good place to shop, price-wise, and the selection is phenomenal. It beats Whole Foods. You know what they call Whole Foods?"

"Oh, I understand. Latinos shop here and they're cheap. No, what do they call Whole Foods?"

"Whole Paycheck." They looked at each and giggled.

❖

"The secret to good vegetarian food is seasoning," Jules said. "People think vegetarian or vegan food is bland, and it's anything but." She was measuring, mixing, and chopping as Sylvia sat at her kitchen table watching her avidly. "I think Millennium does that very well."

"The food there was great, don't get me wrong," Sylvia said. "I could see eating vegetarian every so often, but I still want my steak and chicken adobo the way Perla makes it. As far as I know, the human body is built to eat everything."

"We eat way too much protein. It's not good for us. We need to eat less or no animal protein."

"I'm not going to argue with you about it. Let's change the subject." Sylvia was chagrined that their good feelings from Rainbow were slipping away. She wanted to go back there and recover them.

"Good idea." Jules fell silent as she continued to assemble their dinner.

"Do your folks know about the polyamory?" Sylvia asked. It was a provocative question, but she was genuinely curious.

"Oh, no. They wouldn't get that at all. I don't discuss it with them. My sister Lydia is the only one who knows about it."

"Are you ashamed of it?"

"Of course not. It's just not something I want to tell them." Jules looked quite uncomfortable, and Sylvia was sorry she'd asked the question and embarrassed her.

"Sorry, I shouldn't have put it that way. I'm a little tactless sometimes."

"It's okay. I think you and I have different relationships with our families."

"Do we need another change of subject?"

"Whatever you want," Jules said, and to Sylvia it sounded like she meant it.

"I guess I want to know about the polyamory because it's so foreign to me."

"Well. I met Toni and Claire about two years ago, maybe a little more." As she cooked, Jules outlined the beginning of their relationship. It could have been the story of a couple, but what was missing was any expression on Jules's part of intense love or devotion. She could be discussing two of her friends, Sylvia thought, except she had sex with them. The concept still floored her. She could maybe comprehend a ménage à trois, although she associated that with two women and a man. The arrangement also left Jules free to pursue other women, and to Sylvia that seemed just plain weird. Her picture of Jules, however, was growing more complete.

"Do you love them?" Sylvia asked.

Jules was quiet, suspiciously quiet. "I do love them," she said, finally.

"Well, love is good." Sylvia meant it.

"They've asked me to move in with them."

"What did you say?"

"I said no." Jules sounded regretful but not distraught.

"Why not?"

"I don't know. I care about them. I enjoy being with them, but it doesn't feel right. At least not now."

"I can understand that. It wouldn't do anyone any good if you moved in with them and it didn't work out."

"Oh, boy. You said it."

"How did they take it?"

"Okay. I guess. We don't have much drama going on, which I'm really grateful for. I had enough drama with my parents."

Sylvia could sense a world of things left unsaid. She was surprised at her reaction to the news that Jules didn't want to live with Claire and Toni. She was relieved. She didn't understand why she found it reassuring that Jules seemed to want to keep some autonomy. On the other hand, it was further evidence of Jules's apparent fear of commitment.

"Do you want to meet them? You could come over for dinner sometime. It would be vegetarian, of course." Jules looked at Sylvia, absurdly hopeful and sincere.

"I suppose I'm never going to be eating any animal flesh in your vicinity."

Sylvia couldn't resist a little sarcasm, but Jules just laughed. "I wouldn't say 'never.'"

And once again, Sylvia got the idea she meant something else.

"Sure, I'd like to meet Claire and Toni sometime." Sylvia didn't know if that was true. She was curious, for sure, but she also didn't want to think about what they and Jules did together. It seemed easier to just try to ignore that part of Jules's life.

CHAPTER ELEVEN

Jules wondered as she rang Claire and Toni's buzzer the following Friday evening why they'd never given her a key. She muttered, "Well, they'd have to give me one if I moved in." The door lock released and she took the elevator up to their unit. As the elevator rose silently, her mind drifted back to Saturday with Sylvia. It had been wonderful. There was no other word for it. They still kept pressing each other's buttons every so often, but somehow they managed to keep going forward.

Were they dating or being friends? It seemed like friends ninety percent of the time, but this nagging little extra layer of feeling kept intruding. It was like the onset of a cold where you don't feel obviously sick but you sure know something's different. Jules shook her head again. She recalled the mild innuendo of some of the things she'd said to Sylvia and almost said aloud, "Stop being such a dumbass." It was a good thing she didn't because Claire was right there at the door, holding it open.

"Hello, sweetheart." She stretched and gave Jules a sexy kiss. Claire rarely used endearments, and Jules wondered what brought the change on.

"Come over and sit with me." Claire wasn't cooking dinner. She'd evidently entrusted it to Toni, which was unprecedented. Jules let Claire take her hand and lead her over to the soft black leather couch.

They settled down, and the precise second they were seated,

Chloe hopped up with an interrogatory meow. A bottle of wine was open on the coffee table, along with two glasses, the table otherwise clear. Claire hated clutter. No magazines were allowed on their coffee table. They couldn't, however, prevent Chloe from leaving her dusty footprints on it, Jules thought with amusement. Cat litter must make Claire crazy.

Since the big question of three weeks before, Jules hadn't detected any difference in their triadic relationship, but she noticed a subtle shift in Claire and Toni's relationship. Maybe they were just a wee bit tenser with each other. Claire's tone was more clipped and Toni seemed more jumpy. Now here was this startling role reversal with Toni cooking and Claire acting all solicitous with her. What was going on?

Jules hadn't talked about her various encounters with Sylvia, not that she was keeping anything from them. There was nothing to disclose. Even if there had been, theoretically it wouldn't be a problem. She didn't want to examine too closely why she was so closemouthed about Sylvia. It was probably because of Claire's attitude when she'd first told them about her, but it seemed to be more than that. She felt protective of her relationship with Sylvia for some reason, which was unlike her; she was usually so open. Their relationship rules encouraged and welcomed openness, and Claire had always told her the secrecy and nutty sneaking around of supposedly monogamous couples made polyamorous people disdainful. Nonconsensual nonmonogamy was how Claire described it.

Claire sat quite close to her on the couch and appeared relaxed and casual, with one leg crossed and her hands around her knee. Jules sat back with her legs apart and watched Chloe perform her little cat rituals. "So. How are you, Jules?"

"I'm good. How about you?"

"Not bad. I'm asking because you haven't said much for a few weeks. We wanted to know if you're all right."

Oh, "we," is it? Jules thought. "I'm fine. No worries."

Claire rubbed Jules's shoulder in a distracted way and smiled at her. What was she thinking? Generally Claire was either overtly sexual or physically distant, and nothing in between.

"That's good to hear. We wondered. Do you want to talk about anything?"

"Nope. I'm okay." She felt guilty about not being more open with Claire and Toni about seeing Sylvia.

"We are so fond of you," Claire said, and hugged her.

Fond? That's nice. I feel guiltier than ever.

Toni came in to say dinner was just about ready. Pushing her guilt aside, Jules followed Claire to the dining-room table. It wasn't as though she was cheating on them, for God's sake. She just didn't want to listen to their criticism. That was all.

❖

Whose move was it next? Although Sylvia had invited Jules to Cinco de Mayo, she had invited Sylvia to dinner. It was a pain because Jules very much wanted to see Sylvia again, but she didn't want Sylvia to get the wrong idea and start backing off, which, to Jules's great surprise and happiness, so far, she hadn't. Jules didn't understand what was going on at all, but she was willing to play along and see what would happen. She no longer even questioned why she thought about Sylvia so much. In the midst of her musings, her phone rang. It said *Sylvia* now, and Jules had set up a special ring tone for her—"La Bamba." It seemed to fit. And when she saw and heard the evidence that Sylvia was calling, she was thrilled. None of her girlfriends had ever had their own ringtones.

"Hello, Jules?'

"Hiya."

"Hey, can you get the day off on Thursday?" Jules heard the undercurrent of excitement in Sylvia's voice.

"Sorry, but probably not. I need more than two days to arrange it with my clients. Why?"

"We got the word the California Supreme Court is issuing its decision on Thursday morning at ten a.m. I'm going to be there and wanted you to come."

Jules gripped the phone, trying to stay calm. It was finally time for the court decision, it was a big deal, and Sylvia wanted her to be there. With her. She was asking her to share in this moment. Jules desperately wanted to, but she could hardly arrange a substitute for her dogs at this point. Well, she could, theoretically, but she'd owe someone a big favor, and she was reluctant to be put in that position.

"I'm so sorry, but I can't. I really wish I could, but—"

Sylvia uncharacteristically interrupted her, so she was obviously *really* excited.

"Hey, it's okay. I kind of thought not, but there'll be a rally at the LGBT center at five p.m. whatever way the case is decided. Can you come to that?"

"Sure. Where do I meet you?"

"I'll be at the center early and try to get us seats."

"I'll be there. Sylvia? Call me as soon as you get the news Thursday. I want to know as soon as you do."

"Absolutely."

Jules snapped her phone shut, genuinely excited for Sylvia and, more than that, elated that Sylvia wanted her there. The politics still didn't much matter to her, but being with Sylvia certainly did.

❖

"I can't *stand* it," Hana said. "The suspense is *killing* me!"

Sylvia, Perla, Hana, and Elspeth were in the midst of a largish crowd in front of the California Supreme Court Building on Van Ness Avenue. It was nine forty-five in the morning, and the day already promised to be exceptionally warm for May. The marriage equality supporters had a few signs and some rainbow flags, but mostly they were gathered in tight little groups, alternately talking and staring at the door through which a court employee was expected to emerge with the court decision.

Across the street, the loyal opposition, mostly overweight, glowering men held signs with charming sentiments like HOMOSEXUALS BURN IN HELL! The mildest sign said, MARRIAGE=1 MAN AND 1 WOMAN, with little silhouette pictures to help explain what gender looked like in stick-figure form.

Hana whispered, "Look." They all turned and watched as a young man with a pile of documents in his arms emerged from the doorway. The crowd surged forward, and he passed out the papers as fast as he was able. Some of the feistier reporters got there first, but Perla, with the judicious use of her sharp elbows, managed to snag one and they gathered around her as she furiously started flipping the pages. Around them people began to scream and shout.

"Hurry!" Sylvia implored Perla. Hana and Elspeth clung together, looking anxiously over Perla's shoulder.

"Here it is!" Perla cried, putting her finger on the page. She read aloud as the other three women scanned the page. "'The Constitution properly must be interpreted to guarantee this basic civil right to all Californians, whether gay or heterosexual, and to same-sex couples as well as opposite-sex couples.' We won, we won." Perla tossed the papers into the air and leaped into Sylvia's arms. Hana and Elspeth kissed and hugged. The crowd around them was jubilant and growing noisier by the second.

"The wedding's on!" Hana shouted, and kissed Elspeth again. "We're gonna get married, we're gonna get married!" When they stopped kissing for a breath of air, Elspeth said, "We got domestic-partnered in 2002, married at City Hall in 2004, and now we'll do it again. We'll do it as many times as we fucking have to!" They excitedly talked to the other people and read aloud sections of the court's opinion to each other. Across the street, some reporters were interviewing the homophobes.

"Wonder what *they're* saying?" Sylvia asked her friends.

"Who cares? I hope *they* burn in hell!" Perla said. "Never mind them, though. Are we going over to City Hall to watch the press conference?"

Hana and Elspeth affirmed they would, and Sylvia said, "I'll catch up with you. I have to call Jules and tell her the news."

Perla laughed. "All righty, sister. You just go ahead and do that."

Sylvia glared at her, even more annoyed by Perla's knowing smirk. She followed a few feet behind her friends and took out her cell.

❖

Jules was pulling herself together to start her day when she heard "La Bamba."

"Hi there. I hope you have some good news." She couldn't disguise her happiness at hearing Sylvia's voice.

"The best! We've won. The Supreme Court says it's unconstitutional to deny us marriage rights. It's right there in black and white and signed by the judge!"

"Oh, wow, you must be so happy. I'm happy for you."

"I'm happy for all of us. It's so tremendous. It's incredible. So, I'm going to City Hall for a while, and then I think we'll have lunch. Can you come to the center later?" Sylvia was so excited, she sounded a little out of breath.

"Sure. Where do we meet? Do you think it'll be crowded?"

"Oh, yeah, it'll be nuts. Perla and I'll go in and get seats. Call me when you get there. I'll be waiting for you."

"Sounds good, see you later!" Jules hung up, thinking the words "I'll be waiting for you" had a great sound. It was even okay that she was going to yet another political meeting. Just being with Sylvia was enough.

❖

Jules was wrung out and sweaty by the time she'd finished delivering all her dogs to their respective homes. Her car radio reported that the temperature was over ninety degrees. In fact, it had been so hot, she'd taken the group to Golden Gate Park, where those who didn't feel up to playing could relax in the shade. She was more inclined to do that herself. As a typical San Franciscan, Jules felt that a temperature of eighty was quite high enough. She was running late, too. Sylvia had said to meet her a few minutes before five p.m., and it was already four thirty. She decided that a bus was the wisest choice and ran over to Lincoln Boulevard to snag the number 71 Haight/Market bus.

Jules got off the bus at the corner of Page and Market. As she crossed Page Street and began to walk toward Market, she saw that a large crowd had already gathered and was spilling out from the sidewalk, where horn-honking motorists had to make their way carefully around the people. It struck Jules that they were honking their horns in solidarity, not because they were angry at the street being blocked. Jules sprinted up the sidewalk, scanning the passersby, looking for Sylvia even though she knew Sylvia must be inside. She pulled out her phone and hit Sylvia's speed-dial number.

"Hello? Jules?"

"Yeah. Where are you? There's so many people here."

"I know. If you can get in, we're near the front of the lobby, by the stage."

"I'll do my best." Jules started to thread her way through the mob. Fortunately, many people seemed to be milling around outside, scanning the street or talking into their phones, sharing their excitement. She got into the main lobby space, but it was far more crowded near the front. She looked over the crowd but couldn't find Sylvia in the throng. As she pushed her way as politely as she could toward the stage, she spotted Sylvia with Perla by her side.

Facing slightly away, she was saying something to Perla. She was wearing blue jeans and a red tank top, with a shirt tied around her waist. Her hair was down but looked a little disordered. As Jules got closer, she saw that Sylvia was a bit flushed from the heat, which gave her light-brown skin a nice glow. She looked incredibly beautiful and infinitely desirable. Desire welled up and she struggled to quash it. When she tapped Sylvia gently on the shoulder she spun around, startled, then recognized Jules and threw her arms around her. Jules held on to her, conscious of both her own body heat and Sylvia's, and a jolt of arousal seared through her, stronger than any she'd ever felt.

"Hi. I didn't mean to startle you." Jules was holding on and practically whispering into Sylvia's ear.

Sylvia said, "Oh, I didn't know how long it would take you, and I couldn't keep twisting around…" She leaned back a little in Jules's arms so they could make eye contact, and Jules tried to keep it together under an onslaught of emotions, happiness, anxiety, and sexual arousal. Hot and getting hotter, she couldn't read the expression that remained on Sylvia's face after her initial surprise drained away and Sylvia gently disengaged from their embrace.

"I'm glad we found each other. Perla and everyone are all here." Perla, Hana, and Elspeth greeted Jules with exuberant hugs. She returned them happily but kept her attention on Sylvia, who was focused on the stage. Jules wasn't disappointed because it gave her the opportunity to scrutinize Sylvia a little more. Her skin was misted with sweat, as Jules had noticed during their all-too-brief hug, and she was practically vibrating from excitement. Jules was nearly speechless with desire, and she was afraid she might pant like a dog and drool soon. She caught Sylvia's excitement as well as the emotions emanating from the crowd. She had been to the pride parade several times and it felt somewhat like that, but more so. Something momentous was occurring, and she was being pulled into it by Sylvia's reaction. She was content to watch as Sylvia rocked on her heels, chatted with Perla or Hana, or grinned happily with anyone who caught her eye.

Jules recognized the man from the EQCA meeting she'd attended a few weeks before as he walked onto the stage. The people in the crowd started to focus on him and their conversations moderated. He tapped the microphone and said "Testing," which reverberated over their heads and managed to get almost everyone's attention.

"Hello!" his amplified voice boomed. "I'm Mark Mahan from Equality California. Is this a great day or what?" The crowd screamed, roared, whistled, clapped.

"In case anyone here did *not* get the news…Today the Supreme Court of California affirmed that denying marriage to LGBT people is unconstitutional!" More noise. Jules fixed her gaze on Sylvia as she hung on every one of Mark's words and waved her arms. It was a remarkable transformation.

Jules had long suspected a deep vein of passion lay inside Sylvia that she took care to hide under a matter-of-fact façade, and here was the proof. Jules had worked hard to quell her attraction to Sylvia, both for her own sanity and so she wouldn't damage their budding friendship, and she'd been mostly successful. But her resolve was cracking. They were both caught up in the emotions of the moment, and even the uncharacteristic warmth of the evening was impelling Jules toward doing something she might regret but that she wouldn't ultimately be able to prevent. They were standing close together and were pressed even closer by the crowd surrounding them. Jules was intensely conscious of their nearness. She was certain invisible sexual signals were passing between their two bodies.

Mark continued his speech but Jules could no longer hear him because she was too focused on Sylvia. She realized that another person had taken the microphone, though, one of the attorneys on the case. She spoke for a few minutes and Sylvia listened raptly. Jules wished Sylvia would direct that adoration toward her. The crowd seemed equally taken by her, if their dedicated attention was any indication. Then a representative from the San Francisco county clerk's office rose to explain that weddings could begin on the first of June. Finally Mark came back and said, "I'm now thrilled to introduce you to the mayor of San Francisco, Gavin Newsom."

The response of the crowd was deafening, and during all that noise, Sylvia turned her radiant smile on Jules. Jules stopped thinking rationally and gave in to the irresistible urge and kissed her. Sylvia kissed her back with equal fervor for a few incandescent seconds before she drew away with an unreadable expression and returned her attention to the speakers.

Jules was breathing heavily both from desire and astonishment at her temerity. She looked around, guiltily wondering if any of Sylvia's friends had seen them and deciding she didn't care one way or the other. She only cared what Sylvia was thinking. This wasn't the time for a discussion, though, and chastened, Jules paid attention to the event and the speakers, although she kept looking at Sylvia out of the corner of her eye. Most of the speeches ran together for Jules until near the end, when they caught her attention because the mood of the crowd changed so radically, as did Sylvia's attitude. She'd gone from ecstatically happy to serious in a moment.

The current speaker was telling the now-somber crowd that a group of right-wing religious fanatics had turned in over a million signatures to the secretary of state of California to amend the California constitution to take away their newly won right to marry. The people were muttering and cursing now. The speaker cautioned them: "We don't know if it will qualify because it takes a while for them to check that many signatures. Even if it does qualify for the November election, we'll fight it and we can win." At this statement, the crowd noise took on a different, belligerent tone, filled with angry mutterings.

The rally broke up shortly thereafter, and Jules accompanied Sylvia and her friends up Market Street as they discussed dinner plans.

"I'm not hungry," Sylvia said. "I think I'll just go home."

They gathered around to hug and kiss her and hugged Jules

as well, who stood awkwardly off to the side, unsure what to do. When they were gone, Jules and Sylvia were facing one another and Jules stared at her, saying nothing because she didn't know what to say. Sylvia stared back at her and seemed about to speak, but all she said was, "Thanks for coming out to this with me. I'm tired and I really need to go home. I hope you understand."

"Sure. No problem." She wanted to ask Sylvia what she was feeling, but Sylvia had withdrawn. "Which way are you going?"

"Back to Eighteenth Street." Sylvia gestured behind them. They stood at the corner of Noe and Market Street. The neighborhood was almost always lively, but on this night with the unusually warm temperature and the events of the day, it was even more crowded. The palpable air of elation contrasted directly with the tension between them. Jules sought a way to keep their connection.

"I'll walk you to the bus stop." They set off on their three-block walk.

"What did you think?" Jules asked, finally.

"About what?"

"About our kiss."

"It was a kiss, what's there to think about? It happened."

"Yeah, but did you like it?" Jules was growing a little desperate. They were walking faster as they rounded the corner and started down Castro toward their agreed-upon end point, and she didn't have much time. She didn't know exactly what she wanted to hear, but this wasn't it.

"Of course I liked it. It was a very nice kiss." Sylvia was being maddeningly vague.

"You're kidding me, right?" Jules was afraid she was starting to sound angry and she didn't like it, but, as with the kiss, she was powerless to stop it. All the emotional turmoil was catching up to her. Sylvia was striding at a blistering pace, weaving among the many people on the street. Jules was managing to keep up with her, but only just.

"What do you mean?" Sylvia turned to look at her, and her blank look disturbed Jules.

"I…I'm not sure. I guess I thought you might have *something* to say."

"Jules. It's getting late. I want to go home." It was only a short time after sunset, seven thirty or eight o'clock at the latest. Jules struggled to keep from either shouting or bursting into tears.

They made it to the 33 Ashbury bus stop at the corner, and there stood the stupid bus, on time. Jules didn't want the conversation to end. She wanted to get on the bus with Sylvia or walk, whatever. Just so they could stay together and talk, and maybe Sylvia would tell her what she thought of the kiss.

"Okay. But I'll call you. Can we get together this weekend?"

"I'll call you." Sylvia hopped up the steps into the bus.

Jules didn't recall ever feeling so bereft as she did at that moment.

CHAPTER TWELVE

Perla glared at Sylvia, who pretended not to notice. It was exactly a week after the big court decision and they were eating lunch at the usual place.

"I *saw* her kiss you and you kissed her back for a second."

This was a repeat of the conversation they'd had on the phone Thursday night. Perla had called Sylvia the moment she walked in the door, with the unerring timing of a nosy best friend.

"Just for a second, and it was an automatic reaction." Sylvia was trying to concentrate on eating lunch, even though she knew Perla wouldn't be deflected.

"Bull. Shit."

Perla was clearly getting angry, but Sylvia couldn't help that and didn't want to discuss it.

"Syl. You might want to talk to her. You just told me she asked you to. You need to be honest. It's not fair to either of you to act like nothing happened."

"That's just the trouble." Sylvia threw down her fork. "I don't know what to do. Yes, she kissed me. Yes, I liked it. I liked it a lot." She slumped back in the grubby vinyl-covered chair. Perla was sitting straight-backed, looking at her with a combination of concern and exasperation. "I'm attracted to her. But it would be monumentally stupid for us to get involved. You fucking know it would!" She sounded desperate but it was the truth.

Sylvia had ridden the bus home from the Thursday rally

feeling Jules's lips on hers. The feeling had persisted into the evening and disrupted her sleep as she replayed the moment. The taste of Jules's lips, the way their bodies felt pressed together, the longing in Jules's eyes all left her confused but full of craving. She remembered that feeling only too well. Her joy at the day's events plus the experience with Jules had all merged into one gigantic swell of emotion. What had been nibbling at the edge of her consciousness for weeks now consumed her waking mind, and she was being inexorably drawn into an affair with Jules.

She had no idea if she was overjoyed or terrified. Probably both. She had to stop denying that something was going on. That was unfair to Jules and wasn't good for her either. She needed to put the brakes on her emotions. Getting involved with Jules would be a bad judgment call. Her vision of an affair didn't include four people. Just one was enough. Talk about baggage, good God.

"Suppose I do sleep with her? What then?"

"Did it ever occur to you that she might want to have a different kind of relationship with you?"

Sylvia looked at her, horrified. "Have you lost your mind? She's polyamorous. I am not going to let myself fall for someone like that. Do you think I could be part of that?"

"Well, you've never tried it, but that's not what I mean, Syl. This isn't the same as Elena. You don't know if the polyamory is permanent or not. Besides, at this point, we're just talking about you dating her. We're not talking about forever."

"It was hell with Elena. I'm so not going through *that* again. This would be simply a different version of hell. Even if she said she would stop being polyamorous, how would I ever trust that she wanted me and only me?"

"You won't know that, and like I said, we're just talking about dating."

"Right. I have to get back to work now."

When Sylvia walked home from work that night she thought about Jules and about the kiss and how it felt. She wasn't ready to jump into anything yet. She had her convictions and was determined not to make a mistake. She did, however, owe Jules an explanation.

❖

"I'm not feeling well. That's all," Jules told Toni on the phone on Friday morning. "It's been really hot the last couple of days and I'm drained."

"That's okay. You can relax here, we'll have dinner."

"I know, Tone, but I'm really not feeling like leaving my apartment."

"Okay. Sweetie, take care of yourself. I'll talk to you later."

They said their good-byes and Jules felt a little guilty. She hadn't lied exactly because she really wasn't feeling well, but it was probably psychosomatic. She'd been waiting for Sylvia to call but she hadn't. She wanted to be home by herself when, if, Sylvia called, and *not* at Toni and Claire's.

The weekend dragged by and the workweek began with still no word from Sylvia. Jules ached to call her and beg her to get together, but she didn't, knowing that could be a fatal mistake. Sylvia was such a straightforward person the silence was evidence enough of what had to be a huge dilemma for her. Jules was convinced she wasn't wrong about what she sensed between them. But she remembered what Sylvia had said during their walk at Fort Funston and knew Sylvia was probably thinking. Still, she had hope, and she dragged through her days on autopilot, waiting for a phone call that didn't come.

It would even be okay if she called to say, "Leave me alone. I don't want to see you." It would be better to just know. If Jules had to let go of her desire for Sylvia, she could do that; at least she hoped she could. It was entirely new for her to be the pursuer rather than the pursued. She didn't want to frighten Sylvia away, but she didn't want to let her go either. The thought of never seeing her again was awful.

Jules was at Fort Funston dispiritedly throwing tennis balls for the ball-chasing members of her group. She was in a funk: the entire week had gone by with no word from Sylvia. It was Friday. Suddenly the familiar notes of "La Bamba" sounded in her pocket, and a tremor composed equally of fear and joy rolled through her body. Her hand shook as she pulled out her phone and flipped it open.

"Hi, Sylvia." Jules was pleased that her voice betrayed none of what she was feeling.

"Hello, Jules."

Jules enjoyed the sound of that slightly low-pitched voice with the barest hint of a Spanish accent, the voice she heard in her head at odd moments, the voice she wanted to hear in her ear whispering endearments during lovemaking. She shivered and gripped the phone tight.

"How are you?"

"I'm well. Sorry I haven't called."

"I think I know why. But I've missed hearing from you."

"No, you probably don't know why, but you might think I'm a classless bitch."

"No, not at all, but could you tell me why you think you are? Actually, I'd rather talk to you in person. Could we do that?" Jules couldn't quite keep the note of pleading from her voice. "I can come over to your house or can we meet somewhere?" Jules prayed during the seconds of silent hesitation.

"Let's meet at the Muddy Waters Café on Church Street. Saturday at eleven okay for you?"

"Sure. I'll be there." Jules closed the phone and took a shaky breath. Maybe there was hope after all. *Hope for what, exactly?*

❖

Jules spent Friday night as usual at Toni and Claire's house. Outwardly, she endeavored to be her usual self, but in her mind, everything was in turmoil. Jules wanted Sylvia more than she'd ever wanted anyone. She'd been happy to have girls chase her, as they sometimes did. The strength of her feelings for Sylvia frightened her. The fact that she didn't want to discuss them with Claire and Toni scared her as well. When they made love, she felt like she was being unfaithful to Sylvia, which was even more insane.

But that was the crux of the problem. Sylvia wouldn't enter a relationship with her that wouldn't lead to absolute commitment, in essence, marriage. Jules wasn't ready for that now, nor did she think she'd ever be. She'd seen marriage up close with her mom and dad, and it seemed ugly and soul-destroying. At one time it must have been different. She and her two sisters were evidence of that, which made it even more depressing. Long ago, her parents had been young and in love, and they'd married and had three children. Then somehow it all went badly sour.

Jules shuddered. It would be worse to start out in love and have it deteriorate than to never start at all. That was most likely the reason she had fallen into the poly relationship with Claire and Toni. She hadn't made a conscious decision; instead she'd let them seduce her into their bed and into their lives. She slid into her role like a foot into a nice, comfortable slipper. It was easy, pleasant, and sexually fulfilling. Until they'd asked her to move in, she'd never even thought about the future with them or what it might look like.

Now there was Sylvia. Hot, gorgeous, passionate, unattainable Sylvia. Her easygoing, no-frills, no-drama life was no more. What had happened to her? She was a fucking mess.

❖

With every step she took on her walk from Bartlett to Church and Fifteenth Street, Sylvia grew less certain what she was going to say to Jules. She was in denial about her feelings. The kiss hadn't been just good; it had been remarkable. Jules, who was usually so calm and laid back, had turned into an entirely different person. The kiss, when it happened, seemed inevitable, like it had been waiting to happen all along, as though their every encounter had been a step closer to that outcome.

Sylvia imagined what another kiss like that would lead to. She imagined the two of them in bed, naked...

When she'd walked away from Jules that night, it had taken all her willpower. Jules had noticed her response as well as her hasty exit; she wasn't stupid. Sylvia was sending mixed signals and had to be clear with herself as well as with Jules.

A few nights previously, she hadn't been able to sleep and had tried a little masturbation, which had always been effective for insomnia. She started touching herself and quickly fantasized what Jules's body would be like, how her hands and mouth would feel. She was so turned on, she came faster than ever before. Lying in the dark panting, she desperately wished Jules had been touching her.

She stopped in front of Muddy Waters and looked in the window. Jules was already there, sitting on a bench near the back, slouching and staring into the middle distance. She was dressed in her usual faded 501 Levi's and hooded sweatshirt of plain blue, a couple of shades darker than her jeans. Sylvia felt guilty because Jules looked so down. *I've gone and confused the hell out of her.*

She took a breath and walked in the door and directly to Jules, who looked up as soon as she reached the table. Her glacier-colored eyes looked even lighter indoors. Her expression was wary and tight, so unlike she usually looked. Sylvia felt worse by the second as she stood before Jules's table.

"Hi."

"Hi."

"I'm going to get a coffee. Do you want anything?"

"Nope. I'm fine."

After placing her order for her usual mocha, Sylvia returned and sat down across from Jules, who looked at her expectantly.

"Are you okay?" Sylvia asked Jules, for lack of anything better to say, but she was truly concerned.

"Depends."

"On what?"

"On how this conversation goes." Jules's lips were generally relaxed and always seemed on the verge of a smile. This time, her lips were compressed as though she was trying to hold something back. Sylvia had never seen her like this, and it unnerved her.

"I see. Well, I'll do my best to be as honest as I can."

"That's a good place to start."

Sylvia, stalling for time, asked what she thought was an innocent question. "Did you stay at Toni and Claire's last night?"

"Yeah. Why do you ask?" Jules was uncharacteristically abrupt.

"No reason. Just a question. Why are you so touchy?" It annoyed Sylvia to think of Jules with Claire and Toni. She fought to stay calm.

"I'm a little over-caffeinated. I've been here a while." Jules seemed almost contrite, but not quite. She paused, staring directly at Sylvia. In the silence, the café noises seemed louder than they should have. To Sylvia, the two of them seemed suspended in time with no obvious next step, no path to take.

"Mocha cappuccino!" the barista shouted, breaking the moment.

"Be right back." Sylvia retrieved her large white mug of coffee and chocolate and whipped cream. It would be better if it was a nice big glass of tequila, but that wasn't possible.

She sat back down in the wooden chair, wrapped both hands around the warm cup, and put her nose over the steam. It smelled great. She looked up and into Jules's eyes, with their dilated pupils. Dilated pupils meant someone was sexually attracted to you. Well, that wasn't news, she thought irritably. Nevertheless, Jules's pupils were exerting a pull on her and making it hard to form sentences. She pushed the thought aside and went on.

"I'm sorry about the other night."

"Are you? I'm not." Jules tented her fingers together and stared intently at Sylvia over them.

"If you mean the kiss, no, then, no, I'm not sorry about that either. I'm sorry about the way I left you."

"Okay, apology accepted. You know, that was so fast, it was almost like you needed to escape me."

"I needed to escape myself." It was true. Jules wasn't the problem here; she was. Her and her stupid ambivalence.

"Why is that?" Jules asked. Her smile had returned, but Sylvia didn't find that especially reassuring. Her expression said, "I want to see you naked."

"All right, you want me to say it and you won't be satisfied until I do. The kiss was terrific, and I'm one hundred percent sure I want to sleep with you." Those few sentences came out abruptly, and, truthfully, Sylvia sounded bitchy even to herself.

Jules's smile became a huge grin, and she spread her arms wide in a phantom embrace.

"But I can't."

Jules's face fell immediately and she dropped her arms back to her sides. "Can't or won't?" Her voice was rough with disappointment.

"Both."

"Why? No, never mind, I know why. You're not going to get involved with someone who's poly. You've said so."

"Yes. Try to understand, Jules. I like you very much as a person, and you're very attractive. I *know* that. I've felt it, feel it right now. But…" Sylvia looked at the ceiling, trying to think of the right words.

Jules raised her eyebrows. "You know if we slept together, it wouldn't be mindless sex? I'm poly but I'm not shallow."

"That's the problem. I might like it too much. Also, I tend to need to marry the woman I sleep with, and I can't marry you. You don't want to marry me either, in the literal or figurative sense."

"You realize that's a very narrow view? It's 2008, Sylvia.

We don't need to get married. As a matter of fact, queers have never needed to get married."

"I know what year it is, Jules. And I know myself. We're not going to have a political discussion about marriage right now."

"You wouldn't bend your rules for me? I'm really into you and I'd treat you right. I'm not a player. I've never been dishonest with you. I never would be."

"It's not about my rules. It's about both of us knowing ourselves and knowing there's no future for us. It's better to not even start. I'm so sorry, Jules. I can't do it. I'd love to, believe me, but I can't. I don't want to have to share the woman I'm with. Not with anyone."

Jules had been leaning forward eagerly, but now she slumped back, seeming defeated. "You're so beautiful, you make my eyes hurt."

"Oh, now you're really reaching. You sound like some Latin lover in one of those bad Telemundo soap operas."

"Ouch." Jules winced.

"Jules, you're sweet and kind. I like you, and if things were different, I'd be happy to date you."

Jules rolled her eyes. "Yeah. Yeah."

"No. I mean it. Don't be like that. We're friends and we're going to stay friends, but we might need a little distance."

"Nope, not me. Distance isn't going to make any difference to me."

"Yes. *I* need a little distance, anyway."

"All right. How long?"

Sylvia looked up at the ceiling. "I don't know. Three weeks, maybe?"

"Fine. I'll call you three weeks from today."

"That would be great. Let's do that." Sylvia stood up and thought for a microsecond before she leaned over and kissed Jules lightly on the cheek. "Bye." She left the café before her true feelings could betray her.

CHAPTER THIRTEEN

Sylvia was annoyed to find herself anticipating the day Jules would call, and she almost phoned her once or twice but refrained. It irked her to have to moderate her behavior so she wouldn't give the wrong impression, wouldn't lead Jules on. It was already bad enough that they'd kissed and she'd admitted liking it. Admitting it to herself was even worse than confessing it to Jules.

She didn't consider herself a prude; it wasn't necessary to have a wedding band or a declaration of love to enjoy sex with someone. But sex with Jules would most likely be unimaginably good, and coupled with Sylvia's existing feelings about her, she would be trapped as completely as she had been by Elena. She couldn't imagine that.

Sylvia didn't want to fall in love with someone unattainable, and she couldn't endure the agony of another failed relationship. Jules was nothing like Elena, but that didn't stop her defense mechanisms. Unfortunately, her brain was active with fantasies, and had been from almost the moment they met. But after that kiss, it had become so much worse. Sylvia had an active sex drive, and though it had been asleep for a very long time, thanks to Jules it was awake and clamoring for attention. In the café, only the daylight and being out in public had made her able to keep her distance. She wasn't doing very well, though, with *really* keeping her distance.

In the meantime, Perla, though she hadn't said anything, was lying in wait for the moment Sylvia admitted defeat and confessed she'd done exactly what Perla had predicted. Sylvia loved her, but her competitive, egotistical side didn't want to give Perla the satisfaction of being right.

She could add *that* to the list of reasons why nothing would ever go anywhere with Jules, along with Jules's already complicated love life and Sylvia's determination to never be caught again in an impossible and painful situation. There they were: three irrefutably good reasons she would never start an affair with Jules.

❖

Sylvia had made one difference in Jules's life: now it was routine for Jules to watch the evening news. At first, she watched so she wouldn't miss a marriage update and look stupid to Sylvia. In spite of her assertion about queers not needing marriage, she now knew that lots of them wanted it desperately. And her experience at the meeting after the court decision had had an impact. Not just Sylvia's emotional fervor, but everyone's happy tears had moved Jules in a way she'd never been moved. It was extraordinary to see those older couples brimming with anticipation about getting married after decades of being together. Jules had felt wistful as she'd watched them during the meeting. They listened to the speakers while holding hands, sometimes kissing. They all looked so happy. The contrast between what she saw at that meeting and her parents' relationship boggled her mind.

Jules flopped into the armchair in her living room and turned on the six o'clock news. As soon as the newscaster started to describe the lead story, Jules sat up straighter and increased the volume. According to the pretty but plastic-looking lady behind the desk, the anti-gay marriage forces had handily managed to qualify an initiative for the November election, a constitutional amendment to stop marriage equality. Jules couldn't imagine what sort of effect this would have on Sylvia, and to her astonishment, it also deeply troubled her. Most likely Sylvia had known before it hit the news. Their three-week cooling-off period wasn't quite up yet, but she itched to call Sylvia. Finally she decided to go ahead and the hell with the consequences. She hit Sylvia's number on her speed dial and waited, growing nervous about what kind of reception she would get. Thanks to caller ID, Sylvia would know who was calling and have the option to not answer, though Jules prayed she wouldn't exercise that option.

"Hello, Jules." She didn't sound overjoyed, but she wasn't angry *and* she had answered, which must be a good sign.

"Hi there. Are you watching the news?"

"I am, as a matter of fact."

"Then you know."

"If you mean about the initiative, yes. I know."

"What does this mean?"

"It means we have to convince people to vote it down. We have to fight."

"That's really awful. We just got marriage equality and now they want to take it away." Jules was surprised to find her feelings behind this were genuine.

"Yes, it's terrible, but it's not 2002 or 2004. Things are different."

"I hope so. What are you going to do?"

"I don't know. We'll see on Sunday night at the meeting."

Jules cleared her throat. "I know we weren't supposed to talk until Saturday, but I wanted to call you about the news. Can I go with you to the meeting?" *Well, I probably have to admit my motives are mixed.*

"Sure. Anyone can go. It's not closed. A lot of folks will be there. This is a big deal." Sylvia sounded unconcerned, but Jules sensed it was a façade.

"I'd like to go to the meeting with *you*. And Perla, too. Dinner before?"

There was a pause.

"Okay. We'll meet at La Cumbre. Six p.m."

"I'll be there."

❖

Sylvia wasn't perturbed that Jules had jumped the gun on their cooling-off time frame. She was glad she'd called, glad they were having dinner. It wasn't a date since Perla would be there. There was nothing wrong with spending time with Jules. Also she'd said, "*We* just got marriage equality," which was terrific. They could volunteer together, take walks, be friends. It seemed harmless enough.

The meeting was so crowded Sylvia, Jules, and Perla had to squeeze in against the back wall. Hana and Elspeth turned to wave at them, but they didn't dare leave their seats. Once again, Jules and Sylvia were forced into close physical contact as more and more people crowded into the room.

Dinner had been pleasant, if not a huge success. Jules had concentrated on not staring at Sylvia and getting to know Perla a bit more. Sylvia hadn't said much; she let Jules and Perla talk. Perla was uncommonly animated and chatty with her, but that was probably due to Perla's personality.

Once again, Jules was struggling with her automatic physical response to being close to Sylvia. The room was heating up, naturally, with all the bodies crammed into it, and, Jules strongly suspected, she and Sylvia were generating their own additional heat.

Mark rose to open the meeting, and with his opening statement, the shouting and hissing started. "I guess you all know what happened. The Protect Marriage people have qualified a proposition for the November ballot. It'll be Proposition 8 in the state initiatives." The noise was almost deafening. When a guy next to Jules blew a metal whistle and nearly pierced her eardrum,

Jules whispered to Sylvia, "Yikes, that was loud. What's up with the whistle?"

Sylvia's face was tantalizingly close, close enough for another kiss, but Jules, after a quick glance at Sylvia's lips, met her eyes and forced herself to concentrate on Sylvia's answer. Sylvia's breath tickled her ear as she said, "The whistle-blowing started back in the eighties. When someone was being gay-bashed, he'd blow a whistle to get help. Now it's a sign of us being attacked."

Jules drew back in surprise. She'd never thought of anything like that, but it made sense. They turned their attention back to Mark.

"Yes, we're under attack. Yes, the homophobes now want to put our right to marry to a vote. No, it's not fair." He paused to let the crowd react. Jules was totally impressed at how well he could handle the crowd and its firestorm of emotion. Mark's face was grim as he held up his hand, and gradually the room quieted down. "I've been in touch with the folks in LA. We've had a conference call with all the marriage advocacy groups, and we have a game plan." He paused, this time for effect. "The polls show that it's almost dead even between those who favor marriage equality and those who don't among California's registered voters. We may have a slight edge but it's within the margin of error." After scattered cheers and more rumbling, someone shouted, "Polls aren't accurate!"

"No, polls aren't perfect, but some are better than others, and there is more than one. The consensus of those on the call is that we can win. But it won't be easy. We had someone from Massachusetts Freedom to Marry on the call. He reminded us that the fundies tried to take marriage away from them after it was passed, but they beat them back. He said it's overwhelmingly emotional and it's horrendously hard work. We're going to have to raise a buttload of money. The other side has the backing of evangelical churches and—"

The sound of outrage threatened to break the windows. Jules

glanced at Sylvia. Her face was set in an angry mask and her eyes flashed. Jules could almost read her mind. She was every bit as alluring as she had been weeks before at the meeting where she exuded joy. The sight made Jules weak-kneed and breathless. *I need to get a grip.*

"We're going to run a professional campaign, bring in the best strategists and political minds we can find. We'll need all of you to step up." Mark paused once more and then began speaking again, his voice becoming louder as he went on. "And don't forget, marriage is legal right now. It stays legal through all of this, and at the end of the day, it will still be legal!" The room erupted once again and Jules clapped along with everyone else, but she was looking at and thinking of Sylvia.

❖

"What've you been up to, J?" Claire asked in a deceptively pleasant tone as she poured them glasses of wine before dinner a couple of weeks later. Jules stiffened and knew Claire would notice her hesitation.

"Not much, really. I've had only four dogs this week. Elvis's daddies took him on vacation with them."

"You know, I was wondering…" Claire sounded way too casual. Normally she asked questions like a district attorney with a murder suspect. "You don't talk about Sylvia at all lately. Do you ever see her anymore?"

"Yeah, we're friends. I've spent some time with her." Jules was glad her tone stayed as neutral as Claire's. She still felt guilty for not being forthcoming with them, even though her involvement with Sylvia hadn't come to anything. She'd gone to a couple more ECQA meetings with Perla and Sylvia but didn't want Claire and Toni making fun of her for chasing Sylvia.

Claire looked at her searchingly but changed the subject, to Jules's relief.

"We're going to the pride parade with a bunch of people

from the network. You could probably find someone to hook up with, at least for the day," Toni said.

"I'm not interested in a hookup." Jules knew her tone was abrupt, but she couldn't help it.

"No one's going to force you to do anything," Claire said, and her slightly superior tone really bothered Jules. "I just thought since you aren't dating anyone right now, you might be interested."

"No, I'm not. I'm not even sure I'm going to the parade." She wanted to wait and see if she could join Sylvia and the EQCA folks. Well, mostly join Sylvia.

Claire's perfect eyebrows went up to her hairline. "Jules, we just wanted to suggest it. Is something wrong?" Now they were both scrutinizing her. "You've been really distant for a while and don't seem to be yourself."

"You've seemed a little, you know, off. Do you think we're upset about the moving-in thing? We're not." Toni's round brown eyes broadcast concern, and Jules felt guiltier than ever.

"No, I don't think you're upset. I've sort of been spending more time with Sylvia." The information withholding was making her crazy, and she couldn't understand why she was doing it.

Claire gave her a speculative look. "Oh, really? How's that going?"

"It's fine." Jules knew she didn't sound very convincing.

"Did she decide to give it a go with you?" Claire asked, which immediately hit Jules the wrong way. She wasn't in the mood for Claire's assumptions.

"No. She hasn't decided to 'give it a go,' as you put it. I've been going to the marriage equality meetings. I have to leave right away tomorrow morning so we can go to the No on 8 campaign headquarters for a while." After a long pause both Claire and Toni looked at her and then at each other again. Some kind of communication was going on.

"You two keep looking at each other. What?"

"Jules, there's no need to get upset." Toni was trying to be soothing, which infuriated Jules all the more. "It's just surprising that you would be interested in politics."

"I'm not upset," she nearly shouted, then got her voice under control to say, "If you have something to say, just spit it out, will you?"

Toni and Claire glanced at each other again, and finally, Toni said, gently, "We've been wondering...ever since we asked you to move in, it seems like you've withdrawn from us. Does that have something to do with Sylvia?"

"No. Of course not. Look, nothing's going on with Sylvia, I told you, and I really don't appreciate you nagging me about her." *Great, I sound like I'm fifteen.*

"We don't want to nag you, we just want to know how you feel." Toni was still doing the talking and Claire was keeping silent, but her expression made Jules want to throw something at her.

"I feel fine. I just want to keep us, our thing, just the same, you know. It's working fine and I don't see why we need to change it. That has *nothing* to do with Sylvia. She's just a friend."

"Ah. Okay. Well, think about going to the parade with us. You could meet someone there, or maybe at the party at Eureka Valley Rec Center after."

"Yeah, I suppose," Jules said unenthusiastically.

Toni and Claire stared at each other, then back at Jules.

"We're not twisting your arm. If you don't want to spend time with us, don't." Claire sounded a little acerbic.

"No. Sorry, I'm just out of sorts. That sounds great. We'll do the parade, then go to the party." Jules realized that she ought to go out on gay day with Claire and Toni rather than waiting for an invitation from Sylvia that might never come.

"All right," Claire said. "You think that casserole's ready? Want to go check on it, Tone?"

"Sure." Toni went to the kitchen.

"It's another one from Moosewood, lots of olives, you'll like it." Claire rearranged the flatware at her place unnecessarily and then held up the bottle of zinfandel. "You want?"

"Yeah. Thanks." Jules stretched out her legs and rolled her neck, trying to relax.

"We're having the usual Fourth of July get-together. Why don't you invite Sylvia to come?" Claire said while pouring the wine.

"Sure. I'll ask her." Jules became uneasy. How would Sylvia react? How would it feel to have Sylvia in the same space as Claire and Toni? She dismissed her unease.

They seemed to have an unspoken agreement that night that no one was going to have any sex, and Jules was unaccountably grateful. Did her distancing herself from Claire and Toni really have anything to do with Sylvia? She dismissed the idea. *Just friends.* Hopefully someday soon, her heart would stop aching every time she looked at Sylvia.

❖

On the Monday after the pride parade, Sylvia was sitting at her desk staring at the pile of client files for the week. She had a lot of phone calls to make but couldn't get started because she was concerned about William Noonan. She still hadn't heard from him, and his mother hadn't either. She left him another message.

She and Perla had marched in the parade with EQCA and then stayed to watch and hang out at the celebration. Perla had noticed that Sylvia seemed to be scanning the crowd rather than enjoying the parade and said, "Really? Do you think you'll run into Jules in the middle of half a million people?"

"No, I suppose not."

"Why didn't you just ask her to come with us?" Perla asked gently.

"I don't know. I figured she'd be busy with her girlfriends.

You know." Sylvia gestured vaguely. She'd almost asked Jules and was now mentally berating herself for not doing it.

"Uh-huh." Perla sounded skeptical but dropped it.

Should she call and ask Jules how her gay day had been? She was trying not to speculate if Jules might have picked someone up. *Maybe for some four-way sex, gah.*

The phone rang.

"Hi, Syl." It was Jules, and Sylvia's pulse fluttered a tiny bit.

"Hello. I was just thinking about you and wondering what kind of day you had yesterday." Sylvia was relieved she sounded cheerful and casual.

"It was fine. Hey, I'm calling to find out if you'd like to go to a Fourth of July barbecue next week at Claire and Toni's. With me, I mean." Jules cleared her throat.

"Let me look at my calendar and get back to you, okay?" Sylvia was taken off guard by the invite and wanted to time to process her feelings about it.

"Sure thing. How was your parade day?"

"Nice. We marched with EQCA and hung out with them a little. We had a good-sized contingent and the spectators were really enthusiastic. I just wish we could translate some of that enthusiasm into working against Prop 8."

"Yeah, I hear you. So that's it. Just wanted to extend that invitation. Claire and Toni really want to meet you."

"That's nice of them. I'll let you know soon."

After a long pause Jules said, "Okay, great. Talk to you later."

Sylvia stared at the phone. She was deeply curious about the sort of women Jules was involved with. On the other hand, being reminded that Jules was involved with no fewer than two other women made her irrationally jealous, which she hated. It made her think about how attracted she was to Jules.

She liked that Jules seemed sincerely interested in the election. She was very cute when she asked her and Perla serious questions. Sylvia had tried to make her opinion sound final when they'd had coffee at Muddy Waters, but even then she'd felt a little like she was just trying to convince herself. When she looked at it from another perspective, such as just dating Jules for fun, it seemed like she was being unduly rigid.

There was nothing wrong with recreational sex. She'd never tried it, but that didn't mean she couldn't. It was all just too confusing, so she forced her attention back to her work.

❖

Sylvia told Perla about Jules's invitation and Perla's broad grin infuriated her, but she said, "It seems ridiculous to refuse the invitation. It would make me look moralistic and snobbish."

"Into the belly of the beast, eh?"

"It's not like that, Perls. They're just her friends whom she happens to sleep with, as far as I can tell. It's not a big deal. You know we've gotten to be really good friends."

"Yeah. You're the most stubborn lesbo on the planet."

"What? What do you mean?" Sylvia knew very well what she meant.

"You like Jules a lot. I haven't seen you so into someone since you broke up with Elena, and that was a long fucking time ago, girlfriend. What the heck is so wrong about dating her? She is, after all, available. She's just not available for a relationship. So?"

Sylvia stared at the table moodily. It was Sunday night and they were, of course, at La Cumbre. Sylvia had come very close to inviting Jules out for the usual burrito and EQCA meeting, but had refrained.

"Perls, if I sleep with her, I have a feeling I'll fall in love with her."

"And if you do?"

"I don't know. What would I do, what would happen?"

"She could fall in love with you, too."

"Yeah, right. No way. She's poly. And even if she did, I'd still have to share her with other people."

"So? That doesn't mean she still couldn't fall in love with you and decide she might want to be different with you."

"Yeah. I don't know. She's really nice and really cute. I just...don't know."

Sylvia still believed it would be a horrible idea to become involved with someone who was sexually available but unattainable. Yet she felt herself weakening. Elena had been a long time ago. Getting into that out-of-control, infatuated state of mind scared her. Maybe she could avoid it if she dated someone like Jules with whom a relationship was out of the question. Maybe it wasn't such a bad idea.

Chapter Fourteen

A nxious thoughts tumbled through Sylvia's mind as she got ready to go to the barbecue. She wanted to make a good impression but felt already behind the curve for being neither vegatarian nor polyamorous. She tried to dismiss this thinking, since Jules had already assured her that Claire and Toni's group of friends included omnivores and non-polys. Sylvia detected some anxiety on Jules's part and didn't quite understand its source.

Jules rang the doorbell at precisely the time she'd told Sylvia she would. For someone who had what Sylvia considered a non-routine job, Jules was remarkably on time. Every time. Sylvia opened her front door to Jules, who was dressed as usual in worn-out 501 Levi's and a hooded sweatshirt, red this time, and the same ratty down vest. Standing there with her hands stuffed in her sweatshirt looking nervous, she seemed young and appealing.

"Hi," she said, and grinned. "Are you ready?"

"Almost. Hey, what's the weather like in their 'hood? Should I bring a jacket?"

"Well, it's not too cold, since it's downtown. But we'll be eating indoors. Typical San Francisco barbecue. Cook outside and eat inside. But you know." Jules laughed.

"I do. I'll get something just in case." In spite of her underlying anxiety, Sylvia was exuberant. She had to admit she'd been curious about Claire and Toni from the moment she found out about them. This party would prove interesting for that reason alone. She was, she knew, also simply glad to spend time with Jules. Jules made her happy, and what could be wrong about that?

"What about the other people there?" Sylvia asked.

"Oh, they're just a bunch of folks we know, some from the network. Some of Toni's coworkers."

"Some of them sleep with each other, though."

"Well, not *all* of them." Jules laughed but sounded a bit defensive, and Sylvia realized Jules was nervous about mixing her with this group. That intrigued her.

"How many of them have *you* had sex with?" Sylvia asked.

"Um." Jules paused as she negotiated a left turn on a busy street. It was another moment before she answered. "Depending on who shows up, between three and five."

"Really?" Sylvia thought of herself in imaginary sexual competition with these three to five as of now unknown women, not to mention Claire and Toni. She was dismayed that "really" came out sounding bitchy.

Jules cleared her throat. "You realize that poly people don't think of sex the same way as monogamists do. It's not a zero-sum game. We don't compete for partners."

Sylvia was startled and felt a little guilty. "Yes, of course. I get that."

"And you know this isn't a play party, right? No one's going to be having sex during the barbecue, that's something way different. That's where—"

"Yeah, yeah, I know the difference." Sylvia was irritated and didn't want to admit that was exactly what she'd pictured: a group of sex-crazed poly people having an orgy while eating grilled vegetables or chicken or whatever.

"Sylvia, really. It's okay. I don't know what's running through your mind, but I swear this is pretty pedestrian and ordinary. Just a July Fourth picnic without the backyard."

"I'm fine, Jules. Don't worry." Jules was, as best she could while driving, peering at her with an expression of concern that made Sylvia's annoyance dissolve and made her want to hug her and tell her not to worry so much.

They rang the bell, and it struck Sylvia as odd that Jules didn't have a key. Before she had time to consider that question too closely, they were buzzed in. In the elevator, Jules smiled at her in what Sylvia could only interpret as encouragement. Before she could say anything, the elevator doors opened and they were walking down the hall to an open door.

"Claire, Tone? It's me." It seemed they were the only guests. Sylvia saw someone in the kitchen whose back was turned.

"Come on." Jules took her arm and they crossed the living room. The woman in the kitchen turned and wiped her hands on a towel and came forward to hug and kiss Jules. On the mouth, Sylvia noted, and endured another spike of jealousy. The woman looked at Jules as though she wanted to tear her clothes off at that moment.

"Hi, Jules. Good to see you." The woman turned to Sylvia with an easy smile.

"You must be Sylvia."

"Sylvia. Toni," Jules said.

"Hello, Toni. Thanks for inviting me to your home." Sylvia, in moments of social anxiety, tended to revert to elaborate politeness.

"Where's Ms. Nakamura?" Jules asked, an undercurrent of amusement in her tone. Jules and Toni exchanged conspiratorial looks, and Toni cocked her head toward a sliding-glass door on the far side of the room. They could see a woman and two grills.

"Ah. She's in charge of the barbecuing," Jules said.

"But of course. Besides ensuring the coals are burning properly, we have to make sure no one contaminates the veggie grill with animal cooties."

"Where should I put this?" Sylvia indicated the dish of marinating steaks she'd brought.

"Does it need refrigeration?"

"Not if we're going to cook it within the next hour. It's better it stay at room temp."

"Right. Then you can put it on the table until you start cooking."

"Come meet Claire." Jules was looking more relaxed, which calmed Sylvia somewhat.

Jules opened the French door and said, "Hey."

Toni seemed to be a genuinely pleasant person, who shared an easy friendship-type relationship with Jules, minus the kiss, of course. When Claire turned around, though, Sylvia was hit with a wave of emotion she couldn't identify. It wasn't outright hostility but it was suspicion. Claire didn't smile with her eyes, although her mouth formed the proper expression.

At the introduction, Claire said, "Hello." That was it, nothing more, nothing less. She seemed curt and unfriendly.

"You want us to leave you be?" Jules asked. She seemed to be treating Claire carefully. Whereas Toni was pretty, Claire was beautiful, with her black hair, black eyes, and sharp cheekbones.

"Go make yourselves comfortable and answer the door, if you wouldn't mind."

"Sure."

Sylvia and Jules sat on the couch, and immediately, the cat jumped up to check them out.

"Is she allowed to do this?" Sylvia asked as the animal got right in Jules's face and sniffed her nose.

"Oh, yeah. Chloe, sweetie, chill." Jules picked up the cat and looked into her face. Chloe began to purr as soon as Jules touched her.

"She likes you." Sylvia stared at Jules's hands as she held the cat. They were strong and capable, not small, not large, just good-looking hands. Sylvia swallowed as she imagined Jules's hands on her. They would no doubt feel amazing.

"We're old friends."

"I bet you are." Sylvia couldn't quite keep the edge out of her tone. Jules looked at her quizzically and started to say something, but the doorbell rang and she leaped up to trip the security buzzer. Sylvia stayed on the couch and glared at Chloe.

"Just keep your distance, kitty, and we'll get along," Sylvia muttered to the cat. She was unaccountably annoyed at how familiar Jules and Chloe were. It was only reasonable, Sylvia told herself. Jules had been with Claire and Toni for two years. Why was she so out of sorts? She had agreed to this party out of fondness for Jules and out of curiosity, and now she was starting to cop a bad attitude.

"Do you want something to drink?" Toni was standing before her. Sylvia, suddenly ill at ease, wondered where Jules had gone.

"Yes, thanks. Can I help you?" Sylvia decided she needed something to do.

"Sure. Come check out the drinks, and you can help me peel hard-boiled eggs for the salad."

Sylvia was more than happy to comply. She mused idly about the couple's odd chemistry. She could see the stark contrast between Claire and Toni's personalities and speculated where Jules fit in their dynamic. She busied herself with the eggs, falling back on the tried-and-true social lubricant, alcohol, in the form of a glass of white wine, and made small talk with Toni.

"The door got stuck!" Jules announced from behind them. Sylvia turned around to see her stride through the door with her arm around a thin strawberry blonde. "Tracy couldn't get in, so I went downstairs."

Sylvia drew a breath and thought, *Aha, this is one of them. One of Jules's past partners.* Together, they had that look of familiarity. In fact, if Sylvia hadn't known better, she wouldn't have pegged Toni or Claire as Jules's lovers as much as this woman, who was smiling at Jules in a lascivious manner. Jules seemed oblivious, but that didn't make Sylvia feel much better. The doorbell rang again, and Jules took care of it as Tracy joined Sylvia and Toni in the kitchen. Claire stuck her head through the door. "The coals are ready. Tone?" Toni stopped in midsentence and hurriedly took Claire a plate of assorted vegetables. That left Sylvia face-to-face with Tracy, who turned her toothy grin on Sylvia and introduced herself.

"Hi. I'm Sylvia."

"Hi, Sylvia. I haven't met you before. You know Claire and Toni?"

"No, actually, I've just met them. I'm a friend of Jules."

Tracy cocked an eyebrow. "Friend of Jules, eh? She has lots of friends." Sylvia took the meaning of "friends" as "friends with benefits," or whatever these poly types called their lovers. Sylvia reckoned the term "lovers" was inaccurate, at least by her estimation. But she wasn't averse to letting this skinny little twit think she was one of Jules's "friends."

"I know." Sylvia looked innocently at Tracy. "She's such a wonderful person."

"Wonderful," Tracy repeated, and narrowed her eyes. Several more people, including a few men and women whom Sylvia would have pegged as perfectly ordinary had she met them in any other context, arrived and forestalled further verbal combat. Some of the people might even be straight, Sylvia mused. That was an interesting thought.

As soon as she got the chance, Sylvia took Jules's arm, pulled her aside, and whispered in her ear, "So is Tracy one of the three or five? And are others here?" Jules stared at her with astonishment that morphed into confusion.

"Uh. Yes. So is Jan." Jules cocked her head toward the African American woman with cornrows. "And Mira." Mira was full-figured and had long, beautiful reddish-brown hair.

"Huh," Sylvia said, thoughtfully.

"Are you okay?" Jules, looking concerned, lowered her

voice. "It's not like usual. There's not this jealousy. No one's—"
She glanced at Mira and then at Jan, and both smiled at her.

"Jules. I'm fine. I'm enjoying myself. Really. I'm just
interested." Jules was so concerned about her reaction, her heart
melted, and that feeling settled uneasily next to the jealousy she
didn't want to verbalize to Jules. Since they weren't dating, that
might make her appear a little crazy. Sylvia took a breath, her
eyes locked with Jules's.

"Okay, Sylvia. Time for steak," Toni called out from the
kitchen. As Sylvia walked past Tracy, she heard her say to
someone, "Eww. Red meat. Gross." Sylvia's blood pressure
spiked but she kept silent, though she considered it the height of
rudeness to comment on other people's eating habits, aside from
discussing food politics with Jules. That was different.

Sylvia busied herself for several minutes with grilling. She
was joined by a few other omnivores, and they exchanged good-
natured jibes with the vegetarians at the next grill.

With the cooking done, the partygoers busied themselves
preparing plates of food and finding places to sit and consume it.
Sylvia gravitated naturally to Jules and sat to one side of her on
the couch. To her chagrin, Tracy took up the other side. Sylvia
tried the grilled veggies, which were delicious. She certainly had
nothing against vegetables; she just couldn't imagine them as her
only diet. Then she ate a bite of steak and knew that, as good as
the vegetables were, the taste of a perfectly cooked good-quality
steak was even better. She was only paying partial attention to
the conversation Jules was carrying on with Tracy. One, she was
hungry, and two, she really didn't want to focus on Tracy, who
on first impression was rude and unfriendly.

"And Sylvia works for UCSF as a social worker," Jules said,
leaning back to include Sylvia in her conversation with Tracy.

Tracy glanced at Sylvia and smiled humorlessly before
she returned her attention to Jules. "So, what have you been
up to lately? Seems like forever since we've seen each other."

Sylvia was sure that "seen" was a euphemism for "fucked." The woman's rudeness was certainly consistent. She wasn't even expressing a polite interest in anything to do with Sylvia, in spite of what was clearly an effort on Jules's part.

Jules put her plate on the table and took a drink. Sylvia wasn't sure, but she thought Jules wasn't particularly happy talking to Tracy.

Jules said, "Oh, not a whole heckuva lot, really. But since I met Sylvia," and again she indicated Sylvia with a nod, "I've gotten into marriage equality stuff. She's very involved and I've gone to some of the meetings. Now they have this Prop 8 thing. We found out about this initiative a couple weeks ago." Jules continued, turning her eye contact from Tracy back to Sylvia. "Well, Sylvia, you ought to talk about it. You know way more than me. You're the expert." She grinned at Sylvia.

Rather than forming an answer to Jules's request, her brain fully engaged with processing Jules's compliment. It sounded to Sylvia a whole lot like the bragging of a proud lover. Jules was also looking at her in a frankly adoring way, and she felt herself start to blush. Jules's eyes widened and her smile became mischievous.

"Oh, this marriage equality crap. That's all we hear about now. I'm so over it," Tracy said.

Sylvia turned her attention to Tracy, who looked as though she smelled a fart. Jules's smile faded and her brows came down.

"What do you mean, Tracy?" It was a good thing Jules had asked the question, because Sylvia wouldn't have been so polite.

"I mean, really, Jules? Gay marriage? That's a ridiculous concept. Queers don't need marriage, especially poly queers." Tracy obviously realized the effect her words might have on Sylvia because she smiled unpleasantly.

"I still don't get it, Tracy. It's the biggest gay rights issue there is." Jules turned to Sylvia for confirmation. Sylvia knew her blush of pleasure and embarrassment had just turned to an angry flush. This idiotic and unnecessarily rude woman had just crossed a line.

Sylvia's response finally came out in a clipped and unmistakably dangerous tone. "And what exactly makes you say that queers don't *need* marriage?"

Jules was clearly taken by surprise at what she'd inadvertently started between Sylvia and Tracy. She leaned back on the couch as though to give them room to have at it, either physically or verbally.

Tracy obviously wasn't as sure of herself as she pretended to be. Under Sylvia's ferocious stare, she looked away and shrugged. "Oh. You *know.* For one thing, marriage is such a patriarchal thing, for God's sake. No self-respecting feminist would support it."

"Really? I think a whole lot of people, including me, would consider themselves self-respecting feminists." Sylvia was pleased she managed to keep her voice even.

"Yeah, but, geez, it's an outmoded construct. LGBTs have had relationships for eons without marriage. It's also that old, tired monogamist shit we hear about all the time. Marriage is all about ownership. Men owning women usually."

Jules had listened without comment, staring at her hands in her lap. When she looked up, Sylvia almost laughed at the how terrified she appeared. *Jules is afraid I'm going to eviscerate this stupid chick.* A few other partygoers nearby had caught the shift of conversational energy and were now looking at the three of them with wary interest.

Toni piped up cheerfully. "Oh, I agree with you, Trace. I just gag every time I hear the mayor talk about gay marriage. I cannot believe how much attention it gets."

Sylvia was so angry and so dumbfounded she didn't know what to say. She was saved by Jules, who suddenly said, "A whole lot of people seem pretty into this marriage deal."

"There's a reason for all the attention it's getting." Sylvia spoke with sufficient force that those within earshot fell silent. She was uncomfortably aware that several pairs of eyes were on her and she wasn't much of a public speaker. "Being married gives you rights for all kinds of things. We haven't had any protections for our relationships. We need to be treated the same, legally, as straight people. It's unbelievably important."

"We're not the same as straight people. That's the whole point of being queer. We're different from them," Toni said, and a few people nodded.

"Not in the ways that count. If your lover is in the emergency room, they can keep you away because you're not 'family.' And don't even get me started if children are in the mix."

"We should just do away with marriage," Tracy said. "It'd be better anyhow. It's all just a religious thing." Some of her certainty had dissipated, however, and she shifted in her chair.

"You're wrong," Sylvia said flatly. "It's not religious, it's civil marriage."

"No, it isn't. You get married in a church."

The conversation had become a loud tennis match between Tracy and Sylvia, and the other guests were riveted.

"Ministers and priests have to be given justice-of-the-peace status or it's not legal."

"Well, it's still a stupid idea for queers." Tracy was clearly losing her steam. "Especially if you're poly."

"No, it's not." Claire's clear voice cut through the murmurs. "Marriage is what you make it," Claire said, leaning back in her chair and crossing her legs. She looked at Sylvia, then glanced around the room. "We make our relationships how we want. They're not some idea of mainstream society's about the way people *should* be. But Sylvia's right. If you want to get married, you need to be able to get married. It's only fair." The discussion opened and several people began to argue.

"Are you okay?" Jules whispered to Sylvia.

Sylvia whispered back. "Yep, but get me away from Tracy."

Jules stood up, took Sylvia's hand, and led her to the balcony where they stood looking across the San Francisco Bay. Their shoulders touched, but neither said anything for a few moments.

"Do you want to go?" Jules looked at her anxiously.

"I don't want to be rude," Sylvia said softly. "But I sort of do." She consciously held Jules's gaze and moved closer to her.

"Well. We could leave after dessert. Say in a half hour?" Jules raised her eyebrows. Sylvia looked at her for what she knew was an unusually long time and nearly kissed her. She was able to hold back only because of their quasi-public location.

"Sounds good."

Sylvia's throat tightened. Jules was looking at her intently. They stood on the balcony silently staring at one another. Sylvia broke the spell first and reluctantly stepped back to get some physical separation. "Want to go back inside?"

Jules merely nodded.

When they reentered, the discussion had moved on and the party had resumed a more normal tone. She found a place to sit next to a young Latino guy, and they fell into an easy conversation. Jules brought her another drink and a piece of pie and didn't leave her side other than to fetch something for her and once to go to the bathroom. When she was gone, Sylvia felt unusually alone and vulnerable. She felt a little wrung out from the tense encounter with Tracy and Toni, but she thought she'd done a good job on her side of the argument.

Her emotions around Jules's current and ex-girlfriends were disturbing. The roiling mess of jealousy and sexual competition in her head made her feel out of control. But instead of making her back off, they seemed to be driving her toward Jules. Every time their eyes met or they touched by accident, she shivered. Her physical attraction to Jules was overwhelming the faint, lingering voice of reason in her head. Every time Sylvia looked at her, Jules looked back at her with a question in her eyes, and Sylvia was starting to think she knew the answer to that question was "yes."

Sylvia caught Jules's eye and she bent close. "I'm ready to go."

Jules whispered, "Okay. I'll just tell Claire and then we can leave." Her breath tickled Sylvia's ear.

Sylvia went to the kitchen to locate her tray, where Toni was standing by the sink stacking dishes. She turned to Sylvia and said, pleasantly, "Here. I washed your dish. You just have to dry it." Sylvia accepted the dish towel Toni proffered and busied herself.

Jules came in and put her arm around Toni. "We're heading out. I'm going to take Sylvia home."

"See you later?" Toni asked.

Sylvia stared as Jules glanced from Sylvia back to Toni, looking uncertain. "Not sure. I might just go home. I'll call and let you know."

"Okay, right." Toni paused. "You know, Sylvia's very persuasive. I may be wrong about getting married."

"Yep. She's kind of irresistible," Jules said.

Toni raised her eyebrows and straightened as though coming to attention. "Whoa. Jules never says that about anyone. She's usually the one who has to be chased."

"Is that right?" Sylvia had been scrutinizing Jules as she spoke to Toni. Their glances held for just a moment, and then Sylvia forced her focus back to Toni. "Thanks for a great party. I enjoyed it."

"Whew." Toni laughed and mimed wiping sweat off her forehead. "For a second there, I wasn't sure it would be okay." They hugged.

"Ready?" Sylvia asked, her heart starting to pound.

"Yep. Let's go."

Sylvia was almost certain they weren't simply speaking of leaving.

CHAPTER FIFTEEN

Jules found a legal parking space a block from Sylvia's apartment building rather than simply double-parking right in front to drop Sylvia off, so they sat in the car. Sylvia made no comment about it. In fact, she was unusually quiet, just staring straight ahead.

Jules tapped her leg and Sylvia jumped like she'd been startled.

"Hey. Is everything all right?" Jules thought it sounded like a stupid question, but she couldn't think of anything else to say.

"Yeah." She finally turned to meet Jules's eyes. They looked at each other silently for what seemed like an eternity. Jules moved her head an inch closer to Sylvia's, and Sylvia moved in the rest of the distance and began to kiss her slowly, tenderly. Their hands came up to caress one another's shoulders and hair and cheeks. Their kiss went on and on, becoming increasingly fervent. Jules's body caught fire and her breathing sped up. They were finally on the path she'd been dreaming of for nearly three months. They broke apart, gasping. Sylvia's eyes were huge, her dark, rosy lips parted.

"Should I come inside with you?" Jules asked, and she had to struggle to get the question out coherently. Sylvia nodded and retrieved her baking dish, and Jules swallowed. Too scared to say anything, she followed Sylvia through the front door and down the hallway to the kitchen. Sylvia dumped the dish on the counter and turned around. Jules had kept so close to her, she had to step back.

Sylvia put her hands on Jules's shoulders and squeezed them lightly. "Don't say anything," Sylvia whispered. "I don't want to talk, I don't want to think." They met in another, hungrier kiss. They had no questions, no answers; nothing made sense or had to make sense. There was only Sylvia, who was now leading her by the hand.

Sylvia's bedroom was dim, even though it was only around five in the afternoon. The shades were drawn and the windows faced northeast. Jules was vaguely relieved. She welcomed the dim light because she was certain this was a dream she would soon awaken from. They crossed the threshold and Jules focused on the blanket that hung over the bed. It seemed to have a talismanic pull on her. Sylvia turned to Jules, threw her arms around her, and kissed her feverishly. Jules closed her eyes and lost herself in the sensation.

Sylvia's body was soft, but her arms clasped her with surprising force. If she'd wanted to resist, she couldn't have. She slipped her hands between them to caress Sylvia's breasts, gasping at how good they felt. Sylvia groaned and grabbed her wrists, holding her hands still but not pulling them away. Sylvia groaned again when Jules pushed her tongue into her mouth and pressed her body closer. Jules wanted to cry out from exhilaration and triumph. They'd finally, finally surrendered to the sexual tension that had flared for so long, and Jules was desperate to find out if all the fantasies she'd spun for herself about this moment were accurate. So far, they were.

Jules backed them toward the bed without breaking contact, and they sat down. It was Sylvia who broke their kiss to make eye contact. At the same time, she put her hand on Jules's cheek in an achingly tender motion and smiled ever so slightly. Jules moaned and turned to kiss her palm. She spoke involuntarily, "Oh, God. Sylvia, I—"

"Don't talk," Sylvia murmured. "Just feel." Sylvia grabbed her and they fell backward with Sylvia on top. Jules relaxed into their embrace, and every nerve in her body went on red alert as Sylvia kissed her neck, her cheeks, behind her ears, even her nose and forehead. Her soft dark hair drifted over her face as Sylvia's head moved, and Jules took in the wonderful, heady scent. She blew slightly as a stray strand tickled her nose. Sylvia must have felt her breath because she raised her head and looked at Jules with a questioning smile.

"Nothing." Jules couldn't keep the triumphant grin off her face. Sylvia grinned in return and resumed her kisses, pressing Jules into the mattress. Their legs crisscrossed, the pressure of Sylvia's thigh on the seam of Jules's jeans almost unbearable. Sylvia slipped her hand under Jules's sweatshirt and T-shirt, seeking flesh, and Jules jerked involuntarily as Sylvia's palm connected with her nipple. She was glad she hadn't worn a bra, not even a sports bra, that would have presented any kind of obstacle to Sylvia's touch. They struggled to get closer, but their layers of clothing were terrifically confining. They were generating considerable body heat and Jules was starting to sweat. She prayed her shower from several hours before would still be in effect, but she knew, somehow, that a little sweat wouldn't stop Sylvia.

Sylvia was, as a matter of fact, starting to unbutton her jeans, not the easiest thing to do with one hand; the six metal buttons on her 501s required some dexterity. Sylvia was, surprisingly, not having too much trouble, but she was by necessity going slowly, which was ramping up Jules's arousal in a most pleasant way. Sylvia's hand slipped partway into her jeans and brushed her stomach; it was maddening. She must have made a sound because she felt Sylvia giggle against her mouth, which made her giggle as well.

They moved apart, their eyes locked together and at exactly the same time began to jerk their clothes off. They flung articles of clothing everywhere and scrambled to get under the covers. At the first touch of their naked bodies, they groaned simultaneously and moved together. Jules thought she might explode, her clitoris throbbing in a steady beat between her legs, a sensation made equally of pleasure and pain. She silently prayed Sylvia would touch her soon. They rolled back and forth, trying to touch one another everywhere.

Sylvia started to laugh and Jules couldn't help but ask, "What are you laughing about?"

"At us. We don't need to rush. In fact, I'd like to slow down."

"Ohhh-oh, okay," Jules said, raggedly.

Sylvia put a finger to her lips. "Don't worry, we'll get there."

Jules gazed into Sylvia's now completely black eyes and felt the unspoken trust between them. She let her body go limp and, as in her dreams, she heard Sylvia's soft whisper in her ear.

"That's better."

Sylvia resumed her incessant kisses everywhere, but this time her mouth settled around one of Jules's nipples while she gently stroked around the other one until it, too, was hard and sensitive. Then she pinched it firmly, but not enough to cause pain. Jules's head went back and Sylvia licked her exposed throat, her teeth barely grazing Jules's flesh. Her hand left Jules's breast and slid slowly down her body. Jules twisted back and forth and spread her legs in silent request. Sylvia rested her hand on her pubic hair without moving for a moment, then inched lower. When she found what she was looking for, she made a small, appreciative sound. That murmur against Jules's breast nearly sent her into the stratosphere.

Sylvia's fingers stroked and probed her gently, her explorations unhurried, almost meditative. At first. She was clearly reading Jules's movements and responding. The more Jules writhed, the faster and more firmly she stroked her clitoris. Inexplicably, she would stop suddenly and Jules would start to become frantic for more stimulation, and then she would resume. Dimly, Jules realized that the stop-start movements were propelling her very close to orgasm. Her leg muscles clenched and relaxed. She willed herself to orgasm, but when she got close, Sylvia would merely rest her fingers against her for a moment.

"Oh, God," Jules choked out. "You're driving me nuts."

"Poor thing. Okay, here you go." She stroked Jules with the absolutely perfect amount of speed and pressure and she came, wave after wave. Sylvia kissed her, whispering unintelligibly but sweetly. Jules managed to open her eyes after a few minutes, and her body twitched like an engine cooling off. Sylvia rested her wet hand on her stomach, moving it in slow circles.

"You with me, love?" Sylvia asked, her voice a combination of tenderness and victory.

"Give me a sec and I'll—" Jules tried to sit up but Sylvia gently pushed her back down.

"Take it easy, this isn't a race to the finish line. Well, maybe it's a race, but it's a marathon, not a sprint."

Sylvia's hair was tangled, her cappuccino-toned skin exquisite. Jules held her paler forearm against Sylvia's body just to see the contrast. Sylvia looked at it, then back at Jules, seeming serious, but not in bad way, only as if she was considering the sight. She ran her fingers through Jules's hair, which felt amazing. What Sylvia had just done to her, what they had shared, awed her. She kissed Sylvia and pulled her close, running her hand from Sylvia's hair down her back to her ass, which she squeezed reverently. Their breasts and stomachs nestled together.

Jules straightened herself to force contact along every inch and then pulled Sylvia on top of her. She liked to top from underneath, so to speak, because she could access the lover's body much better. Sylvia didn't seem to object. She shifted just enough to get Jules's hand between them, then sat astride Jules and gently guided her fingers inside. She nodded, her eyes closed, and whispered, "Fuck me."

And Jules willingly obliged her, watching Sylvia's lovely body move through all stages of arousal and finally release as she rode Jules's fingers into what was clearly a mind-blowing orgasm. Jules felt the echoes of it in her own body. Sylvia slid off her and rolled over on her back with her arm over her eyes.

Jules propped herself on one elbow and put a hand on her. She didn't know what to say, but perhaps it wasn't important to say anything. She wanted Sylvia to know she was there and to see her face when she opened her eyes, which she did after a few moments, with a lovely smile. Her face was soft, her eyelids heavy. She looked even more beautiful, if possible. Jules kissed her on the cheek as Sylvia smoothed her short blond hair.

"Wow," Jules said, "I'm blown away. In more ways than one." She knew, instinctively, that Sylvia would understand what she meant.

"You know," Sylvia said, lazily, her eyes closed. "I haven't had sex in almost four years. I think it was worth the wait."

"Hmm. Good to hear."

"I wondered if I would remember how to do it. Looks like."

Jules stroked her cheek. "Oh, you remember." She was used to discussing her physical encounters. The endless negotiations and disclosures were necessary because poly people had such complicated sex lives. She wanted to let Sylvia take the lead in that area, as she had finally made the move that propelled them into bed. For now, though, it seemed prudent not to ask any questions or say much of anything, but just to let her touch speak for her. She'd made it into Sylvia's bed as she had so desired. It was enough.

She put her arms around Sylvia and they cuddled together for a few minutes, neither one moving. Eventually, however, they recovered physically and started all over again, exchanging touch for touch, sigh for sigh, and orgasm for orgasm far into the night.

❖

Sylvia woke up early, an ingrained habit. No matter what time she went to sleep, she always awoke at the same time. She was in bed with Jules, a place she'd vowed not to be. But she certainly didn't regret it, since she considered regret a futile emotion and had nothing to be ashamed of, nothing to feel bad about. In fact, she felt very, very good. It had been an incredibly long time, and she'd let herself forget precisely how wonderful sex could be. The last miserable year with Elena hadn't helped. Sylvia looked at Jules, still fast asleep, then at her bedside clock. It had been maybe three hours, no more, since they'd fallen asleep. After moving quietly out of bed, she found a bathrobe and walked to the bathroom, enjoying the slickness between her thighs, incontrovertible proof of a night well spent.

In the kitchen making coffee, she purposefully emptied her mind. She had no desire to start asking the hard questions, not yet. She wanted to be in the moment. She walked back to her bedroom, two fresh cups of coffee in hand and inordinately pleased to remember exactly how Jules liked her coffee. A touch of milk, no sugar.

When she sat down, Jules rolled over and rubbed her eyes. In the morning light, she looked young and innocent. She didn't say anything, although her mouth formed a slight grin.

"Good morning," Sylvia said cheerfully. "Hope you want coffee."

"Hey. That's great. Sure. Be right back." She got out of bed and walked to the bathroom. In her clothes, Jules was androgynous. Nude, she was far more feminine. Her hips were subtly rounded, slightly larger than her waist. And her butt was perfect. Sylvia's breath caught as she remembered squeezing it. She had really cute breasts, too, smallish but not mere mosquito bites. Sylvia's palms tingled at the memory of how her body felt in her hands. She got into bed and sipped her coffee, waiting for Jules to come back.

Jules took up her coffee cup and drank deeply, then put her

head back and sighed. "Ah, that tastes magnificent, like you." Her blue eyes twinkled and Sylvia's clitoris thrummed at the memory of Jules going down on her at some point in the night for what seemed like forever and making her come like a freight train.

"I'm glad to hear that. I'm very particular about coffee."

"Sylvia?"

Sylvia's heart turned over. *Uh-oh. I don't want to talk about anything right now.*

Jules set her coffee cup down and reached over and put Sylvia's cup on her nightstand. She took Sylvia's hands in both of hers.

"I just wanted to tell you how much last night meant to me. I don't want you to feel like you have to be a certain way or even say anything at all now. I'm speaking for myself. No matter what else happens, I'll always be super happy we could share that. It was wonderful."

Sylvia relaxed—no questions, no processing, no demands. Jules couldn't have been a more exquisite lover, and this morning she was proving to be tender and perceptive. Those qualities had really helped change Sylvia's mind. Jules made her feel safe and cared for. For Sylvia, at that moment, it was enough, and she hoped she could just stay in the present and not worry about the future.

Sylvia kissed Jules slowly, enjoying the coffee flavor of her lips and the subtle remnant of her own sex scent. "You don't have to worry. I don't have any regrets."

"Good. I don't ever want to make you feel bad. Ever. For any reason."

"You don't. I can do that to myself on my own. But I'm not feeling bad this morning."

"I'm relieved to hear that." Jules eyes were very blue and sincere, and Sylvia wanted to hug her again. Well, she wanted to do a little more than that. The caffeine was having an effect she could never recall experiencing—making her horny.

"Drink your coffee."

"Aye, aye, boss. Are we in a hurry?" Jules asked.

Sylvia nuzzled her neck, muttering, "Maybe."

Jules squirmed and snickered. "Oh, boy. Can't wait."

Sylvia broke away to drink some more of her coffee, and Jules kissed down her back to her butt crack, making her wiggle. Then they put their coffee cups down and made love again.

❖

Sylvia made the same breakfast she'd served on the day of Cinco de Mayo—scrambled eggs and beans. Jules happily consumed every bite, lard notwithstanding. As they sat in the kitchen, Jules recalled her fantasy that day. They ate slowly with small kisses between bites of food.

"So you slept with Tracy and Mira and Jan," Sylvia said. "Are there others?"

"Sylvia."

"I'm not mad. I just want to know."

Silence filled the room.

"Yeah, there are others." Jules wondered where this was leading but decided the less she talked, the better.

"I didn't talk to Mira or Jan, so I have no idea what they're like, but I thought you'd have better taste than that Tracy chick."

Jules relaxed and grinned. "It was only once and it was sort of a fluke. I didn't much like her in bed. Or out of bed, for that matter. You know how some women sort of get creepy after you have sex with them? She's not especially bright either."

"I noticed," Sylvia said acerbically.

Jules grunted. "Tracy isn't that good at the poly thing. She does this passive-aggressive, jealousy shtick."

"I suppose I owe her, though."

"How so?"

"She finally nudged me into sleeping with you. You were so

worried I wouldn't have a good time at the barbecue. It was just so sweet."

Jules raised her eyebrows.

"I was this close, anyhow. I just needed a little push." She flicked her index finger.

Jules laughed. "I didn't think of that. I should let her know about her good deed. That'd drive her crazy, but then she'd probably want a three-way."

"Ewwww." They both laughed.

Sylvia said, "I thought Claire and Toni were cool. But I don't think Claire likes me."

"That's just her. I'm sure she likes you."

Sylvia looked out the window. "So now you're going to discuss what's just happened with them?"

"It's not what you think. We don't talk about sex in that dirty, high-school gossip fashion. It's part of our agreement that I can sleep with other women, but I have to be honest. That's also part of our agreement."

"I don't like the idea of you discussing us, but I guess I have to accept it. It's not like I didn't know about you and them. I guess it's really no different than me talking about you with Perla. Well, one difference."

Jules watched Sylvia's lovely face, imagining her internal struggle, then tentatively touched Sylvia's hair. Sylvia finally turned to face her and, to her great relief, said, "No, you're right. I have to adjust my thinking and try to accept. This is all new territory for me."

"I know. I don't want you to be unhappy. It's different for you. I hope it's okay."

"You're so sweet." Sylvia kissed her again and the awkward moment passed.

Later, after Jules got dressed, they stood at the door.

"Bye. I had a great day yesterday," Jules said, and kissed Sylvia gently.

"See you tomorrow with Barney."

"Right. Land's End. Then the meeting."

"Yup." They kissed again.

"I have to *go*." Jules moaned. "Bye." She turned and waved as she walked down the sidewalk. Sylvia waved back and blew a kiss.

❖

It was strange, Jules thought, how she and Sylvia had finally given in to their mutual lust without any freak-outs or drama, no one being clingy or weird. It was all spookily easy. And they were getting together Sunday, although they hadn't mentioned sleepovers.

Jules turned on her phone before starting her Saturday errands and saw a message from Claire. *Oh, fuck. I totally forgot to go back.* Jules was aghast. She called right away as she cursed herself. She'd have to tell the truth. That was the rule. She talked to herself as the phone rang. *It's not as though I cheated. Am cheating. On anyone.*

"Hello?"

It was Claire. "Jules! Are you all right? When you didn't show up, we got worried."

"Yeah. I'm sorry I didn't call. It was kind of unexpected, but I, er, spent the night with Sylvia."

There was the barest pause, and Claire said, "Oh, good. Kind of thought you would. Well, that's nice. Hope you had a good time."

"Yeah. I did. It just got too late to call and I, uh…" Jules hoped she didn't sound as lame as she thought she did. This had never happened before. Friday nights were dedicated to Claire and Toni, and she rarely needed to cancel. She'd certainly never ditched them to sleep with someone else. If anything, Jules thought ruefully, poly relationships were *less* spontaneous than others. When she was interested in someone, she told Claire and Toni all about it, and they were encouraging and supportive.

"Jules, it's fine. You don't need to explain. We'll talk later this week. Take care."

Claire was pissed, even if she was trying to sound like she didn't care. *Shit*. Was it time to end her connection to Claire and Toni? She didn't want to, necessarily, but would she really be able to be up front with them, particularly since Sylvia wasn't at all poly? Sylvia would want an exclusive relationship. Monogamy. The thought staggered Jules. What *did* Sylvia want? After swearing up and down that they couldn't be sexual, now here they were, and what the fuck did that mean? *What does it mean to me?* She decided sitting in place and thinking about it wouldn't do any good, so she started moving, doing her shopping and going to yoga class, after which she felt more focused and hopeful.

As she drove home, she couldn't keep the speculation about Sylvia's state of mind at bay, nor could she stop obsessing about what sort of discussion she'd have with Claire and Toni. *Shit*. She would have to discuss her sexual encounter with Sylvia in detail because they had had oral sex, and poly rules didn't allow any fluid exchange with people outside the triad, for health reasons. She'd been so focused on Sylvia, she'd forgotten. That had never happened to her before. *Ha, another reason not to get involved with non-poly women. You get so caught up in the moment, you forget to lay out the ground rules ahead of time. Not cool.*

"Oh, boy, next Friday's going to be a blast."

CHAPTER SIXTEEN

Jules sat next to Sylvia in the booth at La Cumbre. Across from them, Perla beamed at her. Jules had her hand on Sylvia's leg, and the physical contact with her sturdy thigh and their closeness were flooding her synapses with hormones. Her spiking sexual arousal was making it hard to concentrate on what Perla was saying.

They'd spent a couple of happy hours at Land's End, strolling from the Sutro Bath trailhead to the Lincoln Park overlook and back, with Barney loping ahead. A few times they'd stopped to kiss at some of the scenic spots. Now, at dinner, on their way to the Sunday night EQCA meeting, Jules was teetering between absolute happiness at being with Sylvia and anxiety about what would happen that night or any night to follow. In the meantime, they consumed their burritos and enchiladas and sodas, and Perla told them about a few developments on the Prop 8 front.

"The legal eagles filed suit to get it off the ballot, but that probably won't work. It's the whole California-initiative thing. I'm sure Mark will have more to say."

"As unbelievable as it may seem, some LGBTs don't get why we have to have marriage rights and why it's terrible that Prop 8 is happening," Sylvia said, and glanced at Jules, who grew uneasy, remembering the argument at the barbecue.

Perla cocked an eyebrow first at Jules, then back to Sylvia. "That *is* hard to believe."

"I know. I mean, how stupid can you be?" Sylvia asked, coldly.

"I don't know, but that kind of apathy won't help us win this election. Oh, did you hear, Obama is opposed to Prop 8?" Perla had changed the subject, much to Jules's relief.

"No shit! That's awesome, isn't it, Jules?"

"Yep. Great." Jules couldn't form sentences because she was remembering her night with Sylvia and wondering if it would be repeated. She was also still obsessing about her phone conversation with Claire. It wasn't just Claire's attitude but her uncharacteristic guilt. She'd had sex with several other women, and Claire and Toni knew about them. They talked about it and it was no sweat. But she was in the throes of an off-the-charts infatuation with Sylvia. That was also brand new and totally terrifying, and she had no idea where it would all lead.

❖

After the EQCA meeting, which was as raucous but informative as usual, they'd dropped Perla off and driven the few blocks to Sylvia's flat. Jules was overflowing with anxiety. She was more than ready, and had been since Saturday morning, to make love with Sylvia again. But she wanted Sylvia to decide if they would spend the night together.

"You're quiet," Sylvia said. "Everything okay?"

"Super."

"Come on. What's going on?" Sylvia stroked Jules's arm, and Jules nearly jumped out of her skin at her incredible touch.

"I'm nervous about whether you intend to ask me to stay with you tonight."

"Oh, that." Sylvia lowered her eyes. "It depends."

"On what?" Jules croaked.

"Did you bring a toothbrush and can you deal with me getting up at six?"

"Sure." Jules pulled a toothbrush out of her vest pocket.

Sylvia laughed. "All right, then. Work your magic and find a parking place, and then you can come to bed with me and work your magic there, too."

Jules was exhilarated, relieved, and very, very turned on. "ASAP. What's that prayer Perla used?"

"Gladys, Gladys, full of grace, please find me a parking place. What about *your* parking karma?"

"I need all the help I can get."

Later, in bed, Jules ran her hand through Sylvia's glossy dark hair, feeling the texture. She looked at Sylvia for a long time, and Sylvia gazed back solemnly but said nothing.

"You're without a doubt the most gorgeous woman I've ever seen, let alone slept with," Jules said, at last.

"With your record, that's pretty high praise." Sylvia smiled to take the sting out, but Jules winced anyhow. It was a good bet Sylvia would always have an issue with her poly lifestyle. But that thought floated through her head and out again as they kissed. Jules silently prayed that they could just keep on like this; it was so sweet. Her intellect ceased functioning as Sylvia squeezed her breasts and their legs intertwined and they kissed over and over.

❖

"Jules, darling, it's really okay that you slept with Sylvia. That's what you wanted, right?" Claire's patronizing tone was driving Jules crazy, especially the way she said "darling."

"Stop saying that. That's not the point."

"No, the point is that you exchanged body fluids. We just need for you and her to get a herpes screening."

"No. I'm not going to ask her to do that," Jules said, hotly. "She hasn't had sex with anyone in years!"

"Now, you know people lie about that stuff."

Clair meant non-poly people were dishonest about sex, and poly people were supposedly much more evolved. *Right.* "No, she's not lying and she didn't give me herpes. I'll get the test."

"Jules. Whether she wants to admit it or not, she's now poly."

"I doubt that."

"Well. You're sleeping with her and you're sleeping with us. Sounds poly to me," Toni said.

"Yes, I know." Jules was tired of the argument. She could imagine Sylvia's expression if she told her she had to get a herpes screening and a chlamydia smear. Probably an HIV test, just for good measure. Sylvia would freak and probably stop having sex with her. Not an option.

"I won't have oral with her anymore," Jules said, knowing that probably wouldn't fly either.

"Be realistic, Jules. She'll know something's up. Besides," Toni grinned, "your tongue ought to be preserved as a treasured relic in the Smithsonian when you die. I'd hate to deprive her of that."

Jules frowned. She didn't want to discuss her and Sylvia's sexual relationship any more. She'd never had a problem with that discussion about anyone else, but that was before Sylvia. She was different. She felt protective of her because she was the only monogamist who seemed willing to fully engage with her. She was, in fact, acting poly by sleeping with someone she knew was poly, but Jules was afraid to try to classify anything. They were simply enjoying a monumentally satisfying sexual connection, and she didn't want to roil the waters by demanding any processing. That wasn't the recommended mode for poly folks, but she wanted to tread carefully.

"Look, Toni, Claire. I'm not going to demand Sylvia get any screening for STD because she doesn't have any. She hasn't done anything to get exposed, and she's not lying about it. So can we drop it? I apologized for not calling and for having oral without prior agreement."

Claire and Toni looked at each other again, and Jules waited.

"We want you to stay with us," Toni said. "We really do, but you need to hold to our agreements."

"I will. I said I would. It was a lapse. I'm human."

"Yes, of course you are." They looked at each other again and Jules almost yelled at them to stop it, but that really wasn't fair. They could communicate nonverbally if they wanted to. They were lovers. They could leave her out of their relationship if that's what they needed to do.

"Sure, Jules. Let's drop it for now."

Later that night, when they were in bed, Jules exerted herself to be especially loving. She and Toni practically had a contest of who could give the other the most orgasms. They also gave Claire a working-over that caused the usually stoic Claire to sigh like a Victorian maiden, and they all giggled a great deal. Jules was relieved that their balance seemed to be restored, but she couldn't help thinking about Sylvia and how amazing the sex was between them.

They'd only had a brief phone call during the week. Sylvia said she'd be going to Bakersfield to visit her brother for the weekend but hadn't said anything about getting together when she returned.

Jules was anxious in a way she'd never been with her various girlfriends. It had never been an issue when they would see each other; things just fell into place. She was on edge about when and whether Sylvia would call after she got back and when they could sleep together. Sex with Claire and Toni had felt oddly like cheating on Sylvia, which was insane. Jules firmly told herself to stop obsessing; it would all be fine.

CHAPTER SEVENTEEN

Several weeks later, Perla, Jules, and Sylvia sat together at the Fog City Diner, which Hana and Elspeth had chosen for their wedding reception. The party had completely taken over the restaurant, and all the guests were having a few drinks as they awaited the arrival of the brides. The Fog City called itself a diner, but it was a lot more upscale than the standard greasy spoon.

Jules couldn't tear her eyes away from Sylvia. She wore a dark-green suit with a fitted skirt and a white shell, and she was also in hose and heels. Jules was looking forward to removing all of it later, very slowly. Sylvia glowed as she laughed and chatted with Perla and other EQCA people.

Jules was more moved by the wedding than she thought she would be. The ceremony was simple and spiritual, rather than religious. It was both like and unlike other weddings she'd been to. She didn't generally feel anything at weddings, but listening and watching the two young women exchange vows was surprisingly poignant and, well, really inspiring. The guests seemed to be cheering as much for the concept as for the two individuals involved.

Hana and Elspeth arrived at the restaurant to great acclaim, and everyone settled down to have lunch. After a time, Hana came over to visit their table. She accepted everyone's hugs and congratulations, then said, "I've been so distracted with the wedding, I've lost track of what's going on with the campaign."

"I was talking to Steve during break last week," Perla said, "and he said the executive committee thinks we've got this in the bag. They're going to run more ads and keep doing the interminable phone-banking. Then the usual get-out-the-vote on Election Day and voilà, Prop 8 goes down!"

Hana said, "Well, there might be something to that. Do you know what the latest poll numbers are? After the attorney general changed the ballot language, our numbers went way up. It's like sixty *no* and forty *yes*, right? Isn't that fantastic?"

"Still," Perla said, "I wonder. I was making calls last week and they were all in the Bay Area and all of them said, no worries, they were voting 'no.' I mean, it's a whole lot better than calling and talking to people who are negative and mean. But remember, the campaign folks said we're trying to reach the undecided. I don't know how you do that with random phone numbers."

"Well, a lot of people say they're okay with us being queer and having relationships and not getting fired from our jobs and so on," Sylvia said.

"Oh, yes." Hana rolled her eyes. "Big of them, isn't it, to be so tolerant! But when it comes to marriage, the tolerance evaporates."

Jules recalled she'd wanted to ask a question, and now seemed as good a time as any.

"Why is this whole Prop 8 thing happening, anyhow? I mean, I don't get it. What's so wrong with people getting married if they want to? Why are they so upset about it?

"Gender roles," Hana said. She was in grad school getting a PhD in political science and queer studies, so she knew what she was talking about. "Those people can't stand the thought of truly egalitarian relationships, which is what two men or two women have. They freak at not being able to tell who's the 'man' and who's the 'woman.'"

"It's almost like they say, or they think or whatever," Sylvia said, "'Okay. You gay people have got everything you want—jobs, social acceptance, everything—but you can't have marriage. You can't, you can't!' It's like they're throwing a temper tantrum." The group laughed.

Perla said, "My friend Magda said the way these people go on and on about how we're going to destroy marriage is stupid, when it's really their own problems with adultery and divorce and illegitimate children of single mothers that are destroying it. Magda says that straight culture is suffering from a massive case of projection." They all laughed even harder.

"It just goes to show you," Hana said, "they wouldn't be fighting this so hard if it wasn't so important. It *is* important." Everyone got quiet.

"The word 'marriage,' the concept of marriage, it's vital. No one says, 'I think, when I grow up, I'd like to get civil-unioned.' When I stood in the Shakespeare Garden and said out loud to everyone who's important in my life that I love Elspeth and want to spend the rest of my life with her, that was the best moment of my life."

They all nodded and murmured agreement. Jules saw that Sylvia's lovely features were somber and wondered what she was thinking.

As they rode the Muni back to Sylvia's apartment, she was quiet and staring out the window. Jules was alarmed and racked her brain for something to say. Finally she asked, "So how did Hana and El come up with their wedding ceremony?"

"They told me they wanted some things that were traditional and some of their own, modern touches. Like they both agreed they'd have the chuppah and the wineglass and all that because those are traditional for a Jewish wedding."

"Uh-huh. Did they write their own vows?"

"Pretty much. Hana said they had a few arguments over what to say, like the 'forsaking all others' part. Elspeth thought it was way too old-fashioned and too much like patriarchal marriage."

"What does that mean exactly? I mean, I think I know what it means but…" Jules looked at Sylvia. She didn't seem quite as sad as she had at the restaurant, but she had a somewhat faraway look in her eye. She met Jules's gaze briefly, then stared out the window. She seemed to almost be speaking to herself.

"Hana convinced Elspeth to include it after she found out what it really means. It's not just about fidelity, although that's part of it. It means your loyalty is always to your spouse, no matter what. Not your parents, not your siblings or your best friend. It's your spouse. Everyone else, everything else, is secondary."

"Oh. I see." Jules couldn't think of anything else to say. That certainly epitomized the opposite of polyamory. *Talk about divided loyalties.* She brooded for the rest of the ride home. That was what Sylvia believed. *What do I believe?* It seemed way too much to ask of one person, far too much to burden one person with, even if you did love her. Jules thought about Claire and Toni, and then about herself and Claire and Toni. She didn't see that concept at work at all, of course. That was the point, to not make one person represent your sole source of companionship, happiness, sex, love.

Yet, lots and lots of people felt that was the right thing to do. Hana and Elspeth, for instance. Sylvia, too, though it was obvious that the lack of agreement between her ideals and her experience truly bothered her. From what Sylvia had told her, her previous relationship with Elena hadn't met those goals either. It saddened Jules profoundly and reminded her again that she wouldn't be able to fulfill that role either, and she regretted it deeply.

When they got back to Sylvia's flat, they kicked their shoes off and sat together on the couch. Jules ran her hand from Sylvia's knee up under her skirt. The feel of panty hose was surprisingly sexy, and she moved her hand higher between Sylvia's legs, seeking heat. She kissed Sylvia under her ear and nuzzled her neck. "You look so beautiful right now, do you know that?"

Sylvia turned and smiled, but it wasn't a sexy smile. It was a somber one. Her dark eyes were dull instead of sparkling.

Jules moved her hand away. "Is something wrong?"

Sylvia looked at her feet and sighed, then tilted her head back and closed her eyes. "No. Yes. Maybe. Not really. Sort of. Ugh." She shook her head. "I'm not making any sense, am I?"

"Well…"

Sylvia stopped her with a finger to her lips. "No, don't try to answer. I know I'm not. I want to try to tell you about it."

"If that's what you want, I'm ready to listen." Jules hoped she wasn't the cause of Sylvia's mood, but she wanted very much to know what was bothering her. In the month and a half since the Fourth of July, they'd spent a great deal of time together, most of it lighthearted. They'd laughed and made love and simply enjoyed life. If that was going to end, Jules thought she might as well get it over with.

Sylvia touched Jules's cheek with her palm and tilted her head. "You're a really good listener. I mean, I know that's a cliché, but when I'm with you, I know you're completely focused on me."

"That's good, right?"

"Yep, it is." Sylvia took a breath and then turned to look at Jules directly. "I started thinking of Elena today at the wedding. I didn't want to, but I did, and it made me sad. I'm happy for Hana and Elspeth, but it made me remember."

"I see." Jules's insides grew cold. Sylvia wanted to get married, she knew that, but she wouldn't be the one, and Sylvia knew that, too. She hadn't uttered a word to Jules about exclusivity or commitment or anything of that nature. Jules braced herself for what she thought was coming next.

"I don't let go of things easily. I guess you've gotten that idea." Sylvia snorted.

"Um."

"Don't worry. I know that I have to let go of *you* sometime." Now Sylvia looked at her with real regret. "But not yet, okay? I'm enjoying myself too much." Her eyes hooded and, to Jules's surprise, Sylvia kissed her sensuously and pulled Jules's hand back to her inner thigh. Jules returned the kiss and gently removed Sylvia's jacket. She kissed her shoulders and neck. Sylvia's head dropped to the back of the couch and she moaned. Jules carefully unzipped the white shell she'd worn and pulled it out of the skirt waistband. Underneath, Sylvia's skin was warm and soft.

Jules put her palm right at the small of her back and pushed her down on the couch, gently. She broke away and rose to her knees. "Turn over."

Sylvia complied and Jules unzipped her skirt and drew it down over her hips. Jules's heart was pounding and she caressed Sylvia's breasts over her white lacy bra. Sylvia put her hands over Jules's and squeezed. Then she reached behind to unhook the bra.

"Let me," Jules said, pulling her close and kissing her hair and neck. She got the bra hooks undone and Sylvia's breasts into her hands. They were perfect, she thought dimly. They were luscious.

She could barely stand to let go, but she wanted Sylvia naked. She wanted her, all of her, right that second. She managed to get the panty hose peeled off and out of the way, then Sylvia's underwear. *So much for slow.* For the wedding, she'd worn silk peach-colored briefs. Jules thought they were overwhelmingly sexy, but Sylvia's body moved her more. She took a moment to take off her own shirt and bra so their bodies could touch unencumbered. Sylvia wrapped her legs around Jules's torso, pushing upward to get closer to her. Jules kissed and stroked her way down Sylvia's beautiful body. Jules could tell by her sounds and by the way she moved her hips that she was ready. She reached between them to stroke her clitoris and plunged one finger in, then another.

Sylvia moaned. "More. Please."

Jules kissed her stomach and stroked her with her other hand. She dropped onto the floor, pulled Sylvia around so she was sitting on the couch, and then reverently kissed the insides of her thighs where the skin was the softest. She could smell how turned on Sylvia was, and she knew it was time. She opened her and touched the tip of her tongue to her clitoris. Sylvia jumped and gave a little scream. Jules grinned and plunged her entire tongue into Sylvia's cunt. She moved slowly at first, tasting, testing, and listening to Sylvia's sounds. She entered her again.

Sylvia's legs were rigid with tension, so Jules decided to stop teasing and go for broke. She moved her tongue firmly to her clitoris and licked up and down steadily. It was hard and slippery, and she was close to coming. Jules fucked her harder and wrapped her left arm around her hips to keep them connected. Sylvia's hips jerked once, then again, and she came in wave after wave, her insides squeezing Jules's finger. She pulled Jules's hair and screamed. Jules would have screamed herself in triumph if her mouth hadn't otherwise been occupied.

"Enough! I can't stand it." Sylvia shoved at Jules's forehead and Jules released her. They both sat gasping, Jules on the floor and Sylvia on the couch.

"Oh, God." Sylvia tugged on a strand of Jules's hair. "Come up here." Jules hauled herself back onto the couch and Sylvia licked the come off Jules's lips.

"Mmm. Jesus. That was unbelievable."

"You're unbelievable," Jules said. "You want some more? I'll do it again."

Sylvia pulled Jules's head onto her shoulder. "Give me a sec here. Then we're going to go get in bed. I want your clothes off and, yes, I want some more." She kissed Jules ardently. "But first, I want you."

"Sure. No argument from me." Jules stood up and took her hand and they made their way into the bedroom. She stayed still except for a few stolen kisses and let Sylvia unzip her pants. Sylvia slithered her hand into her underwear and pulled her pubic hair gently. Jules was so turned on from making love to Sylvia, she twitched. Sylvia took first one nipple, then the other into her mouth, biting down a tiny bit. Then she pushed Jules down backward and ripped her pants and underwear off.

Jules loved Sylvia when she was in her commanding sexual persona. Sylvia's face was rapt, her eyes fixed in concentration. She fell on top of Jules and rammed her thigh between her legs. Jules thrust back and nearly knocked Sylvia off, but Sylvia wasn't about to be dislodged or dissuaded. Her silky hair fell over Jules's face and neck, and Jules inhaled deeply, burying her nose in the dark waves. Sylvia slipped her hand between them and probed for her clitoris. She stroked slowly at first but then sped up, her leg thrusting in the same rhythm. The top of Jules's feet tingled and her thigh muscles tensed until she was nearly in pain. She thrust back in unison with Sylvia, her entire being focused on the point of unbearable pleasure. Her body gathered itself and then exploded.

❖

Sylvia woke up with a start. She looked over at Jules, who was sound asleep, then settled the quilt under her armpits and tried to relax, intending to fall back asleep. The images of the wedding floated by behind her eyelids, followed by images of Jules and her. Hana and Elspeth's marriage reminded her far too clearly of the failed relationship with Elena. She felt more strongly than ever that she would never be able to achieve that with anyone, and certainly not with Jules. It was futile to even continue, she told herself, and she should stop. It was completely unfair that Jules was such a perfect lover—sweet, funny, and effortlessly sexy. *If only.* Sylvia scrunched her eyes shut. She had to stop thinking that way; she was smarter than that. Sylvia knew the facts. If she got hurt, she had only herself to blame. She wouldn't let it get out of hand. *I can stop when I need to.*

Jules murmured in her sleep and turned over. Sylvia looked at her face, soft and serene in sleep. Her hand was tucked under her cheek and she looked adorable. Sylvia thought of them making love a few hours previously and, before that, Jules's concern over her feelings about the wedding. She was getting in over her head. She sighed and gritted her teeth. She wasn't ready to stop, to let Jules go. It was just going to get harder, and when the time came, as it would, it would be that much more painful. But she wasn't ready, not yet.

CHAPTER EIGHTEEN

It had taken a few tries, but Sylvia had to admit she didn't mind doing yoga with Jules. It was much like the vegetarian routine in that she resisted and then felt silly for being close-minded, and after a few experiences, she actually found she liked it. She refused to go to yoga class but didn't mind them practicing for an hour in Jules's living room. It was relaxing in somewhat the same manner as sex, but it had a mental component that surprised Sylvia. After an hour of stretching and meditation, she felt serene. She grew to love the sound of Jules's soft voice reading or just free-associating as they lay still in rest position, *savasana*.

It was early September and the weather had turned warm. Outside Jules's flat in the Haight, the sun was shining brilliantly. Sylvia was drifting to the sound of Jules reciting something from the *Upanishads*. After a beat of silence Jules whispered, *"Namaste."* They revived themselves and went to the kitchen, where Jules got them some water, and as she handed the glass to Sylvia, she said, "I have a question for you." Something about her tone put Sylvia on alert.

They went back to sit in the living room, and Jules uncharacteristically looked at her feet instead of directly at her. Usually after yoga, they talked and laughed, went out to eat or cooked something.

Sylvia took a long drink of water and waited for Jules to collect herself. In the silence, she finally asked, "What's up?"

"Claire and Toni have asked me to bring you over for dinner next week."

"That's it? That's the question? You seemed really scared to ask."

Jules looked uncomfortable. "Well. After July Fourth and now that we're, you know, I wasn't really sure how you'd feel." This uncertainty, while a little baffling to Sylvia, was somehow endearing. So much for the sophisticated polyamorists, she thought, amused.

"Hmm. That's a good question. Let me think about it. I don't see why not."

"I thought you might not like to be reminded of them and who they are," Jules said, and once again, Sylvia was struck by her sensitivity.

"You're right. I suppose I like to pretend they don't exist, even if I know that's silly."

"No. Not so much. I can understand that, since you're not into polyamory and you don't want to think about it."

"Sort of." Sylvia agreed but felt like she was being delusional, and she'd always considered herself a realist. After all, Claire and Toni were Jules's lovers, and trying to make believe they didn't exist was stupid. Their "don't ask, don't tell" dance seemed ridiculous. She made up her mind then and there. She was neither a small-minded nor a closed-minded person, and it was time to act accordingly.

"I'll go. Thank them for the invitation for me, please."

❖

"Is she going to expect us to serve prime rib?" Toni asked Jules as they finalized the dinner plans.

"No. She's not like that," Jules said, a little annoyed. "She eats veggie with me a lot."

"Could have fooled me when she was here on the Fourth," Toni said. "With her steak and all."

It occurred to Jules that this was a typical Toni-type reaction. Whenever Jules was seeing someone, Toni, as sweet as she was, could seem a little passive-aggressive. Jules thought it was subconscious jealousy, but Claire didn't seem to notice, and Jules tried to ignore it, as she normally did any hint of conflict. This time, however, it continued to bug her.

"Just promise me you won't try to get us to have a four-way," Jules said.

"Oh, for God's sake." Toni sounded exasperated. "You really think we'd do that? You must be crazy. Or crazy about this woman."

"Nope," Jules said stubbornly, but she wondered. She and Sylvia spent more time together than she spent with Claire and Toni, a lot more. She was almost as nervous about this dinner as she had been about the Fourth of July party. The aftermath of that occasion had turned into something far different than she would have imagined, but she didn't know what to expect this time. She had decided not to probe too deeply into Sylvia's reasons for agreeing to it and to just accept it as a good thing. It would, after all, start to bring the two parts of her life together, which would be helpful, because she didn't really feel good about the separation. Perhaps if she could integrate everyone, she would feel more at ease.

Toni's crack about being crazy about Sophia bothered Jules because she suspected it was true. She had simply never felt this way about anyone. If she went more than a few days without seeing Sylvia, it was far too long. She was addicted to Sylvia's laugh and her lively brown eyes and curvaceous body. She would happily sit and listen to Sylvia talk about her clients for hours. It was feeling more like an obligation to go over to Claire and Toni's every Friday. She didn't want to examine any of it too closely, however. She didn't want to start any troublesome conversations with Sylvia, either. They were doing great, and once Sylvia and Toni and Claire all got to know each other better, it would be easier. Things would be completely in sync and life would feel normal, Jules was convinced.

❖

Sylvia dressed carefully for dinner. She chose black trousers and a red blouse, both tight fitting. The blouse even showed a little cleavage. She not only wanted to feel good in her skin, she wanted Jules's girlfriends to notice and be impressed. Why had they asked her to dinner? Maybe they were just being friendly, Sylvia thought, although it was hard for her to believe it was that simple, no matter what Jules told her about polyamory. It was astonishingly idealistic to think no one would be jealous of anyone else. Humans weren't made that way.

She considered her own agenda. She'd successfully ignored Claire and Toni's existence for the past two months. She knew they were there and she certainly knew where Jules went every Friday night and what she did. She and Jules didn't talk about it, though. They talked about everything but Claire and Toni. *Well*, Sylvia thought, *they're there and I may as well acknowledge them since they're not going away.*

Jules's eyes widened when Sylvia answered the door. She stepped inside, kissed Sylvia, and looked her up and down. "Wow."

Her reaction gratified Sylvia. "I guess you approve."

"That's putting it mildly. You look wonderful. Luscious, delicious. I'm speechless."

Sylvia beamed. "Thank you. So should we go?"

Jules nodded and held the door open for her.

❖

Claire put dinner together and served them with impressive efficiency. Sylvia remembered Claire's clear, crisp voice cutting through all the babble of argument at the barbecue. Now Sylvia could see how gracious she was as she focused on making Sylvia welcome. She might have been wrong about Claire being distant and cold.

"It's nice that you could come over for dinner. After we met you on the Fourth, we wanted to get to know you better."

"Thanks for inviting me. The food's great, really." Claire's features softened a great deal when she smiled, her eyes crinkling at the corners. "Jules has gotten me into vegetarian eating. She's a good influence." Sylvia grinned across the table at Jules, who grinned back. Toni was almost entirely focused on Jules and hadn't said much to Sylvia after her initial greeting.

"Coffee and dessert in the living room?" Claire asked.

"Yep. Jules, can you help me?" Toni asked.

"I can do that," Jules said amiably, and followed Toni to the kitchen.

Sylvia and Claire took seats in the two large armchairs. Sylvia admired the furniture and asked Claire some questions about it.

"Jules hasn't really told me what you do," Sylvia said.

"Oh. I'm an architect."

"What sort of buildings do you design?"

"Office buildings. I've always been interested in the spaces where people work, since we have to spend so much time in them."

They stopped talking as Toni and Jules came over with a tray of coffee. They set it down on the coffee table and sat next to each other on the couch. The cat, who'd been asleep there, woke up and walked over their laps. They busied themselves pouring coffee from the carafe and retrieving plates of peach cobbler. Sylvia stirred cream into her coffee and sipped it. It was perfect, the right temperature with strong, full flavor.

"Mmm, this is wonderful," she said to Toni. "What kind of coffee is it?"

"Free trade from Guatemala," Toni said, and turned her

attention back to Jules, who was petting the cat. "Do you want me to pour your coffee since Chloe's got you?"

Sylvia heard a mild note of flirtation in Toni's voice and had to quell a stab of jealousy.

Jules was sitting back and letting the cat crawl all over her, encouraging it with her petting. She looked relaxed, comfortable, and very sexy. She was wearing the usual jeans, but she'd put on an ironed button-down shirt in a nice salmon shade. Her long legs were crossed and she was smiling at the cat who, as before, purred loudly under her hands. "Please."

Sylvia watched as Toni made Jules's coffee with elaborate care and then scooted close to her on the couch and handed her the cup. As their eyes met, Sylvia saw the heat in their expressions and her stomach twisted with anger.

"Jules told me you're a social worker and you work downtown." Claire's clear, even voice tugged Sylvia's attention away from the two on the couch, and she turned back to her.

"It's the old Sullivan Building on Mission Street, one thousand block."

"Oh, I know that one. It's one of the few in that area that survived the 1906 earthquake. The exterior could use a little work. What's it like inside?"

"I haven't seen the other offices in the building, but ours has been modernized. It's a clinic that the city runs and UCSF staffs." Sylvia wanted to converse with Claire, but her eyes kept wanting to slide over to watch Toni and Jules on the couch. Toni was snuggled into Jules's side, and they were both playing with the cat. It looked like they were a couple rather than Claire and Toni, which infuriated Sylvia. She struggled not to leap out of her chair, throw herself between them, and push Toni onto the floor.

Claire didn't move or even turn to look at them. "I'm interested in interiors, especially how they're designed to accommodate and use natural light. You've heard of that research?"

"No, I haven't. Please tell me about it." Sylvia wanted to

keep it together and carry on a civil conversation with Claire, but it was almost impossible. Toni was using the excuse of petting the cat to touch Jules's hand.

Claire started talking and Sylvia attempted to follow her clear, if technical, explanations.

When she was done, Sylvia said, "That all makes a lot of sense. My clinic's got bright, contrasting colors. It's not puke green or bureaucratic beige." She enjoyed how Claire laughed. She took a sip of coffee, trying to keep her focus on Claire, but she could see Toni and Jules in her peripheral vision. "We're not all lucky enough to work outside, like Jules."

At the mention of Jules's name, both Toni and Jules looked at Sylvia. Jules tilted her head, and Toni stared at Sylvia as though issuing some sort of wordless challenge.

"Sorry, I missed that, except I heard my name."

"I only said you're lucky to work outside," Sylvia said. "Instead of in a building."

"That's how we met Jules." Toni sounded like she was purring, much like the cat, whatever its name was. "Because of what she does. Pet-sitting, I mean. She was *wonderful* with Chloe."

Ah. That's its name, Sylvia thought. And then she thought about strangling Toni.

The evening ended pleasantly enough, and Sylvia and Jules said their thank-yous and good-byes and drove back to Jules's flat. During the twenty-minute drive through downtown San Francisco, Sylvia could barely contain her explosive feelings. She knew it wasn't appropriate to be jealous of Toni because Toni was acting perfectly natural. It was normal to be touchy-feely with the woman with whom you slept. *Except she's the same woman I sleep with.* She wanted Jules to say something, but she didn't know what she wanted to hear. Jules was silent, as usual, concentrating on driving. The silence was weighing on Sylvia this time, and she felt like screaming.

But if she started talking, she was very much afraid

everything she was thinking would come out. She gritted her teeth and kept quiet.

While they were getting ready for bed, Sylvia watched Jules take her clothes off and her anger started to recede. She didn't want to start a fight. "Was the dinner what you expected?" she asked finally.

"Yep. Pretty much. How about you?"

"I don't know what I expected, but it was fine." *No, it wasn't. Not with Toni crawling all over you, but I can't say that.*

"Good. Well, are you sleepy?'

"Not really. You?"

"With that strong coffee? Not hardly." Jules laughed. Then she kissed Sylvia's neck. Sylvia got aroused in spite of her stew of feelings. She shivered as Jules nibbled her way down her throat and decided to keep her thoughts to herself.

❖

The Thursday after their dinner with Claire and Toni, Sylvia took a deep breath and called Jules. After their usual greetings, she said, "I wanted to ask you something."

"Sure."

"Will you spend next Friday night with me? I want to go to a play at the Mission Theater that a friend of mine and Perla's involved with, and I'd like if you went with me."

"Well…"

"I know it's not the usual day for us, but I thought you could make an exception." Sylvia kept her voice calm and uninflected, but inside she was nervous. She wanted to see what Jules would say, what she would do. It mattered more than she wanted it to.

"Can I get back to you?"

"Soon, because I need to get tickets for it."

Sylvia mentally crossed her fingers. Sure, she wanted Jules to go with her, but she also wanted to see who Jules would choose.

She wasn't proud of her underlying motive, but she needed to know.

❖

"Sylvia asked me to go to a play next week. On Friday."

Claire was absorbed in putting dinner on the table and Toni was still in the kitchen. Neither of them responded.

Jules took the bowl of rice from Claire and watched her face as she surveyed the table critically and said, "We need tamari." She turned toward the kitchen, called, "Toni, bring in the tamari," and started to open a bottle of wine.

Jules waited as long as she could. "You don't have anything to say?"

"What's there to say, Jules? You told me what you're going to do."

"What's she going to do?" Toni asked as she brought in the rest of the food and Claire's requested condiment and sat down.

"I'm not sure yet *what* I'm going to do. That's why I mentioned it." Jules fought to keep the irritation out of her voice. She wasn't sure why she was irritated or what she expected from Claire and Toni.

"What?" Toni looked alarmed.

"Sylvia asked me to go to a play with her next Friday."

Toni poured a glass of wine and took what Jules considered a pretty big mouthful. "Oh. So what are you going to do?"

"That's the point! I don't know what to do."

"If you're asking permission, Jules, I'm not sure why. You can do what you want," Claire said, coolly. "We've never tried to control you and we're not starting now."

"You do usually spend Friday night here," Toni said. "Except that one time you forgot," she added with just a trace of reprimand.

"I said I was sorry!" Jules said, more irritated than ever. She didn't know what she wanted them to say, and she was becoming incensed that Sylvia had basically forced her into making a decision about her time and who she would choose to spend it with. *It's not supposed to be a goddamn either or proposition.* Jules fumed silently. She wanted to spend time with Sylvia, but she wanted Claire and Toni to be okay with it, to give her permission, when it came right down to it. They took precedence because they were there first, but Jules didn't want to have to decide. She shouldn't have to choose.

"You should see Sylvia if that's what you want to do," Toni said.

It sounded like she'd said, "You can jump off the Golden Gate Bridge if you want to."

In despair, Jules focused on Claire, who was thoughtfully chewing baked squash. "We do have an agreement but it's not written in stone," Claire said. "We're willing to be flexible."

Toni was silent but looked at Jules like she was mortally wounded, which made Jules feel terrible. Toni was no good at disguising her feelings, but she also hated to get Claire mad at her for being overemotional.

"You're right. I should tell her no." Jules felt worse than ever and had no idea if she was making the right decision. She hated being put in this position, and although Sylvia hadn't made a big deal out of it, it somehow seemed momentous. Jules once again was irritated that she was put into emotional turmoil. *Don't get involved with monogamists.* Well, here she was; she'd gotten what and who she wanted. This was all part of it and it sucked.

CHAPTER NINETEEN

A few weeks later, Sylvia took her time getting her first cup of coffee at work and stood at the counter stirring the coffee with the little wooden stick and staring into space. The kitchen was empty, which was just as well because she didn't feel like chatting with any of her coworkers. She threw the coffee stick away and went to her desk, telling herself to get busy, that it would be good for her. People needed her help, and that had always been the best way for her to cope with emotional turmoil. After she broke up with Elena, she'd worked harder than ever before.

She opened her e-mail and read through it slowly. She wrote answers, deleted the unneeded e-mails, and saved the ones she might need later. Then she looked at her calendar. Three people to see. It was the first of October, which was a busy time for her clients since they got their checks. That could be problematic for the ones with drug and alcohol problems.

None of her determined diligence was helping, though. She couldn't stop thinking about Jules and their predicament. She'd been thinking of it nonstop for the last month, ever since the dinner at Toni and Claire's house. Jules probably didn't consider it a predicament. Sylvia said "lover" to herself. When she connected the word to Jules, it sounded right on one level. She and Jules shared the physical connection of sex, a big part of being a lover. But what about the rest of it? Jules was kind, reliable, affectionate, generous. She had all the right qualities. There was just one problem: her loyalties were divided. She had two other women in her life who were also her lovers. Four was certainly a crowd as far as Sylvia was concerned.

The reality of her situation hit Sylvia hard. She thought about the dinner with Toni and Claire. She thought about Jules and Toni together on the couch. She visualized Jules making love to Toni the same way Jules made love to her, and her head ached with jealous fury. She thought about Jules declining to go to the play with her. The conversation had been tense:

"I can't go with you to the play. I don't want to disappoint Claire and Toni."

"It's just one night!"

Well, that's the name of that tune, Sylvia thought. I guess I understand Jules's priorities. As much as she wanted to be an adult, she couldn't quite tamp down her anger. She'd gone to the play with Perla and had pouted so obviously that Perla had reproved her.

Sylvia had done what she'd sworn she wouldn't do. She'd fallen in love with Jules.

She had no one but herself to blame. She certainly couldn't blame Jules, who'd been completely honest from the beginning. It had been her own idea to start something with someone she knew wasn't available. She supposed she could blame Perla for encouraging her, but that would hardly be fair either. She'd made the choice, although she felt like it had somehow been inescapable. *She made me fall in love with her*. Sylvia slammed her file folder shut and put her head in her hands and closed her eyes. *Fuck*. Her first appointment was in fifteen minutes. She reopened the file and forced herself to concentrate. She'd have to make some sort of move soon because she was driving herself crazy.

❖

Jules made her way across town delivering her dogs to their respective homes. For the first time, she wished she had work that was a bit more absorbing mentally. She had way too much time to think when she was out with the dogs, and her thoughts were going in circles. She and Sylvia had reached some sort of crossroad. Sylvia hadn't said anything. Yet. But Jules could feel it in the air. There'd been a shift after that night at Toni and Claire's. She sensed something was wrong, but she hadn't asked any questions because she hadn't wanted to hear the answers. Sylvia's face after Jules told her she wouldn't go to the play with her had said a lot. There'd also been that discussion after the wedding. With someone who was definite and vocal about her feelings about just about everything, it was a bad sign when Sylvia wasn't talking. Here, again, was the obvious consequence of getting involved with a monogamist. They got possessive, they got jealous. It hadn't happened right away but eventually it would. It was happening now with Sylvia.

Why hadn't Sylvia broken up with her before now? She didn't want things to end, but each day, each week that went by would just make it harder. Should she say something, maybe ask Sylvia how she was doing, have a heart-to-heart? She was afraid of what might happen and of what Sylvia would say. Jules had never worried about anything like this before, and it was a new and unpleasant experience. She felt stuck, like she was in quicksand. She truly didn't know what she wanted. That was a lie. She did. She wanted things to stay the same.

❖

A week later, Sylvia tidied her living room while she was waiting for Jules to arrive to go to dinner. They were trying out a new California-cuisine place in the Avenues, the numbered streets west of Twin Peaks. Sylvia had decided to ask Jules an important question. She rolled her head, trying to release the tension in her neck as she walked around dusting and straightening tchotchkes, something that usually calmed her, but it wasn't working this time. Jules's face kept popping up in her consciousness.

They talked about inconsequential things on the drive to the restaurant. Sylvia waited until they'd put their order in so they'd be free of the waiter for at least twenty minutes. She thought suddenly of another dinner conversation at another restaurant on the evening of their first date. *That didn't go well either*, Sylvia thought, *and here we are. Maybe this will be different.* She was trying hard to keep her mood light and focus on what Jules was saying.

"Lydia wants me to fly back East in December for our parents' fortieth anniversary."

"Are you going to?"

Jules looked unsure. "I don't know. I hate flying and I *really* hate flying during holidays."

"It might be nice, for them, I mean, if you were there," Sylvia said, carefully.

"Maybe." Jules didn't sound convinced.

"Jules," Sylvia said, and reached across the table to take her hand. "Can I ask you a question?"

Jules looked uneasy, like a cornered animal. Her eyes widened and her posture stiffened. "Yeah."

"Where do you see our relationship going?"

"What do you mean?"

Sylvia couldn't believe Jules was being purposefully dense, but she held on to her temper. "I think you know. We've been dating for what, three and a half months?"

"Something like that. I'm not sure. I really don't have any reason to try to figure out where we're going. We're doing fine, right?"

Jules didn't sound as though she really believed that. She looked freaked out, so she must know what Sylvia was really asking. Trying to talk around it was ridiculous. It was time to get to the point. "I want to know how you feel about me."

"I like you a lot. Is there any doubt in your mind about that?" Jules's face was still and blank.

"No. I know that. That's not what I'm asking."

"Then what are you asking?"

"I want to know if we have a future."

"We have a present. Isn't that good enough?"

"Goddamn it, Jules. I'm crazy about you. These last few months have been terrific, just wonderful, but…" *She's going to make me say it.* "You have got two other girlfriends. That I know about," she added, and immediately regretted it.

"There's no one else," Jules said quickly.

"Well. Good. But that's still two too many."

Jules looked astounded. "But why? Why is this suddenly a problem?"

"Because I think I'm in love with you."

Sylvia paused to let her declaration sink in, then continued. "I'd like to find out more about that, about how you might feel. And if it is love, then I wonder if you feel differently about our situation." She watched Jules's face carefully, trying to gauge the effect of her words.

"I love you, Sylvia. I do. Without question. But don't ask me to break up with Claire and Toni," Jules said, and Sylvia knew she meant it.

"Why not? If you love me, then…?" Sylvia was now fully awash in despair and, as she feared, it was going to come out as anger.

"Monogamy is not my thing. You knew that from the start."

"I did. I'm not saying you misled me in any way. I just thought you might feel different now. I know I do." Sylvia fell silent and just stared at Jules, whose face was stiff with what looked like pain. She seemed distraught but didn't speak. "So you just want to go on, la la la, just like we are. All's well. Nothing's wrong." Sylvia knew she sounded furious. She *was* furious. And hurt and disappointed. All her hopes were completely dashed. Her head hurt from trying to keep her emotions under control, and she'd lost her appetite.

Jules shifted in her chair, apparently trying to keep calm, but it wasn't working very well.

"Yes."

"Well, I can't do that!" Sylvia managed not to shout, and her words came out in a fierce whisper instead. "I'm not made like that. If I'm with someone, I'm with that person. Period, end of story. I wanted you. I wanted to have a fling with you and so I did. I didn't reckon it would turn out like this. But that's the way it goes. You are who you are. I know you've never tried to present yourself as anything different. I hoped, well, I hoped you would see things differently. I see that's not possible. I made a mistake."

Jules said, quietly, "Please don't say it was a mistake. It's wonderful to be with you. I admire you, I adore you. You're amazing, incredibly sexy. I don't want to lose you. But there's something else. How would we know it would last?"

"We don't know that, but I'm willing to take a chance, Jules. But if you're not willing to meet me halfway, I have to protect myself. If I stick around, it'll just make me feel worse. It's better I go."

Jules stared at her with a stricken expression.

"Did you hear me? I've fallen in love with you. I want to be with you. But just you, no one else."

"I hear you."

Sylvia stared at her for a long time, hoping she'd say something else, but Jules only looked at her, her face blank. Sylvia slumped back in her chair and kept her eyes on the table. She felt like crap. She wanted to find the right words that would convince Jules to change her mind. She wanted, desperately, to have a different conversation. But that clearly wasn't going to happen. She looked up at Jules and said, tonelessly, "When they bring our food, let's get it to go and get the hell out of here. I want you to take me home."

"This is really what you want?" Jules drank half of her wine in one gulp.

"No, it's not, but what choice do I have?"

"Right." Jules drained her wineglass and nearly slammed it on the table.

They sat in silence for a few minutes until their dinner appeared, and Jules calmly told the puzzled waiter to pack it up and bring the check.

They had a tense, silent car ride back to the Mission and Jules double-parked. "This is really it?" she asked plaintively. "You really don't want to see me anymore?"

"It's not that I don't want to. I can't. Not and keep my sanity. No, I need to get over this. Do you have anything in the house I can bring out to you?"

"No. Yes. I'm not sure." Jules stared at the steering wheel.

"Okay. Well, I'll look around and mail it to you."

"Sylvia. We really don't have to do this."

"I'm sorry. I have to. It was good, it was fun. You're a wonderful woman, that's why...oh, never mind. It doesn't matter."

"It does matter," Jules said, forcefully.

"I fell in love with you. That was my bad. It's not your fault. But I can't go on like this."

"Sylvia..."

Sylvia wanted to take it all back, tell Jules she'd made a mistake, invite her in, make love with her. The tears were starting and she hated to cry. Her head was pounding.

"No. I can't stand it. You have to go. It's better if this is quick." Sylvia bolted out of the car, leaving her dinner behind. She ran to the front door and tried to unlock it, but she was crying so hard, she couldn't get the key to work. She looked back and Jules hadn't driven away. She could see her staring at the windshield. She finally got the door open, stumbled inside her flat, and rushed into the bedroom. She threw herself on her bed and cried herself to sleep.

❖

Jules sat still, unable to move, barely able to breathe. She glanced at the door through which Sylvia had just disappeared and wondered if Sylvia would reappear and say it was all just a misunderstanding and they could go back to how they'd been.

No such luck. This was the end. Jules gripped the steering wheel and looked out over the street. It was still light outside, not late at all. She looked at the bag with the two cardboard food containers. Sylvia had forgotten all about dinner. *I could take it to her.* Jules sighed. Nope, that wouldn't be a good idea. Sylvia was decisive. Once she'd made up her mind, that was that. Except when it wasn't. She'd changed her mind quite decisively on the Fourth of July.

She was right, of course, and that was the most painful part. Jules had heard this all before from other women. It was nothing new. It just was excruciatingly painful to hear it from Sylvia. It was like a shotgun blast to the stomach. This was different than before, like everything about Sylvia was different. *She said she's in love with me. Am I in love with her? Is that why I feel so horrible? I love her. Is it the same thing?* Jules put her hands over her face. If that was true, it was even worse. She couldn't bear the idea of replicating her mom and dad's relationship. Being in love, then having it disappear, would be much worse than never having it at all. *Am I in love with her? Is this what it feels like?* What would happen if she told Claire and Toni they were done and she was going off to live happily after with Sylvia? Ha. They'd find that humorous. Well, Claire would. Toni, maybe not so much.

She put the Volvo in gear and numbly drove back to her flat. She wished she had a pet to go home to, but they weren't allowed in her building. That's what made her appreciate other people's animals so much. The flat seemed so cold and empty. She put the restaurant food away since she didn't feel like eating. She found a beer, sat down in her favorite chair, and drained half of the bottle. It didn't help. *Sylvia.* She spoke the name in her mind and immediately it summoned visions of her face and body. Torturous images of them together walking Barney, at the Prop 8 headquarters, and making love. *Oh, shit.* She wouldn't be able to show up as a volunteer anymore because of Sylvia. Surprisingly, that realization disappointed her. She'd come to care about the cause.

Jules groaned. She didn't know what to do; she'd never had to break up with anyone like this. When you didn't have much of an investment, the end of an affair just didn't matter that much. Not this time. *I need to talk to someone.* Who the heck would that be? Sylvia would be the logical choice, but that was obviously out of the question. Lydia? Jules looked at her cell-phone display. It was only ten back in New York. Not too late. She hit Lydia's speed dial. Darn. It was Saturday night and she was probably out somewhere.

"Hello? Jules?"

"Hey, Lyd. Is this a bad time?"

"Kind of. What's up?"

"I need to talk."

"Are you okay?"

"No."

"Are you sick? Hurt? Street crime?"

"Nope. Nothing like that." Lydia was such a New Yorker. Jules smiled in spite of her emotional turmoil.

"Well. I don't know when I'll be home tonight, but I'll call you first thing in the morning, okay?"

"Right. Bye, Lyd."

She clicked the phone shut and drained the rest of the beer bottle, then decided to go for a long walk to try to clear her head. The Haight Street neighborhood was buzzing, but the excitement didn't move her like it usually did. She walked until almost ten o'clock and finally went home and fell into bed. Her dreams were frightening in a formless, incomprehensible way. Her cell phone jolted her awake and she was nauseous, with a pounding headache. She was confused. She'd only drunk one beer. Oh, and that glass of wine. And of course she'd forgotten to eat.

"Hey, Lyd."

"Jules. Kiddo. What's wrong? You sound awful." In her tenderer moments, Lydia called her "kiddo" even though she was a year and half older. *Maybe I'm really the youngest and not the middle child.*

"Yeah. I'm not so great. Sylvia broke up with me."

"So sorry to hear that. What happened?"

"She wants a monogamous relationship. She says she loves me."

"Wow. What do you think?"

"I don't know. I told her I loved her but I couldn't change."

"Hmm. Why not?"

"Well. For one thing, I'd have to break up with Claire and Toni."

"Yep. So what's the big deal about that? I thought it was all good when you're polyamorous—no possession, no jealousy, all that crap."

Lydia's sarcasm grated on Jules's already frayed nerves.

"I suppose, but it would probably hurt Toni's feelings at least."

"Yeah, so? She'd get over it. What else?"

"Well. You know, the whole till-death-do-us-part thing. We don't have the greatest example, and I just don't see myself doing it."

"Jules. You're rationalizing. In the first place, you don't spend any time around Mom and Dad, and they're not that bad. They went through a rough period but they're much better. They're still fucking married, you know?"

Jules felt put upon and uncomfortable. She wasn't certain what she'd expected Lydia to say, but this wasn't it. She felt horrible and she wanted sympathy. "Why are you being so mean? I called you to talk because I'm hurting."

"Well. What does that tell you, sis?"

"I don't know. Sylvia gave me the boot. It feels like shit. *I* feel like shit."

"Do you want her back? What does she mean to you?"

"I love her but I can't be what she wants."

"Really? You've never tried, have you?"

"I…" Jules was at a loss for words, but she had to admit it was true. She'd never given any kind of long-term relationship a real chance. She'd never made promises, never declared undying love for anyone.

"As far as I can see, you kind of fell into the scene with Claire and Toni. You never expressed much feeling one way or the other before that. You like them, they were there. They invited you. It's enjoyable, easy and fun. Right?"

"Yeah. Right. What's your point, Lyd?" Jules had already thought of this, but she hated having Lydia verbalize it because it made her sound shallow.

"Sylvia's not that easy. She resisted you for a long time, but then she finally changed her mind. What does that tell you? What do you really feel about her? Come on, J, for once in your life do something positive—be an actor, not a reactor."

"But—"

"No buts, no excuses. You just told me you love her. So do something. Make a decision. Is she someone you just want to let go? Is she someone you can't live without? Can you live without Claire and Toni? Who means more to you?"

"I don't know," Jules said miserably.

"Think about it and I'll talk to you soon. Really, I'm sorry you're in such a state, but it seems like you can do something about it."

CHAPTER TWENTY

They sat in La Cumbre on Sunday evening. In between bites of her burrito, Perla stared at Sylvia, her expression compassionate. Sylvia's burrito sat untouched in front of her.

"I was almost certain she only answered my question the way she did out of habit. She told me her parents' marriage was lousy. She's never committed to anyone. She likes polyamory for that reason."

"That makes sense, I guess. I could have sworn she would change. The way she was with you." Perla shook her head. Sylvia knew she felt bad for even suggesting that Jules might change.

"I thought so, too, but I was wrong. Really wrong. She wouldn't even discuss it."

"Well, you need to take care of yourself, Syl. You did the right thing. Time to move on."

"Yep. I'm devastated, though. It didn't even feel this bad when I finally left Elena."

"That's because you needed to leave Elena. The Princess of Darkness was the worst thing that ever happened to you."

"I know. It's ironic, isn't it, Perls? Me, the big believer in marriage, falls for someone who believes the opposite. I thought I was dating the anti-Elena and I was. But she wasn't right for me either."

"Yeah. You could have fooled me, though. Whenever I was around you two, I could have sworn she was totally in love with you."

"She still kept going with Claire and Toni. I should have known. Jeez. I'm a dope."

"No, you're not. She made you happy. You were great together."

"We were. Ah, well. Let's go see what's happening with EQCA. I need some distraction."

"You sure do. Let's go. I'll eat the rest of this later. We've got just enough time to walk to the LGBT center."

When they'd found seats, Hana came over, her face tense.

"Hi, girl. What's up?" Perla asked. She and Sylvia embraced Hana.

Sylvia said, "Where's El?"

"She's talking to the publicity guy, Steve. You heard what happened, right?"

Sylvia hadn't watched any news. Other than working some volunteer shifts, she really had been focused on Jules. Time to get back in the swim.

Perla said, "It was something about a schoolteacher getting married."

Hana rolled her eyes. "It was so bad. It's going to play right into their hands. This first-grade teacher got married and all the kids in her class came to the wedding."

Sylvia thought that sounded sweet. "Aww. How cute."

Hana stared at her. "Yeah. Real cute. Queers indoctrinating kids? Hello?"

"Oh, get serious. No one believes that. I heard they threw rose petals and it wasn't the teacher's idea. One of the parents thought it up and surprised her!"

"Yeah. All true," Hana said. "But our opponents don't focus on the subtleties."

Elspeth came over and hugged them briefly. "Steve says we're screwed. This is going to—"

Mark spoke from the front of the room. "Okay. Quiet down, everyone. We're going to get started."

The room settled. Sylvia couldn't help thinking it was odd

to not have Jules sitting next to her, holding her hand or rubbing her shoulder. She used to look over to catch her eye and Jules would smile in that slow, sexy way that made her melt. Not anymore. Sylvia mentally shook herself and looked up at Mark. He looked more somber than she'd ever seen him.

"We're less than a month away from the election. It's time for the rubber to meet the road." The group murmured.

"It was never going to be a cakewalk. Now things are harder. We don't know what the real effect of this news story will be. We won't for a week or so. The next poll isn't scheduled until a week from Tuesday. That's a week and a half before the election. It's going to have an effect. Not a huge one, we hope, but we don't know. There's nothing anyone can do about that now. We can only keep going."

Perla whispered to Sylvia, "Want to do the phones this week?"

She nodded. Anything to not have to sit and think about Jules and what she was losing.

Mark continued. "We're planning to have some house meetings. Some of the plaintiffs from the case will go around and talk to people, we'll collect donations, etc. We've got the sign-up sheets in the back. Now. The biggest organizing task coming up is Election Day. Get out the vote. We're going to need everyone. We'll need you starting at four in the morning and throughout the day at the polls all over the Bay Area. Andy'll talk about that some more."

Sylvia tried to concentrate, but Jules's image filled her mind, along with their last sad conversation in the car in front of her house. Jules had looked really hurt, and she'd been torn between wanting to comfort Jules and shake her to make her change her mind. It was useless. Sylvia felt another headache coming on. She took a breath and refocused on the meeting. Something must have shown in her face, because Perla patted her on the shoulder. It helped. A little.

❖

Jules begged off going over to Claire and Toni's, pleading a touch of the flu. She was on the phone with Toni and, just as she feared, Toni said, "Oh. Let me come over and take care of you."

"No, really, Tone. I'm totally fine."

"If you say so." Toni sounded like she didn't quite believe her. "Who's taking care of your dogs?"

"Amanda from A Walk in the Park. I'm losing two days' worth of money."

"Oh, Jules, darling. I'm sorry."

"Yeah. Me, too. But what can I say?"

"We'll miss you. Hope you feel better soon."

"Thanks, Tone. Hug Claire for me."

Jules didn't feel very good, but it wasn't the flu. She'd never felt more at sea, more unsure. Lydia's words kept bouncing around in her head. Was it true? *Have I never really made a decision about anything?* That hardly seemed possible. She *was* a "go along to get along" kind of person. It came naturally to her. Was this really the first big decision she'd had to make? How did she really feel about Sylvia? Maybe she couldn't recognize love when she was feeling it. That was a depressing thought. On the other hand, Sylvia's "me and only me" forever kind of love completely terrified her.

She mulled over her feelings for Claire and Toni and her feelings for Sylvia. It was like Lydia said, being with Claire and Toni was easy. She showed up on Friday. They had dinner, they had sex, they went to sleep. Occasionally they went to parties, or they went to the parade or some other event. They weren't demanding; they were pleasant, intelligent, and both were very attractive. It was...*nice*.

Sylvia was another species of woman altogether. Jules recalled the day they met and how difficult and stressful it had been. Then she saw Sylvia in her backyard in that decrepit sweatshirt washing Barney, focused on him like he was the only other creature in the universe. At some point, Sylvia started to look at her like that. *Was that before or after we slept together?* Jules hit her forehead, not remembering the exact time; but somewhere in the past couple months, Sylvia had started looking at her like that, and she'd liked it. She loved it, but she just didn't fully grasp what was happening.

Then Sylvia wanted something more. Jules agreed that Sylvia had the right to expect more. Sylvia wanted someone she could marry someday; that was fair, that was natural. Like being with Claire and Toni was natural for her. But she'd known from the beginning they wanted different things from life, yet she didn't let go. Stupid. Why didn't she just walk away? *Because I couldn't.* Sylvia had gotten to her in some way. Somehow that passion had just grabbed her by the throat or by the heart. *Or the soul!* That was Sylvia. All or nothing. She would never be half-assed or noncommittal. *Like me.* Unlike Claire and Toni, Sylvia wasn't just nice. She was passionate, intense, compelling.

Jules rolled over and put an arm over her eyes. She saw blackness, flashes of light, Sylvia's beautiful, expressive face. She looked sad. Jules groaned and flipped over on her stomach. *I'm a wreck.*

❖

Jules wasn't sure why she was so reluctant to go over to Claire and Toni's on Friday as usual. The breakup with Sylvia should have made her eager to connect with them and have the comfort of routine and normality. Another girl would be along soon. Just like the Muni. You only had to wait a bit. The thought didn't amuse Jules anymore. She couldn't conceive of being with someone else. She was dismayed at how reluctant she was to see her girlfriends. She supposed she was afraid of their judgment, especially Claire's. She could be so cold and sarcastic. Jules didn't want to be subjected to that. And putting her feelings about the breakup with Sylvia into words would make her feel even worse. But she owed them an explanation because this situation was untenable. They were her lovers, and as a human and as a responsible polyamorist, she had to be honest. She owed them truth, never mind how they reacted.

She'd always treated her relationship with Claire and Toni respectfully, but she'd never been too emotional about it. They were at some sort of flex point. The situation with Sylvia and her feelings around it seemed to dictate that something was going to change. She struggled with the concept that she had to make some sort of decision, finally. There didn't seem to be a way to just return to the status quo as though nothing was happening.

She took refuge, as usual, in playing with Chloe before dinner. Toni only came to the door to let her in and kiss her hello. Then she went back to the kitchen to help Claire. Jules cuddled Chloe and thought of what she would say. Chloe, at least, was dependably loving and sympathetic.

At the dinner table, after they all settled and got their food and glasses of wine, Toni said, "We've been a little worried about you, honey. You've been absent and it's unusual for you to be sick. You're practically the healthiest person I know."

"Yeah. I know, sorry. I've been going through a tough period." Jules played with her rice pilaf, pushing it around the plate. She wasn't really hungry.

"Oh? What's going on with you?" Toni's eyes were round and worried. Jules met her gaze, then looked at Claire. Claire looked back at her, inscrutable as always.

"I'm…ah. Shit. Sorry." Jules had never had so much trouble saying something. She saw Toni look at Claire then back at her. Neither said a word. They waited.

"Sylvia broke up with me week before last and it hit me pretty hard."

"Oh. Right. I'm sorry." Toni put her hand on Jules's arm. "That's too bad. We're sorry to hear that."

Jules detected a note of insincerity in her tone. She looked at Claire, who was looking back at her intently, seriously. Jules waited, braced for the "I told you so" lecture.

Claire said, "You know, Toni and I have noticed that for the past couple months you've seemed a little distracted. Off on a cloud somewhere. I wondered if Sylvia had anything to with that but didn't want to pry. I wanted to wait and have you tell us when you were ready."

"Ah. That's good. I'm sorry I was so uncommunicative."

"Was that because of Sylvia or because of us?" Claire asked.

"A little of both, I guess. I started to spend a lot of time with Sylvia and knew you didn't approve—"

"It's not that we didn't approve," Claire said. "We don't think that way. You know that. This is about your feelings, not about us."

"Right. Well. I don't really know about my feelings. That's what's gotten to me."

"What about Sylvia?" Toni asked. "Did she ask you to break up with us?" Now Toni's eyes blazed and she looked like she was ready to start yelling.

"No, not exactly," Jules said. They fell silent again. So Jules told them the story.

"I still don't know how you feel," Claire said. "She's given you an ultimatum and you backed away. So what's the problem?"

"I think I'm in love with her, too," Jules said, surprised to hear herself say it. "But I'm a poly person and she's not. So that's that."

"Is it?" Claire's look held her, challenging her in some fundamental way.

Toni said, in the pause, "Oh, Jules. Honey. It's too bad, but that's the way it goes with monogamous people. They don't like to share. That's their big thing. They like to own their lovers, their time, their bodies, their feelings."

"Is it that you don't want to be monogamous with Sylvia?" Claire asked.

"I don't think I'd be any good at it. I don't think it's a bad thing."

"Monogamy is a valid way of life, just like polyamory. You've never tried it, have you?"

"Uh, no. I guess not. I never wanted to be that involved."

"So you chose to be polyamorous?"

Jules thought for a second. "Well, I sort of just fell into it."

"And we're glad you did, Jules, and that you fell into it with us," Claire said. "But it looks like you're miserable now. Does that have something to do with Sylvia?"

Toni stared at Claire, speechless. Then she looked back at Jules and said, "We don't want you to leave. We really don't."

"Toni. We talked about this. We're not trying to talk you into anything one way or the other, Jules. We want you to be happy, whatever you do. You seem really unhappy right now. You can make a choice, you know. If you want to stop seeing us, it would make me sad, but I would feel better knowing you're happy. But you have to figure out what's going to make you happy. You have to decide what to do."

Jules stared at Claire, utterly astonished. She'd expected Claire to say what she usually said about people being too possessive around sex and relationships, the poly philosophy. "My sister Lydia said something really similar. She told me I have to be an actor, not a reactor."

"She's right."

"I love you guys. I really do, but when I put my feelings for you beside my feelings for Sylvia, there's just such a huge difference. I'm afraid, though. It's such a weird thing to contemplate breaking up with you. I don't want to hurt you."

"Oh, Jules, you don't have—" Claire held her hand up and Toni clamped her teeth shut, though she looked hurt. Claire looked back to Jules, her face softer than Jules had ever seen it. She looked compassionate but stern, if that was possible.

"Jules. *You* have to choose. It's up to you. And fear of the future? Christ, if that had been the ruling emotion for me, I'd never do anything."

"But Sylvia has these high expectations, not just the monogamy. *Everything.*"

"Well. You have to decide if you want to try to fulfill them. You either will or you won't." That was the old Claire for sure. Something started breaking apart inside Jules, some sort of blockage dissolving. *I want Sylvia. I choose her. I'm in love with her.*

"It's been wonderful with you the past couple of years. But I think it's time for me to do something else."

"Jules. I can't believe this. We've had such a good time." Toni was starting to tear up. Claire stood up, came around behind her and looped her arm around her chest, and said in her ear, "Sweetheart. It's okay." Toni grabbed her arm and nodded and wiped her eyes. Jules had never seen this side of Claire, and she liked it.

Jules said, "Wow. This is so unreal. I'm grateful to you both. I can't stay tonight, you get that?"

Claire waved her hand airily. "Sure. We know. You go do what you need to do."

Jules rubbed her hands over her eyes. "Shit. I don't know if she'll even talk to me. She was way upset. She said she didn't want to hear from me."

Once again, Claire astonished Jules by coming over and kissing her cheek and squeezing her arm.

"Well. You won't get anything if you don't try. I hope it works out for you."

"Thanks so much. Don't cry, Toni. You're making me feel bad. I feel crappy enough."

"I'm sorry." Toni sniffled. "I'm going to miss you so much."

They shared a tight three-way hug. Even Claire seemed to be a little misty. Jules left them and ran down the stairs and out to the street. Leaning against her car, her hands shaking, she pressed Sylvia's speed-dial number and prayed. It went to voice mail so she typed out a quick text: *Need to talk 2 u. pls call me back. xo*

CHAPTER TWENTY-ONE

Sylvia dragged herself into her flat. She was beat, and she wanted to be so she didn't have to think. Hana had dropped her off after a long three-hour stint at the No ON 8 office, putting together packets for the Election Day volunteers, as Election Day was only four days away. She'd declined to go out for a drink. That would just wake her up and make her talk, and she didn't want to talk anymore. She'd been over everything with Perla for hours. It was time to accept reality and move on. She was glad an election was coming. After it was over, she'd have to see. One thing for sure. She was glad she still had the capacity to care, to fall in love, to be intimate. Too bad it was with Jules. She was so perfect. Why the fuck did she have to be poly? What was she going to do about someone like that? *Not fall in love. Right.*

She'd seen one or two of the other No ON 8 volunteers giving her that sizing-up look. She didn't picture herself responding. Not yet, anyhow. God, she was tired. She didn't bother turning her phone on; she just collapsed into bed and fell into a dreamless sleep.

The next morning, Perla picked her up and they raced over to Noe and Market. The activity was going to be nonstop, practically twenty-four seven now. It was crunch time. When they got upstairs, they found out the coffee was gone, so Sylvia volunteered to go downstairs to Café Flore for more. The No ON 8 campaign was, unsurprisingly, fueled by caffeine and sugar.

Sylvia had ordered a long list of drinks so she sat down with her own cup to wait. She turned her phone on and found one text message in her inbox. After she opened it her insides froze when she saw the words and who it was from. She flipped her phone shut, her heart pounding. She didn't know whether to be hopeful or angry. *I told her not to call me. God damn it.* She wanted to call back right away, but to say what? To scream, "I said I didn't want to talk to you!" Jules was probably just feeling guilty. She'd dismissed Sylvia pretty harshly. Not much discussion. *Fuck her.* She erased the message.

When Sylvia went back to the campaign office with coffees stacked up in three trays, it took all her concentration to not spill anything. She found Perla, Elspeth, and Hana sitting on folding chairs in the far corner of the office under a hand-lettered sign:

WHEN TIRED GIVES UP, EXHAUSTION FALLS TO THE SIDE OF THE ROAD. WHEN SURRENDER WAVES THE WHITE FLAG, WE'LL STILL BE HERE. ORGANIZING.

Sylvia handed around the coffees and sat down, her nerves jangled. She wanted to talk to Perla, but it didn't look like now was the time.

"—the overnight polls suck. It's tied, dead even." Sylvia caught the end of Hana's sentence.

Perla wiped her mouth and said, "We've got to not let this bother us. Let the coordinators worry about the polls. We've got to get ready for Tuesday. We have to get people out with signs, and they want at least two people near every polling place." Perla referred to the California law of no politicking closer than one hundred feet from a polling place.

Elspeth said, "Well, we're going to the East Bay. That's where the real action is. In SF, meh." She waved her hand dismissively. She meant that the vote was assured in the city. It was the suburbs, with their mixture of voters, that needed attention. "Who's with us?"

Sylvia leaned close to Perla and whispered in her ear. "Guess who texted me last night?"

Perla, leaned back, eyes wide. "No shit!"

Sylvia nodded glumly. "Can we go outside and talk for a minute?" Before Perla could answer, Hana jumped up and started waving her arms and saying, "Oh my God, oh my God." They all turned, and there at the door was the mayor and his entourage, his famous sleek, black hair perfectly in place and with a large grin. Mark and the other coordinators were shaking hands with him, trying to keep their jaws from hitting the floor. Sylvia, Perla, Hana, and Elspeth joined the crowd of volunteers in the middle of the room. The feverish campaign work abruptly halted as the volunteers gathered. Mark handed Mayor Newsom a microphone.

The mayor surveyed the room, his black eyes bright and piercing. He looked so relaxed he could have been sitting at a pool having cocktails with his friends.

"I'm blown away to see so many of you here. I know we have support for this fight. But I wasn't clear just how much." The crowd cheered.

"I'm confident that we'll win. They may think they have it all sewed up, but they'd be wrong."

He said a lot of other encouraging things, his speech full of compliments and reassurances. Sylvia had been momentarily pulled into the excitement of the mayor showing up, but now her mind drifted back to Jules's text message. What should she do? She was mostly angry because she truly wanted to not think about it. It was cruel of Jules to text her. They were done and Jules needed to let her alone. Finally Mayor Newsom left and Perla was back on earth. Sylvia honestly marveled at the way the mayor of San Francisco could hypnotize everyone, including lifelong lesbians. It was uncanny.

"Let's go outside," Sylvia said, and they walked out to the street where the bright sunny day belied the November date.

She showed Perla the text message, and Perla looked at it then back to her, apparently perplexed. "What do you think she wants?"

"I've no idea, but she's got some nerve texting me when I told her no contact. I meant it."

"Well, sweetie. You need to take care of yourself. You don't have to answer, you know."

"I know. Screw it. I'm not calling her back or anything. We've got to get back upstairs, and I've got to get to work and get my mind off Jules."

"That's right. Let's go." Perla took her arm and they returned the office where, with the mayor gone, the election preparation was back on full force.

❖

Jules was a pile of nerves as she waited for word back from Sylvia. She'd decided to give it a full twenty-four hours before she started to panic. It was now eight p.m. on Saturday and she'd heard nothing. *What am I going to do now?* She didn't have an answer. Sylvia was probably going to be extremely busy as the election was coming up, and she hoped that was the only reason she hadn't responded. Jules was watching the evening news religiously, and it wasn't good. No one knew if Prop 8 would win or lose. She really wanted to be there with Sylvia, Perla, and all the rest, but she didn't like the idea of invading Sylvia's space in such a way without her consent.

Jules paced her flat. She might as well wait until tomorrow, even if it killed her. Maybe she would try a voice mail next. It wasn't much of a surprise that Sylvia didn't want to talk to her. *I wouldn't want to talk to me either. I'm such a shit.* But that was then. Now she'd had an epiphany and needed to get Sylvia to listen to her. Jules had never had to persuade anyone to do anything, so it was an entirely new concept for her. It was a heady feeling, though. She'd made up her mind about something for once in her life. Of course, it had to be this do-or-die sort of scenario. She was going to lose the one woman who'd finally cut through all the bullshit and captured her heart. She'd come very close to letting her go forever, but it wasn't going to happen. Jules steeled her nerves and told herself it was just a matter of getting her to meet face-to-face so they could talk. Sylvia would come around. She just had to.

❖

Sylvia listened to the voice mail on Sunday evening and heard Jules speak in a plaintive tone that reminded her of the early summer when Jules was trying to get her in bed. *I'd like to see you. I need to talk to you in person. You name the place and the time, and I'll be there. Please. Thanks.*

Once again Sylvia could sense her will weakening. This was what had gotten to her in the first place. Jules wasn't pushy; she wasn't a player or a big talker. She was charming in a quiet way, not a look-at-how-cool-I am kind of way. She was just who she was, which was the problem. She was poly and had said no future, no exclusivity, no commitment, and she meant it.

All or nothing. When it came to love, that was what Sylvia needed, wanted, and she saw no reason to settle for less. She was desperate to call Jules back to just hear her voice again, which was every bit as dangerous as a sober alcoholic who decided just one little drink wouldn't hurt. *Not going there.* She squeezed her eyes shut and erased the message.

Sylvia went through her Monday workday on autopilot. It was a busy first day of the month so she had to be there and present, and that was helpful on one level. In fact, she felt empty. She was anxious about the election, but missing Jules diluted her attention, which normally would be consumed by such an event. It was almost a physical pain, and it was getting worse instead of better. Whenever she had a moment, her fingers itched to call Jules, who she knew would be walking through some park with her dog group trailing alongside her and her phone on.

It was almost a relief when, in the middle of the day, William finally showed up, completely out of it. Sylvia had to spend the rest of the afternoon dealing with the police and getting him checked back into the psych ward at SFGH. She was relieved he was still in one piece physically and that he had actually come in to the office. It was a shame, though; he had to start all over. Sylvia steeled herself against despair, calling upon those reserves of patience she'd developed over the years. If she could only be so resolved about her breakup with Jules, it would surely help. It wasn't working that way, it seemed.

❖

Jules sighed as she picked up the sandy, soggy tennis ball and threw it into the surf at Crissy Field beach. Elvis, Maggie, and Snips dove into the gentle waves. Snips got there first and came trotting up to her in triumph and dropped his prize at her feet. She had no energy, but she forced herself to throw the ball again. They walked down the beach, the dogs trotting along happily, chasing and play-fighting with each other. Jules sat down on a log and looked at her phone, hoping for the thousandth time she'd somehow not heard the ringtone she knew so well. The phone was maddeningly, depressingly, silent. At three, she called everyone in and loaded them into the car.

A half hour later, she made her last stop at Perla's. As soon as she opened the door with her key and took off his leash, Barney scooted past her at warp speed. She looked up and saw Perla standing in her living room. She bent down to greet Barney, who was leaping ecstatically. Jules was flummoxed. She had no clue Perla would be home.

With Barney under her hands, Perla looked up at her, her face expressionless.

"Hi. How are you?" Jules said, lamely.

"Fine, how's my boy doing these days?" Perla looked at Jules closely.

"He's good. Is he behaving on the leash with you?"

"Yep. He's very good. Aren't you, baby?" Barney licked her face.

"Well. Good to hear."

"Tomorrow's the election, you know," Perla said. "So I came home early. I'm on my way over to NO ON 8."

"Yes. I did know that. How's it going?"

"We don't really know. We probably won't until really late tomorrow."

"Yeah. So." Jules stood, her ring of keys dangling in her hand, ill at ease and wondering what to say.

Perla said nothing, just continued to gaze at her and rub Barney's belly.

"Can I ask you something?" Jules said, tentatively.

"About Sylvia?"

"Yeah."

"You can ask but I might not answer. You broke her heart, you know. I'm not crazy about you right now. I trust you with my dog and I'm happy to continue paying you to be his dog walker, but we're not friends anymore." Perla's voice was cold and hard.

Jules swallowed. "I understand how you feel. I made a mistake, though, and I need to talk to Sylvia to make it right. She won't take my calls."

"That's the understatement of the year, girlfriend. I'm not sure why you think anything you have to say will make any difference."

"Look. I need to talk to her. Will she see me if I show up at the campaign headquarters?"

"Don't know."

Jules was getting more desperate, if that was even possible. "Help me. Please. I love her. I need to tell her that."

"That's nice, but what the fuck difference does that make to anything, I mean, really?" Perla spread her arms in a gesture of skepticism.

"I know you're angry with me, but I don't want to try to explain to you what's going on. I want to tell her."

"Hmm. Okay. We're going to be incredibly busy tonight, and I have no idea where we'll be tomorrow. We may be out in somewhere in the East Bay, but around eight thirty or so, everyone's going to be down at the Westin St. Francis for the victory party. Show up and talk to her. I'll be there, and if she doesn't want to see you, I'll try to get her to change her mind. She's one stubborn chick, though, so I won't make any guarantees. But I promise you, what you say had better be pretty damned good or I'll personally tear you limb from limb, which is what I feel like doing now."

"Tomorrow night at the St. Francis. Got it. I'll be there. Make sure she's there, please. I know you don't owe me a thing, but I'm pleading for you to just help me out this one little bit."

"I'll do that much for you, but the rest is up to you."

"Thanks."

❖

Jules pulled into the underground garage at Union Square, her heart pounding and her mouth dry and cottony. It had been a tortuously long day. She'd gone to vote and then home to force herself to eat something, even though she wasn't hungry. She flipped on the TV and watched for a few minutes, but at sixish in the evening, none of the news would say anything about the California election. Jules noted that the returns were looking good for Obama and she was mildly pleased at that, knowing that Sylvia and her friends favored him over the other guy. She knew it was no good showing up at the No on 8 party before eight thirty because the polls closed at eight. Sylvia would be out doing whatever she could for as long as possible. She looked at her phone for the twentieth time. Only seven thirty. She went out into the cold evening anyhow and drove downtown.

Union Square was crowded. In the center was an art exhibit,

and Jules made her way through it as slowly as she could. At eight fifteen, she'd seen all the art twice and was starting to lose her mind. She obsessed about what she would say. She didn't know the magic words that would convince Sylvia that she was for real. She wasn't in the least religious but found herself praying as she crossed Powell Street and walked up the steps to the entrance of the St. Francis Hotel. A board in front announced the No on 8 Party in ballrooms one and two. She strode past the front desk, squaring her shoulders and trying to breathe evenly.

She found the room, which wasn't difficult as dozens of people were there already. In the rear was a giant video screen behind a podium. People stood around with drinks in their hands, talking and watching the CNN election coverage. The screen was a blur to Jules as her eyes adjusted to the dimness. She didn't see Sylvia or Perla anywhere, or Hana or Elspeth or anyone else she knew, for that matter. She settled uneasily into a chair to wait.

CHAPTER TWENTY-TWO

Perla and Sylvia pulled into the same Union Square garage some forty minutes after eight o'clock. In the backseat, Hana and Elspeth were bouncing up and down with excitement. They traded stories about their day. Perla told them about the time she and Sylvia had spent at a poll in Concord.

"The place was so suburban, it was ridiculous. The Prop 8 people were there. We wanted to talk to them, but you know we were told not to. I gave them the evil eye like my grandmother taught me," Perla said. "You should have seen Sylvia, though. She was talking to the voters like it would be the end of the world if they didn't vote no. She was unbelievable."

"Perls. Shush."

"No, you were. I was awed. *I* would have been convinced."

They entered the St. Francis Hotel, and Sylvia stopped Perla with her hand.

"You promise we can leave after one drink. I know we're not going to get the results soon, and I'm beat. I just want to go home." Sylvia was so tired she thought she might keel over. The adrenaline rush was gone and she just felt dead inside. She wasn't sure she cared what happened at this point.

"Sure, Syl. But we have to at least see everyone for a few minutes. This is the end of the campaign. We've been working on this for months."

"Yeah, I know, I know, but what's got you so keyed up?" Perla was easy to read, and she'd been acting a little strange all day. She kept asking Sylvia if she was still going to the Election Night party, because at one point, Sylvia said she wasn't sure.

"Nothing. It's just the election. Come on, let's go."

"Hey, I've got to hit the bathroom first, okay? Jeez."

Perla dropped her arm. "Fine. I'll go with you."

They located the women's room and then made their way to the rear of the lobby to the ballrooms. Sylvia peered into the room. The noise was deafening, and she was terminally exhausted and wanted to go home. *Why*, she wondered, *do I now care so little about the results of this election?* She knew why: Jules.

Sylvia surveyed the room and turned to say something to Perla, who was staring off to her right. She followed Perla's line of sight and almost jumped out of her skin. Jules was walking toward them. Her throat closed and her palms started to sweat. Jules looked just the same. Her blond hair was messy and she was wearing the same worn-out jeans and tennis shoes and hooded sweatshirt, and she looked terrific. Sylvia held her breath.

Suddenly she was directly in front of them. "Hi, Sylvia."

"Hello." It was a standoff. Sylvia didn't know whether she should turn and run, yell at Jules for violating the no-contact order, or throw her arms around her and hold on for dear life.

"Hi, Perla."

"Hi, Jules. Sylvia, I'm going to go over and talk to Mark and the others. See you in a minute."

Sylvia glared at her. "You knew she would be here, didn't you?" She was suddenly unreasonably angry at Perla.

"I did," Perla said, steadily. "I want you to hear what she has to say and make up your own mind. I'm leaving now."

Sylvia bit her tongue and turned back to Jules. "All right. What do you want? We don't have anything to say to each other, as far as I know."

"Could we go somewhere more private?" Jules asked.

"No. This is fine. Just get on with it." Sylvia knew she

sounded testy and didn't like it, but she couldn't change her tone. This woman wasn't at fault for Sylvia's distress; she'd caused it herself by being so naïve. She'd fallen for the wrong person, someone who couldn't love her the way she needed to be loved. It was unreasonable to expect that, but still…it would have been nice and would have restored Sylvia's faith in love.

"I wanted to see you in person so I asked Perla how to do that. Please don't blame her. This is about me. And you."

"Jules. You've already told me how you feel. What more is there to say?" Jules looked tired and haggard, and Sylvia felt a bit sorry for her but didn't want to give in to that feeling because she was hurting too much.

"I have more to say. A lot more. That's why I'm here. That's why I came to talk to you. Would you hear me out?"

Reluctantly, Sylvia said, "All right. I'll listen." Jules appeared relieved. Sylvia was glad she seemed to be suffering. It was good to know she wasn't alone in the post-breakup blues.

"Could we at least go outside and a little away from the crowd, where it's a little more private?" In the intervening few minutes, the room had filled up even more. Everywhere, people were talking and drinking. As they struggled to hear each other, they all spoke louder, increasing the noise.

"Yeah, okay. We can go down the hall." Sylvia was bone-deep exhausted and not just from her long day of electioneering. The aftermath of breaking it off with Jules had sapped her energy, and she was only just fighting off despair. Jules showing up now was the last thing she needed, and yet, in spite of it all, she was glad to see her and her curiosity was piqued.

They found a bench out in the hallway. A lot of people were walking around, but at least it was quieter so they didn't have to shout to hear one another and there was fresh air.

They sat next to each other and Sylvia waited. Jules gazed at her so intently, she thought *she* would burst into flames.

"I love you," Jules said.

Sylvia inhaled sharply and almost rolled her eyes, but

stopped herself. "So you said a couple of weeks ago, but I have to ask, what does that matter to me, really?"

"I know I said that and I know what else I said. You asked me for something and I said no. That I couldn't. Or wouldn't. I know that hurt you."

"Yes. It did, but I'm trying to go forward and get on with my life, and you cornering me down here tonight is really not cool."

Jules put her hand on Sylvia's cheek and Sylvia closed her eyes. It felt so good, that simple gesture. It also broke her heart again.

"Wait," Jules said. "I need to tell you more. I love you. I adore you. I'm in love with you. You're the one, Sylvia. I can't live without you."

Sylvia finally grasped Jules's wrist and lowered her hand. Her eyes filled with tears.

"That's all very nice, but I've told you what I need. You can say the words all you want, but you have other women in your life, other lovers—"

"Not anymore. I broke up with Claire and Toni a few days ago."

Sylvia stared at her. "You what?" A tiny spark of hope lit in her soul.

"It's done. I broke up with Claire and Toni." She took a deep breath. "And I'm prepared to give myself to you completely. If you still want me, that is."

"What about the polyamory?" Sylvia was skeptical that Jules had truly had a change of heart.

Jules smiled with a trace of wistfulness. "I've never, in my whole life, made a conscious, positive decision about anything. I went to college because my parents expected it. I got a degree in psychology for no special reason. I moved to San Francisco because I took a vacation and it seemed like such a nice place, so I figured I might as well stay. I started walking dogs as a favor for someone. When I met Claire and Toni and got to know them, they seemed nice and all that, so when they asked me to sleep with them, I thought, what the hell. And that was that. I've never done anything where I thought about it for a while, weighed my options, and then chose what to do. Until now."

She paused.

Sylvia's cold skepticism started to melt, although a stubborn block of doubt remained. She waited for Jules to continue.

"I had to have it spelled out to me and, oddly, it was what Claire said that made the difference."

"Oh? And what was that?"

"She said something like, 'We all get to choose who we love, what we want. If it's right for some people to choose polyamory, then it's just as right for some to choose monogamy.' That is what I choose. I choose you."

"Are you promising that you'll never ever sleep with anyone else?" Sylvia didn't like the way she sounded, but there it was.

"I promise. I don't want to and I won't because that's what you want."

"I don't know if you're serious. How do I know if I can trust you?'

"You don't. I think I read a quote from someone once that said, the only way you know if you can trust someone is to trust her. I'm switching the pronoun but you get the idea."

Sylvia stared at Jules as though she could tell something just by looking at her. Elena had made all sorts of extravagant promises, none of which she kept. Jules wasn't like that; she was honest and loyal. In a funny way, it was almost a comfort to Sylvia that Jules hadn't immediately broken off with Claire and Toni just to date her. There was perverse kind of logic to it, but still, this was a big leap. She wanted Jules so much, but she wouldn't settle for a third of her. Now here she was, with a change of heart. That, at least, made sense. Perhaps it was time to take the leap into the unknown. There was really no other way.

"Okay."

Jules eyed her. "So you'll take me back?"

Sylvia grinned. "I'm not sure I had you before, but I'll take you now. I said I love you and I meant it." Jules's eyes widened and sparkled, and she grinned back and sighed a little.

Sylvia leaned in and their kiss was full of love and full of promise. It was the best kiss Sylvia had ever had. They kept at it for some time, and although Sylvia was vaguely aware of people walking by, she didn't care. She moved in as close as she could. Her body caught fire as though she were a pile of dry wood and Jules's kiss was the spark. They only stopped because they needed to take a breath.

Sylvia's exhaustion ebbed and she no longer thought about going home to sleep. She wanted to go to bed with Jules. As soon as possible. But her interest in the election had also returned. It wouldn't take long to get an update. She said, "I'd like to leave now, but I really want to find out what's happening with the election."

"Sure, I understand. You want to go back in?" She gestured down the hall.

"I do." Sylvia stood up and stretched out her hand. Jules took it and they returned to the ballroom. As they entered, a cheer went up from the crowd. The news had just called another state for Barack Obama.

"I wonder if we've gotten any news on Prop 8?" Sylvia asked no one in particular.

They stood pressed together, with Jules's arms wrapped around her from behind, holding her tight, her nose buried in her hair. "You smell better than ever," she whispered into Sylvia's ear, making her shiver.

Sylvia glanced to her left and spotted Perla, who walked over to them with a triumphant grin. "I see all's well now," she said. "Sorry for not telling you she was coming. She swore me to secrecy."

"I'll forgive you. This time. What's up with the news? The polls closed," she checked her watch, "an hour and a half ago."

"I honestly don't know. I'll go find Mark. You two okay while I do that?" She arched an eyebrow.

Jules and Sylvia looked at each other and Sylvia said, "Sure. But I'm dying of curiosity."

Perla went off through the crowd, which was quite thick now. Sylvia's mind was split between anxiety about the vote and her deep happiness to be back in Jules's arms. Her fatigue no longer mattered. She was happier than she'd ever been.

She and Jules stood in the middle of the chaos, an island of two. Sylvia watched the TV monitor, but it didn't seem to make any sense as her brain only had one thought: *She's here. She's mine.*

She pulled Jules's arms tighter. Jules chuckled and the vibration in her body was arousing.

"What are you thinking?" Sylvia asked.

"Don't get mad at me. I know this is a really important night for you. I'm anxious, too, but honestly, what I want to do is go home and make love to you."

At the words "make love," Sylvia's heart lurched and she got wet. She turned and nuzzled her nose against Jules's cheek. "Soon. I just want to get an update."

Perla materialized out of the crowd. "Mark's going to make an announcement soon. It's close."

A few minutes later, Mark came onstage and called for quiet. "I know you're all anxious to hear. At this point, with only a few precincts reporting, we can only say it's too close to call." The crowd moaned.

Sylvia thought quickly. It might be hours before they heard any result. The last few weeks the news had reported that the polls were even. She was torn between wanting to stay to the bitter end and needing to be alone with Jules. She'd worked so hard for so long and yet...

This was a momentous night. Jules had come and declared her love and faith and loyalty. That was unbelievable, and it deserved a sacrifice from her.

"Let's go home," she said to Jules, whose eyes lit up. Then Sylvia called over her shoulder, "Hey, Perls, we're splitting."

Perla walked up to them and then kissed her cheek and squeezed her arm.

"I'll talk to you tomorrow. I'll call *you*. Don't call me. I'm not leaving until this is over, one way or another."

"Right. But if I don't answer, you'll understand?"

"Sure will. Bye, sweetie."

"Are you working tomorrow?" Jules asked while they drove up Market Street.

"Hell, no. I'm wiped out. I've been up since three this morning. I knew it would be an incredibly long day, so I took Wednesday off."

"Good. So would you mind coming over to my place? We don't have to get up until around ten. I have to walk the dogs tomorrow. Would you like to come with me?"

"I can't think of anything I'd want to do more," Sylvia said. "Except…"

"So you're not too tired?" Jules asked a bit anxiously.

"Oh, no. I've gotten my second wind," Sylvia said, her voice lowered. "Could you drive faster, please?" She played with the hair on Jules's neck and giggled when Jules trembled and gripped the steering wheel, her eyes forward and her lips parted.

❖

They crashed through the front door, tearing at each other's clothes but not wanting to stop kissing. Jules managed to pull Sylvia's sweatshirt off and clawed frantically at the clasp on her bra. She couldn't get it loose, so Sylvia reached behind and did it herself. They both pulled and yanked it until it came off and Jules could get Sylvia's breasts in both of her hands. Sylvia pressed her hands as she squeezed them and palmed her nipples.

"Your breasts, God." Jules panted. "They're so, so…" She couldn't find the right word so she just dropped her head and licked Sylvia's nipple until she squealed.

"Let's go, hurry. I'm going crazy here." They finally got the rest of their clothes off and dove into bed, both gasping when their bodies touched. Sylvia had ended up on her back, and Jules pinned her arms and sucked her earlobes and neck. She kissed her cheeks and nose and then went back to her mouth. They both moaned as their tongues and teeth met. Jules's clitoris was throbbing so hard she thought it might explode, but she tried to ignore it and concentrate on Sylvia. Sylvia ceded her the upper hand easily. Jules struggled to keep control and go slowly, to tease her and arouse her little by little, but that didn't seem to be what Sylvia had in mind.

She grabbed Jules's hand and shoved it between her legs. "Fuck me. Now."

Jules obliged her with first one finger, then two, and was rewarded by seeing Sylvia's head go back and her hips rise. Jules longed to taste her, to lick her, but she decided to let Sylvia make that choice. She thrust into Sylvia hard, her thumb rubbing against her clitoris in rhythm with Sylvia's movements. Then she came, the contractions squeezing Jules's hand. Jules watched her face dissolve in ecstasy. When she was still again, Jules kissed her cheek and whispered in her ear, "I love you." Sylvia turned to face her, her eyes shining in the dim light. Her chest was still heaving, and Jules had never seen anything or felt anything as profound as she did at that moment.

"I love you, too," Sylvia said, simply, clearly, and firmly. Jules was lying on her side, her head propped up on one hand. Sylvia pulled her on top, and once more they dissolved into pure passion.

❖

"Ugh. What time is it?" Jules muttered. She was about one-quarter awake as she felt Sylvia slip out of bed, taking the warmth with her.

"Eight thirty. I'm going to turn on the TV, okay?" Sylvia, wrapped in a blanket, dropped back on the bed, snuggled close for a moment, and kissed her before leaving the bed again.

Jules turned over and grabbed for her. "Come back to bed, it's too early."

Sylvia slipped away. "I have to find out about the election. I have to call Perla. You can go back to sleep." She seemed to Jules to be supernaturally awake in spite of how late they'd stayed up. Jules figured they'd only been asleep for about two hours.

"I'm up," Jules said. She tried to get her brain to function.

In the living room, Sylvia huddled on the couch and switched on the TV with her shoulder propping her phone up and her other hand holding the blanket closed.

Jules sat next her as she spoke into the phone. "Yeah. No. Fine. I'm turning on the TV right now. No. Tell me!" Sylvia's tone was commanding, and Jules thought she would certainly obey if Sylvia used that voice on her. She would submit happily.

She watched Sylvia's face fall and thought she knew why.

Sylvia closed her phone and turned to Jules. "We lost." She looked bereft. Jules didn't say anything, but just put her arms around Sylvia and held her.

Sylvia was dry-eyed but grim. They found the news.

"Obama won," Sylvia said, dully.

"That's good, right?" Jules asked, unsure how much she should try to put a good spin on the election. She felt like it might be a test.

"Good. Yeah." Sylvia stared at the TV newscast. The news anchor intoned, "and Proposition 8 lost by a high margin."

"It wasn't that fucking high," Sylvia said between clenched teeth. "Only 52 to 48. Asshole."

"I'll go make some coffee," Jules said, seizing on something practical.

She returned to the couch and handed Sylvia her cup and watched her take a sip. It was always a joy to watch Sylvia consume anything; her whole being concentrated on the experience, the taste. Her eyes closed and she said, "Mmm. This is so good."

Jules touched her hair gently and asked, "You okay?"

Sylvia looked at her for a long moment. "Yeah. I really am. You make it okay. When you told me last night that you chose me, then I was fine. This election? I'm sad, really sad, especially for all the people who were waiting to get married. That's hard on them. But for me, I worked hard, I gave it what I have."

"Which is quite a lot," Jules said, and Sylvia smiled slightly.

"I'm not going to want to get married immediately."

"That's good. Let me get used to a monogamous relationship first before we talk about that."

"You don't have to answer, but I think you know that's still something I want in my future." Sylvia's eyes were dark and serious.

"I know that." Jules paused, wondering what was in her own heart and in her mind. To her surprise, she said, "It might be something I'd consider, someday."

"Wow." Sylvia's eyes widened. "It's incredible to hear you say that. That's not what I expected."

Jules took her hand and kissed the back, then kissed her cheek. "That's because of you. If it weren't for you, I would've probably managed to ignore this whole thing. But you got me into it, and once I was there, once I heard what people said and I saw the people. God, the people. They just broke my heart, they wanted to be married so much. What's going to happen to them?" Jules started crying a little bit, which astonished them both.

"Oh, honey," Sylvia said, and she hugged Jules and stroked her hair.

"You've changed my life," Jules said, partially muffled by Sylvia's shoulder.

"Well, I'm glad."

"It's not only about being with someone or about marriage. It's everything. I've been thinking and talking to Lydia some. I want to go back to school. I like walking dogs, but I need to do something else. I'm getting bored. And like everything else in my life, it was just something I fell into."

"You can literally do anything you want. You know that, right?"

"Now I do. I feel like I can. I never cared before, but now, because of you," she stopped to swallow, "I want to be worthy of you."

"Oh, Jules, you are. You're the best thing that ever happened to me. I'm so happy now."

"All right, beautiful, time to get ready to go to work." Jules took her hand and pulled her off the couch. "There's about five dogs who need to go to the park."

"I need a shower."

"Of course, so do I. Let's go!"

❖

Two weeks later, Jules, Sylvia, and Perla stood in yet another crowd, this time in front of San Francisco City Hall. EQCA had called for a post–Proposition 8 rally. In the wake of the defeat, bitter arguments had erupted at the campaign headquarters among the volunteers. Everyone was looking to lay blame. This rally was meant as a healing occasion.

Perla was scanning the crowd, looking for Hana and Elspeth. Jules and Sylvia stood close together, arms entwined. They hadn't spent a night apart since the night of the election. Sylvia was enveloped in a gauzy, dreamy cloud, truly surprised how much it meant to have Jules with her. It made the Prop 8 situation so much easier to absorb. An emotional shock absorber, that's what Jules was. Also just as cute as she could be with her messed-up blond hair and muscular body. Sylvia enjoyed a lovely hit of sexual arousal that made her turn to grin at Jules, who grinned back.

Jules's phone rang. She answered and Sylvia watched her face go from surprise to elation. She said, "No shit! You're kidding me. Where are you?" She craned her neck and tried to see over the heads of the other people.

"Okay. The Lincoln Statue. Yeah. We're coming." She snapped the phone shut and took Sylvia's arm.

"Perla, please come with us," Jules said, and turned to walk through the crowd. Sylvia let Jules lead and shrugged at Perla's inquisitive look. They threaded their way around the people until they came to a stop at the left of the City Hall where the seated statue of President Lincoln held many No on 8 and Freedom to Marry signs. To Sylvia's shock, Claire and Toni stood in front.

They all exchanged friendly hugs and introduced Perla, whose expression said she'd gladly do bodily injury to either Claire or Toni or both.

"Gosh. I'm surprised to see you two," Jules said.

Claire raised her eyebrows and grinned devilishly. "Yes, well, we thought it was time we got involved." They were holding hands. Sylvia moved closer to Jules, instinctively establishing her ownership. She was nonplussed to see them on what she considered her territory.

"Was it the election?" Perla asked.

"That had a lot to with it," Toni said. "And we had other reasons."

Sylvia said, "Well, if you're looking for someone to replace Jules, this probably isn't the place to find her."

Claire actually laughed out loud. Sylvia hadn't meant it to be funny. "No one could quite replace Jules," she said, and Jules blushed. "And you're right. But that's not why we came down."

Toni's eyes moved from Sylvia back to Jules. "You two seem happy."

Jules and Sylvia looked at each other. Sylvia saw what she wanted to see in Jules's expression.

Claire said, "I think I heard somewhere that no one's free until everyone's free. We talked about it and decided if we're serious about people being able to live their lives the way they want to, we need to support the freedom to marry. If we're going to be consistent, it's only right."

Sylvia could see Perla was impressed. She was nodding sagely.

Then they heard a voice on the loudspeaker and all turned around to listen. "I know you're mad, I know you're devastated. I know I am." Everyone got very quiet.

"We did the best we could. They ran a better campaign, even if it was a dishonest one. They won, and we can't change or deny that." He paused for a long time. "But that part's over now. The election is done and it is what it is. We have to go forward." The people started to murmur.

"This fight is *not* over!" Mark shouted. "I need you and you and you over there. We need all of you because this fight is just beginning." The crowd went nuts. "We're going to regroup and we're going to get back to work and we're going to get the freedom to marry in California."

Sylvia looked at Jules. *Just beginning.*

About the Author

Kathleen Knowles grew up in Pittsburgh, Pennsylvania, but has lived in San Francisco for more than thirty years. She finds the city's combination of history, natural beauty, and multicultural diversity inspiring and endlessly fascinating.

Other than writing, she loves music of all kinds, walking, bicycling, and stamp collecting. LGBT history and politics have commanded her attention for many years, starting with her first Pride march in Cleveland, Ohio, in 1978. She and her partner were married in July 2008 and live atop one of San Francisco's many hills with their pets. She works as a health and safety specialist at the University of California, San Francisco.

She has written short stories, essays, and fan fiction.

Books Available From Bold Strokes Books

Trusting Tomorrow by P.J. Trebelhorn. Funeral director Logan Swift thinks she's perfectly happy with her solitary life devoted to helping others cope with loss until Brooke Collier moves in next door to care for her elderly grandparents. 9978-1-60282-891-9)

Forsaking All Others by Kathleen Knowles. What if what you think you want is the opposite of what makes you happy? (978-1-60282-892-6)

Exit Wounds by VK Powell. When Officer Loane Landry falls in love with ATF informant Abigail Mancuso, she realizes that nothing is as it seems—not the case, not her lover, not even the dead. (978-1-60282-893-3)

Dirty Power by Ashley Bartlett. Cooper's been through hell and back, and she's still broke and on the run. But at least she found the twins. They'll keep her alive. Right? (978-1-60282-896-4)

The Rarest Rose by I. Beacham. After a decade of living in her beloved house, Ele disturbs its past and finds her life being haunted by the presence of a ghost who will show her that true love never dies. (978-1-60282-884-1)

Code of Honor by Radclyffe. The face of terror is hard to recognize—especially when it's homegrown. The next book in the Honor series. (978-1-60282-885-8)

Does She Love You by Rachel Spangler. When Annabelle and Davis find out they are in a relationship with the same woman, it leaves them facing life-altering questions about trust, redemption, and the possibility of finding love in the wake of betrayal. (978-1-60282-886-5)

The Road to Her by KE Payne. Sparks fly when actress Holly Croft, star of UK soap *Portobello Road*, meets her new on-screen love interest, the enigmatic and sexy Elise Manford. (978-1-60282-887-2)

Shadows of Something Real by Sophia Kell Hagin. Trying to escape flashbacks and nightmares, ex-POW Jamie Gwynmorgan stumbles into the heart of former Red Cross worker Adele Sabellius and uncovers a deadly conspiracy against everything and everyone she loves. (978-1-60282-889-6)

Date with Destiny by Mason Dixon. When sophisticated bank executive Rashida Ivey meets unemployed blue-collar worker Destiny Jackson, will her life ever be the same? (978-1-60282-878-0)

The Devil's Orchard by Ali Vali. Cain and Emma plan a wedding before the birth of their third child while Juan Luis is still lurking, and as Cain plans for his death, an unexpected visitor arrives and challenges her belief in her father, Dalton Casey. (978-1-60282-879-7)

Secrets and Shadows by L.T. Marie. A bodyguard and the woman she protects run from a madman and into each other's arms. (978-1-60282-880-3)

Change Horizon: Three Novellas by Gun Brooke. Three stories of courageous women who dare to love as they fight to claim a future in a hostile universe. (978-1-60282-881-0)

Scarlett Thirst by Crin Claxton. When hot, feisty Rani meets cool vampire Rob, one lifetime isn't enough, and the road from human to vampire is shorter than you think... (978-1-60282-856-8)

Battle Axe by Carsen Taite. How close is too close? Bounty hunter Luca Bennett will soon find out. (978-1-60282-871-1)

Improvisation by Karis Walsh. High school geometry teacher Jan Carroll thinks she's figured out the shape of her life and her future, until graphic artist and fiddle player Tina Nelson comes along and teaches her to improvise. (978-1-60282-872-8)

For Want of a Fiend by Barbara Ann Wright. Without her Fiendish power, can Princess Katya and her consort Starbride stop a magic-wielding madman from sparking an uprising in the kingdom of Farraday? (978-1-60282-873-5)

Swans & Clons by Nora Olsen. In a future world where there are no males, sixteen-year-old Rubric and her girlfriend Salmon Jo must fight to survive when everything they believed in turns out to be a lie. (978-1-60282-874-2)

Broken in Soft Places by Fiona Zedde. The instant Sara Chambers meets the seductive and sinful Merille Thompson, she falls hard, but knowing the difference between love and a dangerous, all-consuming desire is just one of the lessons Sara must learn before it's too late. (978-1-60282-876-6)

Healing Hearts by Donna K. Ford. Running from tragedy, the women of Willow Springs find that with friendship, there is hope, and with love, there is everything. (978-1-60282-877-3)

Desolation Point by Cari Hunter. When a storm strands Sarah Kent in the North Cascades, Alex Pascal is determined to find her. Neither imagines the dangers they will face when a ruthless criminal begins to hunt them down. (978-1-60282-865-0)

I Remember by Julie Cannon. What happens when you can never forget the first kiss, the first touch, the first taste of lips on skin? What happens when you know you will remember every single detail of a mysterious woman? (978-1-60282-866-7)

The Gemini Deception by Kim Baldwin and Xenia Alexiou. The truth, the whole truth, and nothing but lies. Book six in the Elite Operatives series. (978-1-60282-867-4)

Scarlet Revenge by Sheri Lewis Wohl. When faith alone isn't enough, will the love of one woman be strong enough to save a vampire from damnation? (978-1-60282-868-1)

Ghost Trio by Lillian Q. Irwin. When Lee Howe hears the voice of her dead lover singing to her, is it a hallucination, a ghost, or something more sinister? (978-1-60282-869-8)

The Princess Affair by Nell Stark. Rhodes Scholar Kerry Donovan arrives at Oxford ready to focus on her studies, but her life and her priorities are thrown into chaos when she catches the eye of Her Royal Highness Princess Sasha. (978-1-60282-858-2)

The Chase by Jesse J. Thoma. When Isabelle Rochat's life is threatened, she receives the unwelcome protection and attention of bounty hunter Holt Lasher who vows to keep Isabelle safe at all costs. (978-1-60282-859-9)

The Lone Hunt by L.L. Raand. In a world where humans and Praeterns conspire for the ultimate power, violence is a way of life…and death. A Midnight Hunters novel. (978-1-60282-860-5)

The Supernatural Detective by Crin Claxton. Tony Carson sees dead people. With a drag queen for a spirit guide and a devastatingly attractive herbalist for a client, she's about to discover the spirit world can be a very dangerous world indeed. (978-1-60282-861-2)

Beloved Gomorrah by Justine Saracen. Undersea artists creating their own City on the Plain uncover the truth about Sodom and Gomorrah, whose "one righteous man" is a murderer, rapist, and conspirator in genocide. (978-1-60282-862-9)

The Left Hand of Justice by Jess Faraday. A kidnapped heiress, a heretical cult, a corrupt police chief, and an accused witch. Paris is burning, and the only one who can put out the fire is Detective Inspector Elise Corbeau…whose boss wants her dead. (978-1-60282-863-6)

Cut to the Chase by Lisa Girolami. Careful and methodical author Paige Cornish falls for brash and wild Hollywood actress Avalon Randolph, but can these opposites find a happy middle ground in a town that never lives in the middle? (978-1-60282-783-7)

Every Second Counts by D. Jackson Leigh. Every second counts in Bridgette LeRoy's desperate mission to protect her heart and stop Marc Ryder's suicidal return to riding rodeo bulls. (978-1-60282-785-1)

More Than Friends by Erin Dutton. Evelyn Fisher thinks she has the perfect role model for a long-term relationship, until her best friends, Kendall and Melanie, split up and all three women must reevaluate their lives and their relationships. (978-1-60282-784-4)

Dirty Money by Ashley Bartlett. Vivian Cooper and Reese DiGiovanni just found out that falling in love is hard. It's even harder when you're running for your life. (978-1-60282-786-8)

Sea Glass Inn by Karis Walsh. When Melinda Andrews commissions a series of mosaics by Pamela Whitford for her new inn, she doesn't expect to be more captivated by the artist than by the paintings. (978-1-60282-771-4)

The Awakening: A Sisterhood of Spirits novel by Yvonne Heidt. Sunny Skye has interacted with spirits her entire life, but when she runs into Officer Jordan Lawson during a ghost investigation, she discovers more than just facts in a missing girl's cold case file. (978-1-60282-772-1)

Blacker Than Blue by Rebekah Weatherspoon. Threatened with losing her first love to a powerful demon, vampire Cleo Jones is willing to break the ultimate law of the undead to rebuild the family she has lost. (978-1-60282-774-5)

Murphy's Law by Yolanda Wallace. No matter how high you climb, you can't escape your past. (978-1-60282-773-8)

boldstrokesbooks.com

Bold Strokes Books

Quality and Diversity in LGBTQ Literature

 victory EDITIONS

 *Drama*

 MATINEE BOOKS

E-BOOKS

SCI-FI

MYSTERY

 erotica

 BSB SOLILOQUY

EROTICA

 BOLD STROKES BOOKS

YOUNG ADULT

 LIBERTY EDITION

Romance

W·E·B·S·T·O·R·E

PRINT AND EBOOKS